# CONFLUX

## THREAT FROM THE TROIKA

## WILLIAM BRAZZEL

BALBOA
PRESS
A DIVISION OF HAY HOUSE

Copyright © 2018 William Brazzel.

All rights reserved. No part of this book may be used or reproduced by any means, graphic, electronic, or mechanical, including photocopying, recording, taping or by any information storage retrieval system without the written permission of the author except in the case of brief quotations embodied in critical articles and reviews.

Balboa Press books may be ordered through booksellers or by contacting:

Balboa Press
A Division of Hay House
1663 Liberty Drive
Bloomington, IN 47403
www.balboapress.com
1 (877) 407-4847

Because of the dynamic nature of the Internet, any web addresses or links contained in this book may have changed since publication and may no longer be valid. The views expressed in this work are solely those of the author and do not necessarily reflect the views of the publisher, and the publisher hereby disclaims any responsibility for them.

The author of this book does not dispense medical advice or prescribe the use of any technique as a form of treatment for physical, emotional, or medical problems without the advice of a physician, either directly or indirectly. The intent of the author is only to offer information of a general nature to help you in your quest for emotional and spiritual well-being. In the event you use any of the information in this book for yourself, which is your constitutional right, the author and the publisher assume no responsibility for your actions.

Any people depicted in stock imagery provided by Thinkstock are models, and such images are being used for illustrative purposes only.
Certain stock imagery © Thinkstock.

Print information available on the last page.

ISBN: 978-1-5043-9176-4 (sc)
ISBN: 978-1-5043-9178-8 (hc)
ISBN: 978-1-5043-9177-1 (e)

Library of Congress Control Number: 2017917590

Balboa Press rev. date: 01/09/2018

A veteran Special Forces officer, now working as an investigative journalist, must contend with an extremist group plotting an attack in the United States in Brazzel's (*The Seventh Holy Man*, 2014) thriller.

For his latest *New York International News* article, middle-aged reporter Sean Carrol, with photographer Wayne Deeter, will be interviewing Carl Dietrich, the leader of a German paramilitary organization called Deutsche Christen, which has members in the United States. Carrol didn't really have a choice; the right-wing organization forced his hand by abducting his 12-year-old niece, Amanda, and 10-year-old nephew, Danny. The journalist obeys, but Dietrich refuses to release the children until he approves the completed article—and Carrol conducts a second interview with the group leader. It's hardly surprising when Dietrich later changes the terms again and continues to hold onto his hostages. Deutsche Christen has multiple camps, but their locations are unknown. Still, Carrol is determined to find his niece and nephew, especially after a military rescue attempt fails. He later reunites with his former elite Special Forces unit for extensive training for another mission. This incenses Dietrich, who sends men to make a direct assault against Carrol. The journalist suspects that the group has something larger in store; then a former Deutsche Christen member warns that the group is planning attacks in America, and the CIA hints that a "foreign entity" may be linked to it. The Special Forces unit prepares for more action when it's apparent that Deutsche Christen's strike could have global consequences.

Brazzel's straightforward prose throughout suits the typically stoic protagonist, who narrates the tale. Carrol meticulously describes everything, even the mundane, such as his morning routine of feeding and/or walking his ever faithful German shepherd, Boynton. This approach occasionally results in moments of suspense: during one of those walks, both Carrol and Boynton spot a man who, it appears, is watching them a bit too intently. But the writing is at its strongest when it comes to hearty scenes of action: "The guard gasps and then collapses after his larynx has been crushed. We deposit his body in the grassy overgrowth just within the camp perimeter and then hurry back to the edge of the river bank." Carrol is an enthralling, well-developed character; it's revealed that he lost his wife, Debbie, a few years ago to cancer and may have a new romantic interest in neighbor Linda Mancuso, an FBI retiree and childhood friend. There are also some effective spy-fiction elements, as when an anonymous caller warns the journalist that he's in danger, and Carrol deduces that someone close to him has betrayed him. The plot can sometimes be perplexing, though; for example, the reasons why Dietrich demands the interviews and corresponding articles are never made clear. Still, Brazzel knows how to escalate tension gradually for optimal effect: Deutsche Christen's plan gets bigger as the story progresses, and by the end, there's a frighteningly good chance of a worldwide conflict.

What this thriller lacks in nuance, it makes up for in copious action.

— *Kirkus Reviews*

# Contents

| Chapter 1 | Abduction | 1 |
| --- | --- | --- |
| Chapter 2 | Waiting for Instructions | 10 |
| Chapter 3 | Decision | 19 |
| Chapter 4 | Meeting at the Camp | 26 |
| Chapter 5 | Meeting of the Parties | 38 |
| Chapter 6 | The Next Step | 54 |
| Chapter 7 | New Information | 70 |
| Chapter 8 | Revisit | 87 |
| Chapter 9 | Planning a Rescue | 99 |
| Chapter 10 | Public Disruptions | 112 |
| Chapter 11 | Preparation | 119 |
| Chapter 12 | Back Together | 125 |
| Chapter 13 | The Team Reunites | 134 |
| Chapter 14 | Unification | 138 |
| Chapter 15 | Mission | 147 |
| Chapter 16 | Rage from the Militia | 159 |
| Chapter 17 | Trexler's Demise | 168 |

| Chapter 18 | Vengeance | 174 |
| --- | --- | --- |
| Chapter 19 | Missing | 181 |
| Chapter 20 | Shame | 191 |
| Chapter 21 | Foreigners at the Door | 195 |
| Chapter 22 | Threat and Betrayal | 208 |
| Chapter 23 | Mounting Crisis | 222 |
| Chapter 24 | Searching for the Traitor | 235 |
| Chapter 25 | Message to the United Nations | 241 |
| Chapter 26 | Retribution | 250 |
| Chapter 27 | China's Threats and Aspirations | 257 |
| Chapter 28 | Special Mission | 260 |
| Chapter 29 | Sino-Russian Plan | 263 |
| Chapter 30 | The Plan | 273 |
| Chapter 31 | Strategy for Combat | 276 |
| Chapter 32 | Preparation for War | 284 |
| Chapter 33 | Hell on Earth | 290 |
| Chapter 34 | Emergence | 295 |
| Chapter 35 | Attack upon Japan | 298 |
| Chapter 36 | The Final Conflict | 303 |
| Chapter 37 | Unbearable Loss | 306 |
| Chapter 38 | Confrontation with Dietrich | 313 |
| Chapter 39 | Odin | 318 |
| Chapter 40 | Finality of War | 323 |

# CHAPTER 1

# ABDUCTION

This April has delivered the harshest and most unpleasant weather Manhattan has experienced in over two decades. Eighteen inches of precipitation has been recorded for the first half of the month. Today, once again, the rain is streaming down the bedroom windows of my condominium severely impairing my view.

When I roll out of bed and get dressed, Boynton, my five-year-old German shepherd, begins performing his usual dance; this is my cue to hurry. After getting dressed, I scurry downstairs to the living room, open the closet, grab my poncho, and walk toward the front door while Boynton runs to get his leash. His lack of traction on the hardwood floor causes his legs to slip out from under him. This unfortunate scene repeats itself on most mornings, but he never seems to learn.

Once outside, we walk briskly to Juniper Valley Park, one of the top ten parks in Queens, located just three blocks away. Boynton seems extremely anxious this morning. He's tugging so hard on the leash that I have to wrap the handle tightly around my wrist and hand to keep him from pulling loose. When I pull back on the leash, he begins choking. I stop walking and stoop to rub his throat in an effort to calm him.

By the time we finish our walk, the sun is shining through the receding black clouds, and the rain has halted. The beautiful foliage of azaleas and freesias manifests in a gorgeous diversity of color and pleasant scents from the fresh, sweet gardens. It's a beautiful morning.

When returning home, I see Mrs. O'Malley sitting in a straight-backed wooden chair on her front porch. She's drinking a cup of coffee while intently surveying the surrounding neighborhood. She's been a resident here for over thirty years, and I've known her since my wife and I moved in fifteen years ago. While Boynton and I stand next to the black wrought iron fence that surrounds the grounds of her two-story colonial, she gets up and leans against the railing of her wraparound porch. "Good morning, Sean. Good morning, Boynton."

"Good morning, Mrs. O'Malley. I hope you're enjoying your day."

"I'm just breathing in the morning air and planning my day. The weather promises to improve this afternoon, so I'll probably take a walk. You and Boynton enjoy your day as well."

"We definitely will, Mrs. O'Malley. I'll talk to you soon."

After tending to Boynton, I have to finish my article about an illegal arms-trafficking ring in Buffalo for the New York International News, my employer. Once it's completed, I'll e-mail it to John Errins, my editor.

When we arrive home, I open the front door, and Boynton dashes to the kitchen. He barks, impatiently waiting for me to feed him. Normally he's very calm, so I'm not sure what's agitating him. When I prepare his food, Boynton continues barking and nervously paces from the center island to the doorway and back. He gets so worked up that he jumps up on my back. As he slides down, his nails dig into my skin, causing me to lunge forward while howling in pain.

"Bad boy! Very bad!" I yell while massaging the burning scratches on my back. Boynton growls in response causing me to step back. I haven't heard him growl since my wife, Debbie, became ill over three years ago. During that period, he was constantly on edge, exhibiting frequent episodes of erratic behavior. He never let Debbie out of his sight though. On the days she was bedridden, Boynton would climb onto my side of the bed and curl up next to her. Sensing she would only be with us for a short time, he was heartbroken.

When I lean over to pet him, he opens his mouth, bares his teeth, and begins snarling at me. Something is really bothering him. I wonder whether he senses tragedy once again.

Just then, the doorbell rings. Boynton charges toward the front door, barking loudly. Through the glass I see two officers from the New York Police Department. When I open the door, they display their badges and introduce themselves as Sergeant Callahan and Officer Caruso. Standing at about five foot ten, the sergeant, who appears to be in his early to mid-forties, is a bit paunchy. Officer Caruso, on the other hand, is in his early thirties and possesses a strong muscular frame. At a height of over six feet, he is a picture of the consummate police officer.

"Sean Carrol?" the sergeant asks.

"Yes, I respond."

After requesting to come in and speak with me, the sergeant asks, "Is the dog friendly?"

"Yes, he's very friendly. Today he's a bit agitated, but I don't think he'll bother you." Boynton watches calmly as they enter. The officers sit on the couch near the front living room window while I take a seat in the lounge chair next to the fireplace. "What brings you here officers?"

The sergeant responds, "Mr. Carrol, have you ever heard of a group by the name of German Christians?"

"Yes, I know that name, however, they use Deutsche Christen, the German version of their name, for public consumption."

"How are you aware of them, Mr. Carrol?"

"I know a little about this group, having previously interviewed some of their members."

The sergeant says, "Your sister Monica received an unsigned note this morning, allegedly from this group. After reading it, she immediately contacted the New Jersey State Troopers. The note demanded that you conduct an interview with their leader, Carl Dietrich, at one of their facilities. Believing that you wouldn't voluntarily cooperate, their organization abducted your niece Amanda and your nephew Danny as insurance. After interviewing your sister, the state troopers notified our office, requesting we contact you."

"Are you serious? Those bastards took my family? I know they're an extremist group, but I never would have expected coercion to be one of their practices." After pounding my fist on the side table, I fall back in my chair while muttering some threatening obscenities. Within a few seconds, I stare at the officers and tell them, "How cowardly these militia are, using my niece and nephew as a pressure point to induce my cooperation!"

"You're right, Mr. Carrol, but you have no choice other than to cooperate. After all, we don't know what will happen to the children if you don't agree to the interview," responds Sergeant Callahan.

"Do you know why they're demanding that I conduct this interview?"

"We really don't know the answer," Officer Caruso states.

"How is my sister? I need to call her right away."

The Sergeant says, "Wait, Mr. Carrol. We need to ask you a few more questions."

"Well, get on with it!"

"You mentioned an interview that you did with some members of Deutsche Christen. Why did you do the interview, and what was the purpose?"

"About three years ago, I did a story for my newspaper concerning violence committed by the Far Right in the United States. As I recall, the Deutsche Christens were one of several militia groups I interviewed and reported on."

"Did you uncover anything they would have been upset by?" Sergeant Callahan asks.

I peer at the officers while I digest their question. Yeah, I reported that their organization is one of the most violent groups of those I'd interviewed.

"That in itself wouldn't create a drop of sweat from those guys. They relish being referred to as bad boys," the sergeant says.

"Did you discover anything they were trying to keep secret?" asks Officer Caruso.

"I really can't think of anything. You've got to realize I was only there for an interview and didn't have the luxury of time to perform an investigation."

Officer Caruso states, "Right now, the Pennsylvania State Troopers, some officers of Homeland Security, and agents of the F.B.I. are searching for the Deutsche Christen camp in an attempt to locate Amanda and Danny." "The search is concentrated in the areas north of Pittsburgh, where the Deutsche Christens have several camps. The search party hopes to find the children alive. In any event, they won't take any unnecessary chances that may jeopardize the kids' safety. This is a dangerous militia with large caches of heavy weapons. In addition, the organization is comprised of thousands of ex-military men from all branches of the service. If necessary, the federal authorities will call in the military to assist them. However, this will only be employed as a last resort."

While impatiently waiting for the interview to end, I say, "I appreciate you telling me all of this. Right now, though, I really have to call my sister."

The sergeant responds, "That's okay. We don't have any further questions for now, but we may need to talk to you again."

I get up, escort them to the door, and shake their hands as they leave. Then I rush to call Monica. The phone rings several times. While waiting for her to answer, I drift off in thought, remembering how close we had been during high school. I recollect her eye-catching beauty and the unending trail of boys who constantly paraded by our home trying to catch a glimpse of her.

Finally, I hear my sister's distraught and shaky voice. "Hello?"

"Hi, Monica."

"Sean, I'm so scared. Did you hear what happened?"

While leaning against the nearby living room wall, I answer, "Yes. The police just left."

"I don't know who this militia group is or why they've abducted my children. How do you know them, Sean? Who are they?"

"Deutsche Christen is a right-wing paramilitary group with members located throughout the United States. I only know them from an interview I conducted previously with a few of their members."

"With Amanda barely twelve years old and Danny only ten, I know how frightened they must be. Experiencing this trauma at such young ages, I worry about how they'll be affected physically and emotionally. Sean, the real question is, how do we get the children back?"

"I'm not quite sure yet, but I do know the authorities are searching for the kids and hope to find them and secure their release soon."

"Why would this group abduct my children? Couldn't they have just requested that you do the interview without taking the kids?"

"They could have, but I think they figured I'd refuse to do it. They want to force my cooperation."

Still crying, she says, "My two innocent children are being used as pawns by a group that has no respect for other lives. They invaded my life and kidnapped my children. I'm so angry that I can't even think or reason clearly."

"I know how you feel. Knowing that the children are being held by this group enrages me too. I feel so helpless and distraught that I'd like to grab a gun, track these guys down, and blow every one of them away. At this point, unfortunately, the only recourse I have is to conduct this damned interview in the hope that the kids will be released once I complete it. In the meantime, are you okay?"

"I'm all right considering the circumstances."

"Is there anything you need?"

She impatiently says, "I don't know. At this point, I can't think of anything other than my children."

"I understand, but please call me if you need anything at all. After all, I'm only forty-five minutes from your home in North Arlington."

"I know, Sean, but I'm okay for now. Goodbye, and thank you."

"Goodbye, Monica."

After hanging up the phone, I notice that Boynton is lifting his right front paw in a gesture of friendship. I cautiously reach over and shake his paw while he licks my hand. Maybe he was acting strangely this morning, because he'd sensed trouble.

# CHAPTER 2

# WAITING FOR INSTRUCTIONS

I put on a pot of coffee while ruminating about Deutsche Christens' motives. My thoughts naturally begin and end with Amanda and Danny, and what they may be experiencing. I'm like a second father to the kids, and I can only think of our weekends together as a family. They love to go the movies, especially original Disney productions. Our times together have always created special memories; I really miss them.

While sitting at the kitchen table, I evaluate the potential impact of the interview with Carl Dietrich. What does he expect to gain from this? I can't fathom why the members of Deutsche Christen would target me, and why their insistence? There are so many other seasoned reporters who would jump at a chance to take on this interview. When I get up to pour a cup of coffee, my phone rings.

An unfamiliar voice with a deep, raspy tone asks, "Is this Sean Carrol?"

"Yes."

"Mr. Carrol, this is John White. I'm a member of Deutsche Christen. My reason for calling is to arrange for an interview between you and Carl Dietrich."

I angrily respond, "Why are you demanding I do this interview, and why have you abducted my niece and nephew?"

"Your reputation as an investigative reporter is impeccable. Besides, your special forces background assures many of us that you share a common understanding of the frustrations and difficulties that we face as ex-military men. No other reporters possess these credentials. With regard to your niece and nephew, be assured they're safe and unharmed."

"They'd better stay that way, or I'll make sure your group pays."

"There's no need to make threats, Mr. Carrol. We have no intention of harming anyone. To arrange the interview, someone from our organization will meet you at a predetermined location. You should bring a cameraman, but you won't be permitted to take pictures of anything outside of the designated area where the interview will be conducted. I'll call you tomorrow to arrange the time and location of the meeting. Goodbye, Mr. Carrol."

After slamming down the phone, I clench my coffee cup and then throw it hard against the wall. It smashes into pieces, while leaving residue on the wall and the floor. In my confusion and anger, I find myself fixated upon exacting revenge against Deutsche Christen. After all, they've violated my family and made unwarranted demands on my life. In essence, they've placed a gun to my head. I learned early on, during my special forces training, that an enemy attack requires a merciless response. Somewhere down the road, I'll have to even the score.

It's now noon, and I have to figure out what alternatives I have to secure the release of my niece and nephew. I'm not overly confident that I can count on the good nature of the Deutsche Christens to voluntarily release them. I get up from the table and walk into the living room, still rattled from the trauma of the kidnapping.

After calming myself, I decide to take a ride to Stan Monahan's house. He's a trusted friend, whom I know will be able to provide an objective viewpoint to my ordeal. He always seems to be able to put things in perspective. Stan lives on Katonah Avenue, near Woodlawn Cemetery, in the Bronx. We've been friends since our special forces days when we were part of the elite Maxim unit. This name was specifically assigned to our team due to our ability to fight with blind ferocity much like the Maxim Czech underground unit who fought the Warsaw Pact troops after the 1966 invasion of Czechoslovakia. The Maxims ambushed the Soviet troops and their mercenaries at will throughout the occupation of Czechoslovakia. Like ghosts they appeared and disappeared without detection.

I recall during Desert Storm how Stan saved my life while we were under attack in downtown Baghdad. After a bullet from enemy fire grazed my temple, I got pinned down in an alleyway. He opened fire on the gunmen and took out three of them. The remaining two fighters ran but were immediately killed by incoming mortar fire. If it weren't for Stan, I would have been another statistic of the war.

At quarter to one, I climb in the car and head to Stan's place. The drive will take about half an hour from my home in Queens. After I travel through the communities of Whitestone and Malba, I cross the Bronx-Whitestone Bridge continuing on through Unionport and Schuylerville. A congested checkerboard of industrial and residential buildings, both communities display the character of their blended histories representing nearly two hundred years in development.

When I finally arrive at Stan's, he's sitting comfortably in a lounge chair on the front porch with a can of beer in his hand. He's still a mountain of a man, standing at six feet four inches and possessing a powerful muscular frame. His red hair has grayed on the sides, and he's gained a few pounds. In spite of this, he still appears to be in pretty good shape. I get out of the car and can see Stan grinning from ear to ear. We haven't seen each other in over a year, but we do manage to stay in touch by phone.

After I climb the porch stairs, Stan gets up, puts out his hand, and then pulls me to him, crushing me with a bear hug.

"My God, Stan. You still have the strength of a Brahma bull."

"It's nice to see you too, buddy. Do you want a beer?"

"Yeah, that'd be great."

"I'll be right back. Just take it easy." Stan walks into the house and eliminate then in a couple of minutes with a Heineken in hand. He tosses the bottle to me and then takes a seat. Stan knows I have a good reason for visiting him. Over the years, having spent so much time together, he can almost read my thoughts. "So what brings you out here, Sean?"

"I have a major problem with an organization called Deutsche Christen. They're compelling me to do an interview with their leader, and I don't want anything to do with it."

"What's the problem with interviewing this guy?"

"He's part of an extreme Far-Right paramilitary group prone to violence. I get the impression that they're using me in an effort to release some bizarre message about their group. Their main goal may be to attract new members."

"Just tell them no, Sean."

"I can't. They've abducted Amanda and Danny and are holding them as hostages."

"Oh, God. What the hell are the authorities doing?"

"The federal authorities, along with state troopers and a number of local police departments, are attempting to find the kids, however, they know they're facing a very dangerous and well-armed militia. They're cautiously searching, because they don't want to jeopardize the welfare of the children. To make matters worse, many of the members of Deutsche Christen are from special forces and other military branches. This makes a rescue even more dangerous."

"What's the name of the leader of this group?"

"His name's Carl Dietrich."

"You know, Sean, I've heard that name before. I recall there was a colonel by the name of Dietrich who was dishonorably discharged from the military. If memory serves me right, he led a special forces team into the towns of al Haditha and al Qa'im in Iraq. They murdered several hundred people without cause. Dietrich was tried and found insane by a military court, and he was committed to Catawba Hospital in Roanoke, Virginia, for a one-year stint. At the conclusion of his treatment, he was to be incarcerated at Leavenworth Prison in Kansas. Unfortunately, while at Catawba, he managed to escape and has never been found."

"The question then comes to mind, why does he want to reveal himself now?"

"Good question."

"Stan, I've never experienced a family ordeal like the one I'm going through. I feel helpless. There must be something I can do to rescue Amanda and Danny."

"Emotion is infecting your thinking, causing anxiety and impatience. You've got to step back, digest what's occurring, and think through everything before taking any action."

"I guess you're right."

While we're talking, I can see Stan's wife, Betty, carrying a bag of groceries as she crosses East 241st Street. She immediately recognizes me and waves while hurrying her pace.

"Let's not mention any of this to Betty," I say. "I don't want her to worry."

"I won't say a word," Stan replies.

After running up the steps of the porch, Betty rushes to hug and kiss me. "It's so good to see you, Sean. We've really missed you!"

"I've missed both of you. I wish we could see each other more often."

"What brings you out here?"

"I had some free time and thought I'd pay you both a visit."

"I'm glad."

Betty is a wonderful person, and unlike Stan, has such a great disposition. Although a great guy, he's very gruff and outspoken. She's a couple of years older than Stan, but she's kept herself in great shape. Standing at five feet six inches, Betty weighs about 130 pounds and possesses the most gorgeous long, flowing auburn hair. She's the epitome of an Irish lass. She asks, "Would you like to stay for dinner?"

"I'd love to. I haven't had a good home-cooked meal in months."

"I'll be back once the groceries are put away."

I offer to help, but she tells me, "It's not necessary."

Stan and I settle back into our chairs. While we're talking, Betty returns and sits on Stan's knee. She asks me, "How've you been doing?"

"I've been good. I have my hands full with Boynton, of course. Otherwise, everything is okay."

"I know you miss Debbie. Stan and I loved her too. She was a very caring person and a great friend."

Betty's eyes begin to fill with tears. She and Debbie had been fast friends from the beginning of my friendship with Stan.

Betty continues. "Unfortunately, Sean, her cancer came on so suddenly and took her from us so quickly. She was always encouraging me to be positive no matter what impediments I faced. Even during her illness,

Debbie was always looking on the bright side of things. It's as though I've lost part of myself. I miss her so much."

"I know how you feel, Betty. The two of you were more like family to her than friends."

She gets up, gives me a hug, and then excuses herself. "I've gotta prepare dinner. It'll take about forty minutes."

When she leaves, Stan and I continue talking about the abduction and my interview with Carl Dietrich. We slowly digress into a discussion about our experiences in Iraq and our short stint in Afghanistan. We both agree that those were dark times, but the brotherhood of our special forces team managed to keep us sane.

"If you remember, Stan, most of our experiences involved intense combat in the outlying desert areas of both countries, where we were under constant attack from the Taliban. Because of the intensity of the battles, every detail resulted in injury or death to one or more of our team members."

Stan falls back in his chair and breathes a heavy sigh when he talks about how our team became trapped in Samangan in northern Afghanistan, just one hundred miles south of Uzbekistan. "As I remember, one of the fiercest battles we encountered was when we were encircled by enemy combatants while we defended our position within the town. I recall that we came under heavy artillery and RPG fire. If you remember, Sean, the battle lasted nearly a full day when—luckily for us—Seal Team X arrived, followed by three F-16 fighter jets. I can still picture how the jets lit up the landscape. They were able to force the enemy from their positions, leaving them vulnerable to our weapons fire. Nearly two hundred enemy combatants were killed. Luckily, only two of our team members were lost."

I nod. "I remember how frightening that was."

After dinner, Stan and I talk about the children and discuss our alternatives with respect to a rescue. Frustrated by our limited options, we agree to mull over some ideas about how to free Amanda and Danny. Impossible as it seems, there has to be a way to rescue them. Hopefully, the military will intercede to make a rescue attempt. I thank Betty and Stan for dinner and tell them that I'll be in touch. I kiss and hug Betty and say goodbye to Stan. While walking to my car, I can see them standing at the top of the porch steps, waving. I wave, start the car, and head back to Queens.

## CHAPTER 3

# DECISION

When I arrive home, Boynton is already pacing at the front door. He's overdue for his walk and gets very excited when he sees my car pull into the driveway. Once inside, I put his leash on and rush to the park. When we arrive, I let him off of his leash and watch as he runs into the nearby bushes. Within a couple of minutes, he rushes back, panting while jumping with excitement. When we return home, I prepare his food and then head upstairs to change.

After descending the stairwell, I suddenly remember I have to call Wayne Deeter. A photographer will be required for the interview with Carl Dietrich, and Wayne is the most experienced and talented photographer I know. I reach into my pants pocket, pull out my cell phone, and dial his number. After several rings, his wife, Doris, answers.

"Hi, Doris. It's Sean. Is Wayne there? I need to speak with him about an assignment."

"No, Sean. Wayne just left for the convenience store to pick up some milk for breakfast."

"When he returns, would you please have him call me right away?"

"No problem."

About ten minutes later I walk into the kitchen and my phone rings. When I pick it up, I recognize Wayne's voice. "Hello, Sean."

"Hi, Wayne."

"Doris told me you called."

"Yeah, I need to talk to you about a serious dilemma that I'm facing." I explain about my niece and nephew, the demands of Deutsche Christen, and the interview. After outlining the entire situation, I hear Wayne let out a loud gasp. I continue. "This group is a dangerous organization with chapters located throughout the country. Many of their members are veterans who hail from various branches of the military. Unfortunately, the ultimate motivations and goals of Deutsche Christen aren't very clear. In addition, I'm not quite sure what Mr. Dietrich, their leader, is attempting to accomplish by mandating this interview, but I have to adhere to his demand."

"Sean, what do you need from me?"

"To complete the interview, pictures will be required. That's why I need you to accompany me and assist by taking photographs of the interview."

"Honestly, your description of this group frightens the hell out of me. I know we've interviewed dangerous individuals before, including criminals and gang members, but this interview may present unexpected dangers. Are you sure that we can trust these people?"

"Of course not. But based upon the fact that they need me to write a favorable article about their organization, I'm fairly sure that no harm will come to us. Right now, they need us more than we need them. Unfortunately, they've got an ace in the hole. My niece and nephew are in their custody, and this guarantees my cooperation."

"Sean, I don't feel comfortable with this assignment. My gut tells me that we could be tempting fate."

"Possibly, but I have no choice. The kids' welfare is my main concern."

"Against my better judgement, and as a favor to you, I'll assist with the interview. If I were asked by someone else to do this, I'm not sure I'd be so willing. However, our friendship and the circumstances involved compels me to participate."

"By the way, when is this interview supposed to take place?" Wayne asks.

"Probably within the next few days, but we may have to leave as early as tomorrow to meet with a representative of their group. Right now though I'm flying blind, but as soon as I hear something, I'll let you know. Hope to speak with you tomorrow, Wayne."

"Good night, Sean."

After hanging up the phone, I head into the living room to watch the news. I take a seat on the couch, pick up the remote, and turn on the television. Much to my surprise, the program features the kidnapping of my niece and nephew. Captain Stacy of the Pennsylvania State Troopers is outlining the situation concerning the abduction of Amanda and Danny, and the tactics the police are employing in an attempt to rescue the children.

Alongside the captain is an inspector from the Federal Bureau of Investigation. Wearing a long black overcoat, he is approximately forty-five years of age, and six feet tall. He's the image of the stereotypical F.B.I. agent. He listens intently while the captain summarizes information and answers questions from reporters about the kidnapping and the search taking place near Pittsburgh, in the areas above the conflux of the Ohio River.

A reporter questions the captain, "How many people are searching for the children?"

"We have approximately two hundred officers, including ten F.B.I. agents and a small team of Homeland Security officers participating in the search."

The reporters pummel the captain with questions, aggressively confronting him and requesting names of the abductors and specifics with regard to the rationale for the kidnapping of the children. After twenty minutes of questioning, the captain suddenly suspends his interview. "We have limited time, and I have to rejoin the search."

Captain Stacy then introduces Inspector Jardine of the F.B.I. The agent steps forward, leans against the dais, and states, "We have much more ground to cover. Based upon information we've accumulated, the abductors belong to the Deutsche Christen organization, but I'm not at liberty to reference individual names associated with the abduction." Displaying pictures of Amanda and Danny, he mentions their ages as twelve and ten respectively. "According to family members," he says, "these are happy and well-adjusted kids, and I am determined to find them."

He explains the difficulties encountered while searching the area. "The mountainous terrain and heavy forests are major impediments to our search." After harshly cutting off a question from a local reporter, the inspector continues. "Our progress has been slow and extremely frustrating. The area being scoured constitutes hundreds of square miles. It will take several days before we can conclude the search in that area and move on. We hope to rescue the children soon, however, I can't offer a timeframe." He terminates the interview by saying, "That's all the information I'm authorized to provide at this time."

I think to myself, *What a hard-ass he seems to be.* Abrasive and gruff, he doesn't exude a very warm demeanor. His emotionless delivery makes me wonder whether he possesses any feelings at all. However, I guess his position as an F.B.I. agent and his experiences in the field, mandate his harsh exterior.

A few minutes later, I pick up the remote and change the channel. The same story is being broadcast. I turn off the television and dial John Errins. "Hello, John. It's Sean."

"Hi, Sean, I just learned about the abduction of your niece and nephew. I'm so sorry. I wish that there were something that I could do to help."

"Thanks for your kind words, but I've gotta let you know that I'm being mandated by members of Deutsche Christen to do an interview with their leader, Carl Dietrich. I don't know exactly when, but I believe they expect the interview to be conducted within the next few days. Quite honestly, I wouldn't even consider doing this interview if it weren't for the children's abduction."

"Is there anything I can do?"

"First of all, I need to take a photographer with me. I've already asked Wayne, and he's agreed to assist."

"Is there anything else you need?"

"Yeah. Do you have access to a small GPS unit that can be installed on Wayne's camera? This way, you'll be able to track us and pinpoint our location when we interview Dietrich. Besides, knowing the whereabouts of the militia camp may enable the military to easily rescue the children."

"We have two GPS units in our storage locker. I'll get one and have it installed on Wayne's camera in the morning."

"That's fantastic, John. Please make sure it's inconspicuous when you install it."

"Don't worry, Sean. I've done this a hundred times before."

"Great!"

"By the way, what's the purpose of the interview?"

"I'm not completely sure. Based upon what I know of Carl Dietrich, I believe the interview will likely be used as an advertising tool to increase the group's membership. Quite honestly, I don't care. My only concern is making sure that the children are safe. Once this damn interview is completed, I hope to bring the kids home, but I don't have any assurances of that."

"Sean, get a good night's sleep. We can talk more about this tomorrow."

"See you in the morning."

I'm worried about the undisclosed interview process and the prospect of rescuing the children. I feel as though I'm heading into a storm with a strong, unrelenting headwind. I'll have to depend on my military instincts and training to guide me. I'll also need to be vigilant every step of the way.

## CHAPTER 4

# MEETING AT THE CAMP

As usual, I awaken the next morning with Boynton licking my face. After having experienced an emotional roller coaster over the abduction of Amanda and Danny yesterday, I feel helpless and depressed. Last night, my dreams were more like nightmares, as I continually tossed and turned, envisioning the images of my niece and nephew and those of the militia from Deutsche Christen. I awoke numerous times in a cold sweat and screamed out for the kids, worried that they were in danger.

I climb out of bed, get dressed, and walk downstairs. While I grab his leash, Boynton waits patiently near the front door. I clip on his leash and open the door. Unlike yesterday, today is beautiful, sunny, and mild—perfect weather for being outside. I watch Boynton as he exhibits a playful puppy-like personality, unlike yesterday, when he was on edge and out of character.

When we arrive at the park, I let Boynton loose and throw a stick for him. Instead of chasing the stick, he stops dead in his tracks. He's fixated on a man who is standing next to a tree about a hundred yards away. Motionless, the man stares unimpeded while we observe him. Perceiving a potential threat, I quickly move toward Boynton. Suddenly, the man turns and begins walking in the opposite direction. Within a couple of minutes, he disappears.

Boynton looks up at me. He seems perplexed, as though he has a sense about something, yet he doesn't grasp the connection. He runs toward me and picks up a stick. This is my cue that he wants to play. I grab the stick, reach behind my back, and throw it about a hundred feet. He runs, picks it up, and deposits it at my feet. We do this several more times. Finally, I yell, "Boynton, it's time to go home. Come on, boy." He rushes back and drops the stick, panting heavily from the exercise; he'll definitely need some water when we arrive home. I clip the leash onto his collar, and we begin walking.

As we approach our condominium, I spot a large white envelope resting on the landing near the front door. I climb the steps and cautiously retrieve the envelope. There are no markings on the outside, however, I can feel documents of various sizes enclosed within.

I rush inside and sit down on the couch while Boynton jumps up and lies next to me. Anxiously, I rip open the envelope and view a manila folder measuring a quarter of an inch thick lodged below a large number of loose documents.

After extracting everything from the envelope, I begin reading a note that refers to plans to be implemented by Deutsche Christen.

> Our intent is to create disruptive actions throughout the United States. Most will involve violence. Critical targets have been pre-selected to create the utmost chaos and maximum damage. Our ultimate goal is to do as much damage to government authority as possible, in the hope that we can slowly dismantle and destroy the governmental structure.

While continuing to examine the contents of the envelope, I discover a series of maps that display locations along the Ohio River. Each location is marked with a small circle and is strategically situated near the riverbank. Inside the manila folder, I spot numerous photographs of storage facilities, with clusters of weapons neatly piled on metal shelving. I assume these weapons are stored within the Deutsche Christen facilities. In addition, there are organizational demographics and charts and graphs estimating membership growth of the paramilitary that have been created for the last two calendar years.

The numbers are impressive, to say the least. Membership of the organization has grown an average of 2 percent annually. While attempting to digest the information, I find it disconcerting to know that so many people are disillusioned with their lives, willing to devote themselves to a paramilitary organization. They must be truly desperate.

As I continue to review the contents of the envelope, my telephone rings. When I answer, an unrecognizable male voice with a light Southern drawl asks, "Did ya look at the documents from the envelope?"

"Yes," I reply.

"Did ya understand what I gave you?"

"No, not completely."

"Mr. Carrol, you've gotta pay special attention to the maps that show the circled areas along the Ohio River. These are the locations of the Deutsche Christen camps in Ohio, Pennsylvania, and West Virginia. They've got quite a few similar camps throughout the country. Unfortunately, I'm not privy to any information about them. You'll notice that the documents also provide construction plans for the bunkers within the camps. The plans are universal. This enables the militia to function effectively no matter where they're lodged."

I ask, "Are you the man who was standing in the park watching me and my dog today?"

"Yes, Mr. Carrol."

"To be honest with you, I'm a little confused about why you're providing me with this information. Don't you think the police would be a more appropriate authority for reviewing and assessing these documents?"

"Not at this point. I'm aware of your background and know from some military pals that you're trustworthy. I'm afraid to pass this information along to anyone else, because Deutsche Christen has friends everywhere. If these documents fall into the wrong hands, some buddies of mine could be in serious danger. They've taken a huge risk by obtaining and smuggling these documents to me. I don't want to jeopardize their welfare."

"Thanks for the information. By the way, who am I speaking to?"

"That's not important right now, Mr. Carrol. Simply heed my warning and familiarize yourself with the information contained in the envelope."

The line then goes dead. I pick up the documents again and continue studying them. Judging from some of the plans, the bunkers appear to be very well constructed. They include a surplus of living and storage space throughout the complexes. Several areas within the bunkers are designated as weapons and vehicle storage. The acreage surrounding the complex is massive, and the topography is rugged, providing an optimal training area.

My cell phone rings again. I pick it up and immediately recognize Mr. White's voice. Sounding more like a robot than a human being, Mr. White tells me that he needs to meet with me to discuss arrangements for the interview. He asks, "Do you know where Saint John's Cemetery is?"

"Yeah, I do."

"I'll meet you at the green gatepost on Metropolitan Avenue. It'll be quiet at this entranceway, and we'll be able to speak freely. You'll recognize me by my black pullover cap. I'll see you at 2:00."

At 1:55, I enter the green gatepost and slowly walk toward a burial marker located approximately fifty feet ahead to my left. Within a few minutes, I see Mr. White enter. I immediately walk toward him. "Good day, Mr. Carrol." After I acknowledge his greeting, we take a seat on a nearby wrought iron bench located under a large, thick maple tree with a cross carved into its lower trunk.

Mr. White begins. "Mr. Carrol, you'll need to make arrangements to meet our representative in Pittsburgh tomorrow. He'll meet you at Market Square in the Golden Triangle area on the corner of Forbes and Market Street. Make sure you're standing in front of the large window at the entrance to the Oyster House. To identify yourself, you should wear a red baseball cap."

"What time should I be there?"

"Our representative will meet you at exactly 2:00 p.m."

"Can you tell me what the purpose of the interview is?"

"Unfortunately, I don't know what Mr. Dietrich has in mind."

"Can you at least tell me where the interview will take place?"

"All I can tell you is that you'll be traveling to one of our camps. Beyond that, I'm unable to provide you with any other information."

Mr. White gets up from the bench, shakes my hand, and then departs. He's a rather unemotional person and appears detached and unconcerned about the events that are unfolding.

I climb into my car and head home to get ready for tomorrow's interview with Carl Dietrich. When I arrive home, I grab my cell phone and immediately call Wayne Deeter. The phone rings twice before he answers. "Wayne, its Sean. I just met with Mr. White of Deutsche Christen. He informed me that we're to meet his representative in Pittsburgh at 2:00 p.m. tomorrow."

"Not a problem. By the way, I met with John this morning. We installed the GPS unit in the camera. It's very small and hardly noticeable. By using this monitoring device, John will be able to activate it for the trip allowing him to pinpoint our location."

"That's great. In the meantime, I'll make reservations for a morning flight out of LaGuardia to Pittsburgh. I'll arrange for a 9:00 a.m. flight. Can you have the company limousine pick us up at 7:00?"

"Consider it done."

"See you in the morning, Wayne."

I hang up the phone and immediately walk to Linda Mancuso's condominium, located a couple of buildings away. I need to ask her to watch Boynton while I'm conducting the interview with Dietrich.

Linda retired from the F.B.I. two years ago after twenty-one years of service as an agent. As a result, we were able to reconnect our friendship. She's been a friend of mine since childhood. We attended grammar school and graduated high school together. During high school, we dated for a couple of years, but I never considered our relationship serious. She was the valedictorian of our graduating class and was even voted prom queen in our senior year. Linda's maintained her beauty for all these years. Possessing a mane of long black silky hair, deep seated brown eyes, and smooth olive skin, she's the quintessential picture of a runway model.

I ring the doorbell a couple of times and wait. Within a few minutes, the door slowly opens, revealing Linda's face. "Hi, Sean. I'm surprised to see you. What brings you over here?"

"I need to ask a big favor."

"What do you need?"

"I was just assigned to a news project, and I need someone to watch Boynton."

"Shouldn't be a problem. When do you need me to watch him?"

"I'm leaving early tomorrow morning and should be gone for about two days."

"Why don't you bring him over tonight? I have all of his food and other supplies. No need for you to bring anything."

"Thanks a lot, Linda. I'll bring him over in a couple of hours. Is that good?"

"See you then, Sean."

I take Boynton to Linda's place. Although he loves her, he's not happy knowing that I'm leaving. While I stand at the front door, he begins whimpering as he sits at my feet. Linda grabs his leash and walks him into the kitchen. She reaches into a drawer, pulls out a dog bone, and places it on the floor. While he's distracted, I wave and throw a kiss to Linda before quietly slipping through the doorway. When I return home, it's nearly 5:00 p.m., and I'm a little bit hungry. I take a yogurt from the refrigerator, quickly devour it, and toss the empty container in the garbage. Leaning over the kitchen counter, I check the land phone for any messages. Clearly listed on the phone screen is a number from the F.B.I. After entering my password, I listen to the message.

"Mr. Carrol, this is agent Jardine of the F.B.I. Please call me whenever you get a moment. I'd like to discuss the kidnapping of your niece and nephew."

Remembering his television interview and his unemotional delivery of the case information, I'm reluctant to call him. In spite of my personal feelings, I believe that the welfare of Amanda and Danny is more important. So I dial his number. Immediately, I hear a male voice answer. "Agent Jardine, may I help you?"

"Yes agent, this is Sean Carrol returning your call."

In a somewhat pompous tone, Agent Jardine informs me, "I'm the lead F.B.I. agent in charge of the investigation of your niece and nephew's abduction. I want to encourage you to keep me abreast of any information that you come across relative to the case."

"At this point, the only thing that I can tell you is that I'm supposed to meet with Carl Dietrich tomorrow. I'll be flying into Pittsburgh International Airport from La Guardia and meeting with an associate of his. We're supposed to rendezvous in front of the Oyster House Restaurant at 2:00 p.m. I'm hoping that our mutual interest in locating the children mandates that we work together. Needless to say, you'll have my full cooperation in the investigation."

"I appreciate it. I'm going to organize a detail of agents to monitor as much of your trip as possible."

"Agent Jardine, don't take any unnecessary actions that may threaten the welfare of my niece and nephew. Just so you know, I promise to provide you with all pertinent information that I obtain from the interview."

"Don't worry, Mr. Carrol, we'll be very discreet."

After hanging up the phone I need to get ready for tomorrow's trip. I head upstairs to the bedroom and begin packing some clothes. To ensure a complete record of the interview, I'll bring a voice recorder and a laptop, along with some pads of paper and pencils.

After making the airline reservations, I take a quick shower and put on my bathrobe. Feeling a bit on edge, I decide to go downstairs to watch the news. When I click on the TV, John Dale, the nightly anchor, is introducing the next story concerning the right-wing paramilitary movement in the United States. He says, "For the past five years there's been a major proliferation of membership among various paramilitary groups. Embedded primarily in the Midwest, South, and West Coast, a dozen organizations have begun expanding their territory. Within the past two years, the paramilitary has established new chapters along the East Coast as well. Spanning from Florida to Pennsylvania, they've become entrenched in rural and semi-suburban areas located near waterways such as the Ohio and Delaware Rivers."

Citing several reports concerning militia groups, Mr. Dale summarizes the reasons for this expansion and growth. "The militia's dissatisfaction with federal and state government policies, as well as the burgeoning tax increases being levied upon the public, inspired their major distrust and anger. The groups have also expressed discontent with the disturbing march toward socialism and the absence of government representation on their behalf. This includes the lack of proper and timely medical care for veterans."

"They cite the substantial growth of government, poor political leadership, and the insurmountable federal debt as major reasons for the decline of American leadership. The demographics of these organizations reveal a disturbing trend: eighteen to twenty-eight year-olds constitute close to 80 percent of new members. No longer open to speculation this information reinforces the fact that the younger generation has lost faith in both the future and the United States."

Continuing, he states, "The history of the right-wing paramilitaries features the standoffs at Ruby Ridge, Idaho, in 1992 and at Waco, Texas, in 1993. These were the catalysts for the formation and growth of the militias throughout the country. Both events galvanized many paramilitary groups and caused them to view the government with disdain. Since then, numerous new groups have formed and flourished, revealing their impatience with and distrust of the U.S. government."

Mr. Dale concludes his report by saying, "The current trends are disturbing. This dramatic evolution has forced the government to carefully monitor all right-wing paramilitary groups in order to weigh the threat they may pose to the United States."

I wonder where our country is headed. With such a fractured national community, our direction is unclear and frightening. That our leaders will actually take the necessary steps to reclaim our country and the principles upon which we were founded is likely a long shot.

I think about my interview from three years ago. The paramilitary groups were fragmented by organizational differences; they consisted of many separate factions and loose alliances of one sort or another. Today, however, my intuition tells me they may have overcome their differences and united under one mantel. If in fact this has occurred, then the United States could be confronted with a major threat within its own borders. Once I interview Carl Dietrich, I'll need to press this issue and attempt to extract pertinent information beyond the fundamental goals and philosophy of Deutsche Christen.

CHAPTER 5

# MEETING OF THE PARTIES

The next morning, I awaken earlier than expected. After shutting off the alarm clock, I rush downstairs to make a pot of coffee. It's now 6:15, and I'm anxious but wary about what awaits me today. After plugging in the coffeepot, I head upstairs to take a quick shower and get dressed. I collect my belongings for the trip, hurry downstairs, and pour a cup of coffee.

As I amble toward the living room window, I stare at the cell phone photo of Danny and Amanda that I recently received from Dietrich. They're standing outside of a small log cabin with their hands restrained by thin rope tied over their wrists. Meant as a threat, the photograph stirs my anger, but more importantly, it ensures my cooperation. In spite of Dietrich's depravity, I'm still hopeful that my niece and nephew will be returning home with me after I complete today's interview. I know my sister will be overjoyed when she sees the kids. What a reunion that will be! I can't wait to have them back home.

Just then, my mind-set returns to reality, as I weigh the questions to be posed to Carl Dietrich. Echoing in my head is the unanswered question: what motivation does Carl Dietrich have for demanding this interview? Knowing I'm being used infuriates me, especially because the interview will support the sinister plans of Deutsche Christen, whatever those plans may be.

The limousine pulls up at exactly 7:25. Wayne climbs out from the backseat and begins walking to the front door. His thin, wiry frame attests to his high school years as a champion cross-country distance runner. Unusual as it seems, he still maintains a regimen of running at least four days a week. Although he's forty years of age, he retains the appearance of someone in his early thirties.

Seeing him approach, I pick up my belongings and open the door to greet him. "Good morning, Wayne."

"It looks like a pretty good day for traveling," He says.

"Sure does."

While I shut and lock the front door, Wayne picks up my bags, carries them to the limousine, and hands them to the driver. After climbing into the backseat, I instruct the driver to take us to LaGuardia Airport. Once we arrive, we head through baggage screening and on to the terminal. Wayne and I take a seat and anxiously await an announcement for boarding.

It's 11:00 when we land at Pittsburgh International Airport. We now have three hours before we'll meet the representative from Deutsche Christen. After hurrying to secure our bags, we walk outside to hail a taxi. Immediately, a black sedan pulls up, and the driver jumps out to assist us.

I direct him to take us to Market Square. He informs me that the trip will take about twenty-five minutes.

In order to take advantage of the quiet time, I close my eyes and rest my head against the rear seat cushion. When we arrive at our destination, I witness the bustling crowds of people. Most are business people who appear to be rushing with briefcases to their next appointment. The shops around the square abound with customers, many of whom are carrying shopping bags while casually stopping to window shop. Once the driver stops the car, Wayne and I get out and grab our bags from the trunk. I hand the driver fifty dollars and then walk toward the Oyster House. Nearly three hundred feet away, I spot the large front window where we're to meet our contact.

Realizing the importance of today's meeting, I'm extremely nervous about the interview, but I'm more concerned about the involvement of the F.B.I., especially since I don't know anything about Jardine and his plan.

While we're walking, Wayne points to his right, indicating the Starbucks on the corner. It's conveniently located just down the block from the Oyster House. "Sean, we have some time. Let's get a fresh cup of coffee at Starbucks and then review our strategy for the interview."

"That sounds good."

After ordering our coffees, we decide to sit under one of the many outdoor umbrella tables in the center of the square. Surrounded by a diversity of specialty shops, restaurants, and department stores, we slowly sip our coffee while digesting the makeup of our surroundings. We have two hours before forging our way to the Oyster House. I ask Wayne, "How will you be able to project the personality of Dietrich through your photos?"

"That's why I'm the best, Sean. Normally, I observe the subject for a short time and slowly absorb his makeup. After understanding the personality, I limit my shots to those moments when the facial features jibe with the subject's real persona."

We continue discussing the information we'd like to extract from the interview, as well as the photo angles we need to capture. I tell Wayne, "Hopefully, Mr. Dietrich won't impose any limitations on my questions. Unfortunately, based upon my limited knowledge of him, I believe he may have already circumscribed the parameters of the questions. In spite of this, I'm going to try my best to broaden the boundaries of our interview."

We review our strategy and decide to question Mr. Dietrich about the need for paramilitary groups such as his. I say, "Similar to a boxer, we'll need to probe for any organizational weaknesses in an attempt to gather general information at first. By delving a little deeper, we'll attempt to obtain more detailed facts about the future plans of his organization. Currently, no one understands the goals of Deutsche Christen. Secrecy has been a hallmark of the group, stymieing any knowledge of its structure or actual membership numbers. All we have is speculation from government and media outlets. If our interview is successful, the information we gather will be critical to the newspaper article I'll write. Although I'm concerned about the interview process, I hope to be able to obtain some hints of the real intentions of Deutsche Christen without jeopardizing the safety of my niece and nephew."

"Sean, you'll likely be walking on eggshells throughout this interview. One mistake could result in unexpected consequences. You'll have to be very careful when it comes to the depth of the questions you ask."

At 1:55, I reach into my bag, pull out a Cincinnati Reds baseball cap, and put it on. Wayne and I begin walking to the Oyster House. At exactly 2:00, we're standing in front of the large window. Immediately, a man approaches from Mc Masters Way at the corner of the Oyster House building. He's approximately six feet tall and is thin but muscular. Stern and businesslike, he exhibits no emotion when he approaches. Wearing a worn black bombardier jacket, leather gloves, and dark mid-rise boots, he appears more like a hit man than a member of a paramilitary group. Judging from his gait, he must have been an athlete. With a wealth of self-assurance, he approaches Wayne and me, introducing himself as Dave Drury.

Mr. Drury requests that we walk behind a barrier of trees near the restaurant. After patting us down for body wires and weapons he says, "Mr. Carrol, I want you and your associate to walk with me in the direction of the Monongahela River. Within a couple of blocks, we'll meet my driver and then ride to the Smithfield Bridge. There's a small boat basin on the other side of the river where a boat will be awaiting us. Once on board, we'll begin the trip to our destination." I walk to the designated location nervously observing every street corner, vehicle, and building I encounter, worried that Mr. Drury will discover some F.B.I. agents lurking about.

I continue walking, convinced that the purpose of this first step of our journey is to allow Mr. Drury to cautiously assure himself that no government agents are involved in observing our movements. When we near Liberty Avenue, a black SUV is waiting. The driver steps from the vehicle and grabs our bags. Dave Drury tells us, "Climb in the backseat." Wayne and I get in and sit quietly. He then instructs the driver, "Head to the bridge and take us across to the boat basin." Within ten minutes, we arrive at our destination. The driver pulls the SUV alongside the river bank and exits the vehicle to retrieve our bags.

We open the doors and quickly negotiate the length of the dock where a fifty foot cabin cruiser awaits. Constructed of fiberglass, the boat is a dual-engine inboard cruiser featuring a twenty-foot-high flying bridge. After stepping onto the deck, Mr. Drury points to a stairway and says, "Go below deck." While following, he orders us, "Enter the large cabin to the right and take a seat at the small circular table." He grabs some heavy rope from the corner of the room and begins to tie up Wayne and then me. I feel uncomfortable about being harnessed this way, but I know that I have to comply if I expect to secure the release of my niece and nephew. From his jacket, Drury extracts two black blindfolds shaped in a figure eight. They're about an inch wide and thicker than a normal blindfold. After placing them over our eyes, he informs us, "We'll be underway shortly."

Within a few minutes, the engines rev up, and the boat begins to move. When we reach open water, the engine suddenly accelerates with an explosion of power. I hear Wayne grunt in pain.

"Are you OK, I ask?"

"I'm fine. I just hit the wall when the boat sped up."

Nearly an hour later the boat begins to slow down. I can feel it pull toward the right. Thinking we've completed our trip, I tell Wayne, "We've arrived at our destination."

"I don't think so, Sean. The boat is just slowing to negotiate some low water levels. From what I've read, shallow areas are created by low tides along the Ohio River. If we don't slow our speed, the boat may run aground."

Suddenly, the engine accelerates, and we continue on. Approximately a half hour later, we slow down once again but angle to the left. This time, I know we've finally arrived at our destination. I can feel the boat slowly gliding over the water. In the distance, I hear voices bellowing. The voices intensify, indicating our close proximity to the shore. I hear people instructing the pilot about the docking position and cautioning him to slow his speed while approaching the bulkhead.

When the engine shuts down, Mr. Drury and a guard enter our cabin and untie us. They usher us up the stairs to the deck. Gently, they guide us up the ladder, where we step from the boat onto the dock. While we walk, Mr. Drury tells us, "You'll remain blindfolded until we reach the staging area where the interview will be conducted."

When we reach the location for the interview and our blindfolds come off, I squint from the sudden explosion of light, unable to get my bearings. Anticipating the interview with Dietrich, my heart is beating like a bass drum. I'm exhausted from the trip, but I've got to rejuvenate my energy so that I can heighten my focus for the interview process. When my eyes finally begin to adjust, I view the interior of the tent. I see a scant ray of light squirting from the small window flap in the front door. The contents of the tent appear rather stark; there are two tables, three chairs, and a small storage cabinet lodged in the corner.

After ordering the accompanying guards to place our bags in the corner, Mr. Drury requests that one of them remain to assist us with the setup. The young man who volunteers is in his late twenties. Standing at a slender six feet three inches, he evokes the image of a boyish physique. Introducing himself as Alfred Carmichael, he says, "How can I be of assistance?" His soft voice and polite mannerisms display a shyness and naïveté while at the same time exuding a character of honesty and sincerity.

Replying, I say, "Set up two tables to accommodate our equipment, and please assist Wayne by holding the camera lights to ensure the proper angles required to provide clear images of Mr. Dietrich during the interview."

While we're preparing the setup, I ask Alfred, "How long have you been a member of Deutsche Christen?"

Leaning against the back of a chair and touching his index finger to his chin he tells me, "Overall, I've been a member for two years."

"Do you know how many members the organization represents?"

Alfred frowns and immediately stops me. "I can't discuss any specifics about our organization. That will be up to Mr. Dietrich."

"Fair enough. May I ask what made you join the organization, and how you believe Deutsche Christen will improve your quality of life?"

"That's not a problem, Mr. Carrol."

While Alfred continues setting up the table, I sit on the edge of a nearby wooden chair. Alfred smiles and quietly responds.

"When I returned from Afghanistan in 2014, there were no jobs. I had some money saved, but it wasn't enough to sustain me for very long. One afternoon while strolling along the Ohio, I caught a glimpse of a Deutsche Christen poster. It advertised a meeting and summarized the philosophy and goals of the organization. After attending, I immediately joined."

"What did you discover?"

After digesting my question, he says, "I found that the group ascribes to the same morals and values with which I was raised. Considering the overall state of our country today, and the political paralysis of our leaders, I think there's no hope among most veterans. We believe the quality of our lives and that of our families will never improve. There are no jobs for us. In fact, employers avoid even considering veterans when they advertise available employment. This organization advocates the rights of the individual and gives us hope that positive change will soon be underway."

"What kind of change are you referring to? And how will it come about?"

"Mr. Carrol, I've already said enough. Please don't ask me any more questions."

Judging from his answer, I conclude that Alfred is extremely intelligent and well versed in current events—something unexpected from most young people today. I wonder whether other members of Deutsche Christen are like Alfred, or if he's an anomaly.

Today, it seems that young people are preoccupied with electronic games and gadgets, as well as violent movies and television. All of this has become like a narcotic, relegating reading, socialization, and religion to the backseat.

As Wayne, Albert, and I complete the setup, Mr. Drury enters the tent and informs us, "The interview will commence in ten minutes." Wayne and I attend to the last details of the setup while Alfred and another guard assist.

Not long after we complete the equipment preparation and lighting adjustments, an imposing figure accompanied by two guards enters the tent. Standing at six feet four inches and weighing approximately 240 pounds, he epitomizes the strength and power of a professional athlete. He's in his mid-forties, has close-cropped black hair, and leather tough facial skin. He exudes discipline and possesses a stern demeanor. Walking directly over to me, he introduces himself. "Mr. Carrol, I'm Carl Dietrich." He reaches to shake my hand. After hesitating for a moment, I reluctantly shake his hand, and then introduce Wayne as our photographer.

He asks, "Are you ready?"

"Everything is set."

"Before you begin the interview, Mr. Carrol, I want to lay out the parameters for your questions. You won't be allowed to ask anything regarding my background, the military tactics of our organization, or our racial beliefs. Is that clear?"

"Yes, it's very clear." Beginning the questioning, I ask, "Mr. Dietrich, how long have you been a member of Deutsche Christen, and what changes has the organization experienced over the past several years?"

"I've belonged to this organization since 2003. At that time, Deutsche Christen was a loose confederacy of chapters scattered throughout the country. About three years ago, we created a compact among twenty-six organizations. These groups span most of the country, from Pennsylvania all the way to Washington State. This unification represents approximately 1.15 million militia. Growing at an average rate of twenty thousand new members per year, our organization is flourishing. No longer a disjointed group, we have now established ourselves as a viable, organized political and military force within the continental United States."

I'm beginning to understand why he wants this interview. It's all about intimidation, targeted at the U.S. government. I ask, "What are the goals of Deutsche Christen?"

"Our initial goals were to recapture the morals, ethics, and character of the original United States by any means necessary. After observing the current state of affairs within our country, we realize there is only one path to achieving our goal."

"What might that path be?"

"I ask you, Mr. Carrol. Other than political actions, what options are available to us?"

Responding, I say, "The only remaining option seems to be an armed struggle."

"Yes. Do you understand why an armed struggle is our only alternative?"

"No, I'm not quite sure."

While smirking, he responds, "The politicians and their parties are so embedded in the fiber of our country that there is no chance of arresting their political power. With so much corruption emanating from the political community within the federal and state governments, it's impossible to make any inroads or changes." Exhibiting an overbearing arrogance, he continues. "The government has stacked the deck against the American people."

I lean forward in my seat and respond, "Mr. Dietrich, we do have the power of the vote."

While laughing, Dietrich says, "You can only vote for the stable of candidates offered by the major parties. Voting for a fringe or independent candidate is worse than voting for a Democrat or Republican."

I roll my eyes and shake my head while pointing my finger at Dietrich. "Your jaundiced rationalization of our system is despicable."

"Mr. Carrol, even if a marginal candidate wins, he'll have no power or influence, because the embedded party politicians will isolate him. With each passing day, we are witnessing the demise of our country. Politicians have disabled our institutions and handicapped the constitutional foundation established by the founding fathers. We're also losing our relevance in the world."

Becoming angry, I begin to raise my voice and ask, "How can that be? We possess the most powerful military in the world. Our country, above all, maintains freedom—something to which most countries only aspire."

"Mr. Carrol, you're extremely naïve. If you've been paying attention to current events, you'll realize that the government is gutting our military power. Due to our debt and trade deficits, we can no longer afford the luxury of fielding a military capable of intervening in other parts of the world, where terrorist threats have become an everyday occurrence. Your claim that we have freedom is absurd."

Livid at his comments, I can feel my blood pressure rising by the moment. Attempting to regain my composure, I stand up and curtly respond, "Mr. Dietrich, the foundations of the country are still intact, and we are able to voice our opinions. You sit here with impunity, spouting your hatred for our government and the institutions thereof. Isn't that freedom?"

Realizing the power and impact of my question, Dietrich suddenly stands and declares, "The interview is over."

I ask him, "Now that I have done what you requested, where are my niece and nephew?"

"They're safe."

"I want to take them with me."

"I'm sorry, Mr. Carrol. Before they'll be released, you'll be required to do another interview after you publish the first article."

Incensed, I grit my teeth and begin rushing toward him. The two guards step from behind Dietrich with their machine guns pointed in my direction. I stop, stare at him, form a fist, and then raise it in a threatening manner. "There'll be no more interviews until I see Danny and Amanda. I want to be assured they're safe."

Dietrich responds, "Very well, I'll have them brought to you. Mr. Drury, secure the children and bring them here."

Dave Drury, accompanied by one of the guards, leaves to get the children. Within ten minutes he returns with my niece and nephew. They appear in good health and are well groomed. Amanda's light brown hair has been combed and neatly braided. Danny's appearance hasn't changed, except for the khaki pants and brown pullover T-shirt he's wearing. Normally, he's in play clothes. Upon seeing me, they scream my name and rush over to hug me. Holding my hands, they kiss and caress my fingers to let me know how much they've missed me.

Amanda says, "We're so scared, Uncle Sean."

"I know, sweetheart. We'll get you out of here."

"When?" asks Danny.

"I'm not sure, but it will be soon."

Mr. Dietrich then signals for the children to be taken back to their quarters. Amanda and Danny begin crying. I say, "Kids, don't cry. We'll figure this out."

"Goodbye, Uncle Sean," they reply. When they turn back to wave, Amanda throws a kiss.

Carl Dietrich then tells me, "Before releasing the children, we'll have to make sure that both interviews have been conducted and that the first article has been published. Within the next couple of weeks, the second interview can be done. My representative will be in touch with you to make the necessary arrangements."

"I'll keep my schedule clear, but I want to be assured that my niece and nephew will be released after the next interview."

"You can count on it. Oh, I almost forgot, Mr. Carrol. Before you publish your article, I want you to forward a copy of the final draft to me so that I can determine its acceptability. You can forward the article to an e-mail address that will be provided to you by Mr. White. I'll see you soon."

Carl Dietrich departs with a guard. When he throws open the flaps of the tent, I view a sign partially blocked by a tree limb. Visible at the top is the word *Wheel*, and the word *Brigade* is inscribed below. I wonder what this represents. Is it a group or a place? I can't determine.

After pulling the blindfolds from his jacket pocket, Drury instructs the guard to place them over our eyes. He secures our arms and guides us back to the boat. The engine is already running when we board. The guard escorts us below deck and seats us. After tying us up and blindfolding us, he leaves the cabin and heads up to the deck.

Arriving back in Pittsburgh at 8:00 p.m., Wayne and I immediately secure airline tickets for the flight home. It's about 10:00 when we arrive at LaGuardia and catch a cab. As soon as I arrive home, I dial my sister to let her know about the kids.

"Hello?"

"Hi, Monica. It's Sean."

"I'm so happy you called. How are my children, and where are they?"

"Unfortunately, they're still being held captive by Deutsche Christen, but they both appear to be in good health and are well nourished."

"Why didn't they come home with you?"

"Carl Dietrich insisted that the children remain until I complete my article and conduct a second interview."

"What a heartless bastard he is, holding my children without concern for anyone else's emotions or needs!" She begins to cry uncontrollably, and mutters several unrecognizable sentences.

"Please stop crying, Monica. Everything will be okay. Unfortunately, at this point we don't have much choice. I promise you that I'll bring the children home safely, no matter what it takes."

She begins to calm herself and tells me, "I'm sorry, but I'm just so frightened and concerned about Amanda and Danny. I haven't slept in two days. The thought of my children being held captive by a group like Deutsche Christen scares the hell out of me."

Feeling a lump in my throat, I hold back my tears. My head is beginning to throb from the worry and anxiety that I'm experiencing, and I feel completely helpless to control my emotions. Finally, I tell Monica, "I have to go. I'll talk to you soon."

# CHAPTER 6

# THE NEXT STEP

Early Friday morning, I hurry to get dressed. Anxious to retrieve Boynton, I rush to unpack my clothes and organize my notes from the interview.

At Linda's, I can hear Boynton whining as soon as I ring the bell. When Linda opens the door, Boynton jumps up on my chest and begins licking my face. Linda says she's just made a fresh pot of coffee, and asks if I'd care for a cup. "That'd be great." I take a seat in the kitchen and watch patiently while she pours both of us a cup. I can't help but notice how beautiful she is with her long, flowing black hair, thin waistline, and beautiful facial complexion untainted by make-up. She awakens my memories of our teenage years when we were worry- free and content with our simple lives.

While I sip the coffee, Boynton lies at my feet, peering up at me without diverting his gaze for a second.

"I guess he missed me."

"He was a very good boy, Sean, but he's lost without you."

Linda inquires about my trip and what I encountered. I relate, "The trip and interview were very stressful. When interviewing Dietrich, I was constantly on guard. His demeanor displayed a very unpredictable and unstable personality. He's the type of person who, I believe, can explode without provocation. His instability worries the hell out of me. The worst part is that I came back without the children. While the kids still remain at the camp, I'm afraid he could lash out at them at any time without reason."

"I understand your concern, Sean, but I wonder what can be done to free the children."

"I don't know. It seems like an insurmountable task, but I won't rest until the children are safely returned home."

"I only hope that happens soon. I can't imagine the fear that Amanda and Danny are experiencing."

"Before I went to Pittsburgh, Agent Jardine of the F.B.I. contacted me. I informed him about my interview with Dietrich. He requested that I provide him with any information I obtain concerning the whereabouts of the children. According to him, a team of F.B.I. agents have been assigned to the case and a few members of the team were to be in Pittsburgh to observe my encounter. Before and during my trip, I was convinced that the agents would be discovered. If so, Amanda and Danny would be in serious danger."

"Based upon your interview, what do you think Dietrich is after, Sean?"

"Your guess is as good as mine. However, he manifests a deep mistrust and intense hatred for the U.S. government. He emphasized the merger of multiple militia groups and recounted the tremendous membership growth within their organization. There seems to be only one possibility."

"Do you mean he wants to go to war with the U.S. government?"

"He hasn't exactly been forthcoming about his intent, but by all appearances, that would likely be his plan. I only hope he'll provide more information about his intent during the next interview."

Puzzled, Linda asks, "What next interview? I thought only one interview was required.

"That's what I thought, but Dietrich mandated another one be done within two weeks."

"How can you be sure he'll release the children after the next interview?"

"I can't be sure. Dietrich isn't a man of honor. He simply strings you along with the hope that you'll continue performing for him like a circus animal. His initial promise to release the kids was an out-and-out lie. From the outset, he had no intention of releasing them after the first interview. Because of this, I wonder if he's being truthful about releasing them after the next one, even though he's given me his word. I'm very concerned about Amanda and Danny. I pray that Dietrich releases them after I complete the next interview, but if he doesn't, something drastic will have to be done."

"Do you think he'll demand more interviews?"

"I'm not sure. With Dietrich, anything is possible. He plays a shell game, daring you to guess his next move. He has a sadistic streak and enjoys the emotional and physical pain he exacts on others. He's a twisted, amoral monster."

I glance at my watch and see that it's 9:00. "My God Linda, I've got to get going. There's a lot of work to be done today. Thanks for the coffee, and for watching Boynton."

"You're welcome, Sean. I'll talk to you over the weekend. Goodbye, Boynton."

I clip on his leash and head home. Before taking him inside, I walk him to the open lot across the street for a quick stop.

After settling Boynton in, I grab my car keys and head out. Before backing out of the driveway, I stop to double-check my briefcase, making sure that the notes from the interview are intact. Reassured, I take the half-hour drive to the office where I'll begin preparing the article. Hopefully, I'll complete it within a couple of days. When it's finished, I'll submit it for publication in the Sunday edition of the paper.

After arriving at the newspaper, I walk up the stairs and pass John's office. I wave to him and head straight to my desk. Unlocking the briefcase, I remove and sort my notes. Before I'm able to begin working on the article, my phone rings. "Hi, Sean, It's John. Will you come into my office for a couple of minutes?"

"I'll be right there."

I head to John's office. After we shake hands, he requests that I take a seat on the couch next to his desk. Immediately, he reaches into his top desk drawer and extracts a Hagstrom map. He walks over to me, unfolds the map, and lays it on the coffee table in front of the couch. When I lean over to view it, he points his finger at the map and says, "Sean, we tracked your trip up the Ohio River from Pittsburgh and determined your destination to be the Wheeling, West Virginia, area."

I think to myself, *That explains the words I saw on a sign at the camp.*

While we're talking, John's secretary interrupts. "Mr. Errins, I have a phone call from a Mr. White, and he says it's important that he speak with Mr. Carrol." John tells her to switch the call to his office.

Before picking up the call, I caution John, telling him that Mr. White is a spokesperson for Deutsche Christen. John then picks up the receiver and turns on the speaker phone.

"Hello?"

"Mr. Carrol, this is Mr. White."

"Yes?"

"I'm calling to give you the e-mail address where you need to forward your article."

"I'm ready to take down the address."

He tells me the address, and I write it down. "One more thing, Mr. Carrol. The article must be finished today."

"Mr. White, I'm just starting to work on it. Requiring me to rush the article may dilute some of its content. Creating a piece beneficial to your organization will require a few days of intensive writing. By rushing the process, you may do your group a serious disservice. As a seasoned reporter and writer, my reputation could suffer severely if I write a lousy piece."

"Mr. Carrol, you will have it finished and sent to Mr. Dietrich today."

Angrily I say, "All right. I'll finish the article today." I slam the phone down and tell John, "I have to get back to my desk. Their demand that I complete the entire article in one day is ridiculous. Most likely, it will take all day and part of the night to complete, if I'm lucky."

"Sean, do you want me to assign a couple of reporters to assist you?"

"Thanks John, but I'm gonna have to finish it myself. Nobody else will be able to incorporate the same emotion that I will."

"Not too much emotion, Sean, because that may smother the effect of the article, not to mention upset Mr. Dietrich. Approach the article with fact-based content, the way you normally do."

I head back to my office and review the interview note. Before I begin writing, I make a call to Agent Jardine. I promised that I'd update him regarding any information I obtained during my interview with Carl Dietrich. Although there wasn't much I could pass along, I did make him aware of the camp location in eliminate where my interview took place, and my suspicion that Dietrich may be planning military action against the U.S. government. In addition, I advised him of the substantial growth of the militia and the major threat they presented to the country. After speaking with Agent Jardine, I hang up the phone and begin writing. Most of what I'll write about is the philosophy and the makeup of the group, as explained by Carl Dietrich. I'll delve into some of the organizations' history and their deep mistrust of the U.S. government, as evidenced by my interview with Dietrich and my conversation with Alfred Carmichael. Attempting to avoid any negative commentary, I won't mention the abduction of my niece and nephew or the violent reputation of Deutsche Christen. I don't want to provoke Dietrich.

While writing the article, I'm presented with some challenges. The contrast of my emotion with fact causes difficulty when attempting to bifurcate the two. My anger, the third ingredient, further muddies my thinking.

I begin writing some of my thoughts for the second paragraph, while rethinking the impact of the article.

> The paramilitary threatens to destabilize the U.S. government and reshape the future of the country.

Thinking that this verbiage could cause Dietrich to become enraged, I decide to revise the sentence and the succeeding paragraphs. Rewriting, I tone down the intensity.

> The paramilitary has been slowly increasing their membership, but their intent is uncertain—something that concerns the government. Maintaining a watchful eye over the militia is a mandatory requirement in order to ascertain its goals and create a military defense, if warranted.

Satisfied, I continue to write.

> Deutsche Christen maintains a membership of some 1.15 million fully armed and well-trained militia.

When I finish this paragraph, I feel a tap on my shoulder. After turning around, I see Wayne smiling while holding several photographs. He shows me the photographs while describing the content and angles of the pictures. He seems quite pleased with the results. After showing me the pictures, he says, "Sean, I know what you told me about Carl Dietrich's background. In the meantime, I did some research and made a few phone calls to gather additional information about this guy."

"What did you uncover?"

"Not only was he convicted of the murder of several hundred Iraqis during Desert Storm, but also he was accused of two murders in the United States prior to going overseas. While living in Pittsburgh in 1988, he was charged with the murder of his ex-wife. Some neighbors in the next-door apartment heard him threaten to kill her. In fact, that evening they heard him punching her. They described the sound of her body violently striking the adjoining wall. In response, the neighbors called the police, but they didn't arrive at the apartment for nearly forty-five minutes. By that time, Dietrich was gone. To gain access, the police broke the door lock and forced their way in but found nothing suspicious. The resulting investigation speculated that Dietrich strangled her with his bare hands.

After she was dead, he was suspected of tossing her body into an old wood chipper he owned. The authorities were unable to convict him, because there were no eyewitnesses and no clues at the scene in the apartment. In addition, comprehensive visual and chemical forensics tests revealed no incriminating evidence on the chassis or in the feed tray of the wood chipper."

"Wayne, I can't believe that the authorities weren't able to uncover any evidence against Dietrich. With all of the potential crime scenes, they have nothing to corroborate his involvement in the murder? Not one scrap of proof?"

"You've got to remember that Dietrich isn't stupid. He apparently leaves nothing to chance."

"I know he's not stupid, but I don't believe anyone has the ability to carry out such a perfect crime without a feather of evidence."

"It doesn't matter what you believe: the results are the results. The second case was just as inconceivable. Dietrich was charged with murder in 1989, involving an eighteen year old woman who was found with her throat slit on the campus grounds of Ohio State University. A male student from the university claimed Dietrich was at a bar near the campus the prior evening. He also told authorities that this same woman had been sitting at a table drinking beer with Dietrich. When the police interviewed him, however, he denied even knowing the woman. Oddly enough, a few days later, the male student withdrew his accusation providing no reason other than that he had made a mistake."

"This Dietrich is some piece of work. Knowing what you've told me, I'm now even more worried about the children's welfare. Wayne, I don't want you to take this the wrong way, but I have to finish this article about Deutsche Christen. My deadline is today. I'll require every minute available to finish writing."

"No problem Sean, I'll make sure that these pictures are delivered to the setup department for the Sunday edition of the paper."

"Goodbye, Wayne."

"See you later."

Around 7:00, I finally finish the article. After proofreading it one more time, I rush over to John's office for his review. I knock, enter, and hand him the article, requesting that he proofread it before I forward it to Dietrich. He quickly reads it and says, "Your article is emotionally charged, but I believe it's exactly on point. Let's see if Mr. Dietrich will allow it to be printed in its present form." I take the article and head back to my desk. After scanning it, I e-mail the article to Dietrich.

I then walk into John's office and ask him if he'd like to grab a quick bite to eat. I haven't eaten anything all day, and my stomach is growling. We decide to head over to the Martinique Café; it's only a few doors away and the food is reasonably good. We descend the stairwell to the street and begin our short trek to the restaurant. Once we enter, the hostess greets us and directs us to our table. Nearly five minutes later, a young waiter approaches and asks if we'd care for something to drink. We both order a Canadian Club and ginger ale. The waiter walks to the bar and quickly returns with our drinks. John tells him we'd like the penne dish. "Great choice", he says. He then tells us that our food should be ready shortly.

John remarks, "Sean, you look really stressed."

"Quite honestly, I'm scared to death. The kids are in such danger, and I don't know what the hell to do. I feel completely helpless. I have nowhere to turn for help."

"The simple fact is that you're walking a tightrope without a net to catch you. Any attempt to rescue the children places them in serious peril."

"I know, but Amanda and Danny can't remain there indefinitely."

While we're talking, the waiter serves our dinners and asks if we would care for another drink. John orders a drink, but I decline because I have to drive home.

After finishing dinner, we both shake hands and say good night. I hurry back to the office to see whether Dietrich has e-mailed his approval of the article. It's as though I'm rushing to class to receive a grade from my professor for a midterm exam—how ridiculous. While running up the steps, I can see Charlie, the night watchman, opening the front door for me. I immediately head for my desk and access the computer. After sitting down, I check my inbox for a new e-mail. Sure enough, there's a response from Carl Dietrich.

> Mr. Carrol, I've read your article and am not overly impressed. The tone more so than the content concerns me. Please change the tone and forward the revised copy to me.

I slam my fist on the desk and hear a loud crash. Looking down, I see fragments of broken glass strewn throughout my office. A large water jar that I kept on the edge of my desk hit the tile floor and exploded when I banged my fist.

After cleaning up the broken glass, I grudgingly rewrite the content of the article, mellowing out the sharp edges of the verbiage. I know exactly what Dietrich is referring to.

> The paramilitary exhibits an aggressive military style, one that leaves no room for negotiation. Everything they undertake incorporates the use of power to meet their own ends, no matter what their needs are.

I eliminate and reword some of the sentences. The words "a unique" is substituted for "an aggressive," and "leaves room for compromise" is inserted in lieu of "leaves no room for negotiation."

The revisions take me an hour and a half. This time, I've eliminated all emotion and have strictly presented the facts with no underlying opinion. I reread the article one more time before forwarding it to Carl Dietrich. Within fifteen minutes he replies. Condescendingly, he remarks that the article is now acceptable. *How wonderful! Dietrich the Great has afforded me his approval.* I think to myself, *Now I can sleep better knowing Carl Dietrich's literary blessing has been conferred.*

I forward the article to the front desk for placement in the Sunday edition of the paper. After packing up my briefcase, I walk to the entranceway of the office and then downstairs. My car is parked in the private parking lot just across the street from the newspaper building. When crossing the street, I take the keys from my pants pocket and click the electronic button to unlock the doors. I then toss my briefcase onto the front passenger seat and climb in.

Just as I'm closing the driver's side door, I hear a man's voice yell to me. "Mr. Carrol, please wait." I turn to see who's calling, but I don't recognize him. As he approaches, I stand and face him. He comes closer, removes the hood of his jacket, and reaches out to shake my hand. I reluctantly shake his hand, unaware of who the hell he is. Approximately forty years of age, he appears to have been involved in some of life's worst turmoil. His eyes are sagging slightly, and his face is rugged and deeply creased, presumably from stress and lengthy exposure to the outdoors. Standing six feet tall, he is well built with the sleeves of his jacket stretched so tightly that one can almost see the vessels protruding through. On his left hand, I catch a glimpse of a tattoo inscribed with the words *Semper Fi* set within a small American flag.

"Mr. Carrol, you don't know me, but I'm the man who left the envelope of information on the landing of your condominium. My name's Jake Trexler, and I'm a former member of Deutsche Christen. The reason I've come here is to talk to you about some secret plans of the group."

"If you want, we can head to my office at the newspaper and speak privately."

"Not now, I've got a number of issues to speak to you about that will require some time. Besides, this isn't the proper venue for having a discussion. Do you know of some out-of-the-way place we can meet and talk tomorrow?"

"Let me think for a second. Yeah, we can meet at the Immigration Museum on Ellis Island by the seawall in front of the museum building. The usual crowds will be present, however, there are several isolated areas where we can talk privately."

"What time do you wanna meet?"

"Is 10:30 a.m. good for you?"

"That'll be fine. See you then, Mr. Carrol."

"Good night, Mr. Trexler."

I return home and know Boynton will be acting out. He hasn't seen me for most of the day, and I'm sure he'll be excited. With the weekend at hand, I'll be able to spend more time with him.

After getting out of the car, I head straight to the front door and open it. Boynton is laying in the entranceway of the kitchen when I come in. I stoop to pet him and notice his food bowl resting on the floor in the middle of the room. It's still full. This is unusual. He appears a little lethargic, and his eyes are red and glazed. He must not be feeling well. When I enter, he usually greets me with excitement, knowing that I'll walk him to the field and then prepare his dinner. I touch his snout to check for moisture; it's dry and crusty. He must be running a fever. For expediency, I grab a container of Gatorade and pour it into his water bowl. This will provide what he needs to supplement the minerals in his body. Boynton strolls to his bowl and reluctantly drinks some of the Gatorade. After looking up at me with such sad eyes, he wanders into the living room, climbs onto the couch, and goes to sleep.

In the meantime, I walk upstairs to change into a pair of shorts and a leisure shirt. I then head downstairs to the kitchen and grab a bottle of merlot from the liquor cabinet. After pouring myself a glass, I head into the living room. I fall back into the plush cushions of the couch and turn on the evening news.

The newsman reports, "Congressman Dellilo of the Albany legislature is slated to be charged with laundering money he illegally received from a local businessman for some favors he provided." Yawning, I can't help but think how mundane this story is. I've heard and read about this subject all too frequently.

The next story, however, immediately piques my interest. The reporter says, "A holdup at a Chase Bank in Cincinnati, Ohio, occurred this afternoon. Four men dressed in green and brown military camouflage fatigues entered the bank at about 4:00. They ordered the manager and all employees to lie on the floor. The thieves wore ski masks and were heavily armed. They made off with $350,000. When escaping, they shot one of the bank security guards. The guard, whose name is McIntyre, was sixty-five years old. He died instantly from the gunshot."

The story switches to an on-scene TV reporter who is standing on the banks of the Ohio River. He states, "The bank thieves drove to the Ohio

River while the police pursued them. Unfortunately, they lost track of the thieves near the river. The police did manage to recover the get-away vehicle, but no evidence was found."

It occurs to me that the thieves may be members of Deutsche Christen. Using the river to escape would be a perfect means of avoiding detection. The maps provided to me by Trexler verify the large number of camps they operate along the Ohio. In conjunction with their knowledge of the areas nearby, an escape would be effortless.

I realize the boldness and viciousness of this militia. There appear to be no boundaries they won't cross in order to further their organizational goals. At this point, I'm worried that my next encounter with Dietrich could be disastrous; meaning that I'll have to approach the next interview more cautiously. I don't want any negative repercussions, especially while Amanda and Danny are being held.

# CHAPTER 7

# NEW INFORMATION

The alarm goes off at 8:00. I roll out of bed and hurry to see how Boynton is feeling. He's never slept this late, and I'm worried. I rush downstairs and get to the landing. I see him comfortably nestled in the corner of the couch. As I approach, I observe one eye beginning to open. Bending down, I touch his snout. Luckily, it's moist, indicating his fever has broken. Boynton rolls on his back when I begin petting him. He appears to be coming alive. Thank God he's all right.

I walk to the kitchen and put on a pot of coffee. Then I head upstairs and take a quick shower. When I open the shower door to step out, Boynton is lying in his usual spot on the bathroom rug. His darting eyes signal that he needs to go out. While I rush to get dressed, the phone rings. I answer and immediately recognize the deep, raspy voice of Mr. White.

"Good morning, Mr. Carrol."

"What can I do for you, Mr. White?"

"We'd like you to conduct the next interview with Mr. Dietrich. It's been scheduled for this Thursday. Instead of meeting in Pittsburgh, we prefer that you fly into the Greater Cincinnati Airport. Our representative will meet you at the front entrance. Make sure you're there by 1:00 p.m."

"Mr. White, I want to be assured that my niece and nephew will be leaving with me after the interview."

"Mr. Carrol, I can't make any guarantees. Mr. Dietrich is the only one who has that authority."

"Mr. Dietrich has made a firm promise to release the children after this next interview. I'm hoping he's not lying to me."

"As I said, I have no authority in matters such as this."

When Mr. White hangs up the phone, I dial Wayne. It rings several times with no answer. I leave a voice mail message for him, requesting that he call me regarding the next interview.

After hanging up the phone, I notice Boynton is holding the leash in his mouth, subtly indicating he needs to go out. I grab my poncho, put on his leash, and take him outside. When we arrive at the park, I let him wander off of the leash. After twenty minutes of play, I glance at my watch. It's now 8:45 and time to head home. I call Boynton, and he rushes back to me. After clipping his leash on we walk home.

Before leaving for the office, I tend to Boynton, making sure he has enough water for the day. I should be home early, because I have to start preparing for the next interview. I also have to remember to call Linda and ask her to watch Boynton again.

Upon arriving at the paper, I rush upstairs to begin outlining some questions I intend to ask during the interview. Hopefully, this time I can probe a little deeper to determine what activities and changes may be occurring within Deutsche Christen. Remembering the phone call and notes from Mr. Trexler concerning the plans of the paramilitary, my suspicions have been piqued. He stated there is always an ulterior motive related to the actions of their leadership. This leads me to wonder whether there is a major event near at hand. After all, why would Carl Dietrich expose himself publicly? He's an escaped felon, and the authorities would love nothing more than to apprehend him. Unfortunately, any attempt by the authorities to rescue the kids could result in serious injury or death to them.

While drafting some questions, I feel a tap on my shoulder. I turn to see Wayne standing behind me. He says, "I got your message. When do we need to leave?"

"We've got to leave early Thursday morning. We're expected at the entranceway to the Greater Cincinnati Airport no later than 1:00 p.m."

"I'll make the airline reservations."

"That's fine, Wayne. By the way, do you still have the camera with the GPS unit?"

"Yeah, I'll make sure to bring it with me to Cincinnati."

"Just for the record, we're not going to Cincinnati, because the airport is located in Hebron, Kentucky."

"I didn't know that. What a great trivia question, Sean. Talk to you later."

It's now 9:35, and I have to meet Mr. Trexler at the Immigration Museum at 10:30. I jog to my car and quickly start the engine. Speeding through traffic, I hope to make the appointment on time without causing an accident. Within twenty minutes, I arrive at Battery Park. After buying a ticket, I board the ferry for the 10:05 cruise. The ride seems to take forever. I'm anxious, but realize that my impatience is causing me frustration. I'm aware it won't hasten the trip, but I'm eager to talk with Jake Trexler.

When the ferry finally docks at Ellis Island, I check my watch. It's now 10:35. I disembark and run in the direction of the museum where I'll meet Mr. Trexler. I'm a couple of minutes away when I spot the museum building. The entrance featuring the overhead red grate suddenly juts out. I stop and glance in the direction of the Hudson River. Just two hundred feet away, a ferry is docked, and passengers are waiting to board the next tour. About one hundred feet farther south, I spot Jake Trexler. He's wearing the same hooded jacket he wore the night before. To avoid unwanted attention, I scan the area and cautiously approach him.

When Jake Trexler recognizes me, he walks in my direction. "Good morning, Mr. Carrol."

"Good morning, Mr. Trexler. Have you been waiting long?"

"Nope. I arrived about twenty minutes ago."

We begin walking along the seawall and settle on a bench under a cluster of trees located in a remote area along the periphery of the museum grounds. Here, we'll be able speak freely without interruption or roving eyes. Jake Trexler removes his hood, revealing his sagging eyes and rugged facial features. He tells me, "I know you're going to do another interview with Carl Dietrich this week."

"In fact, I'm meeting him on Thursday."

"I know him very well. Dietrich's extremely volatile, and he's got a hell of a temper. You've gotta be very careful with what you say—and definitely watch your actions. Dietrich is so thin-skinned that the slightest provocation may cause him to erupt in violence. As an example, I saw him slam a guy to the ground for simply dropping a glass of water."

"I'll make sure that I control my behavior, because my actions could affect the welfare of my niece and nephew." I get to my feet and look down at Jake Trexler. "Can you shed any light on what might be taking place within the Deutsche Christen group? I get the strong impression that a major event is about to take place."

"What makes you think that?"

"The fact that Carl Dietrich has suddenly emerged from hiding seems too coincidental. He must believe the government is fearful about apprehending him. After all, he has a standing army of over 1.1 million troops providing him with the latitude to undertake any actions he wishes with impunity."

While nervously peering about, Trexler says, "Mr. Carrol, I'm not quite sure about your analysis, but I do know Carl Dietrich is calculating. He takes actions on sure bets, not on chance. I can't corroborate your observation, but based upon Dietrich's history, it's possible that something significant may be in the works."

While talking, we're interrupted by the loud whistle of a passing tugboat located about a quarter of a mile out from where we're sitting. The tug is heading south along the Hudson, most likely scheduled to rendezvous with a passenger ship somewhere within the New York Harbor. Several succeeding whistles delay our conversation, providing me with a few minutes to digest Mr. Trexler's comments.

When the tugboat moves farther downriver, I ask, "Are you aware of the makeup of the weapons arsenal possessed by Deutsche Christen?"

"I know they possess a large cache of arms. Most of their arsenal consists of grenades, Kalashnikov assault rifles, bazookas, machine guns, and other small arms. The weapons were smuggled into the United States by cargo ships and then off-loaded onto barges. This took place over a period of one year. The shipments were secretly transported twice a week at selected drop points throughout the country. There they were loaded onto trucks and delivered to designated paramilitary camps."

"Have they attempted to acquire anything larger such as cannons, antiaircraft guns, or surface-to-air missiles?"

Jake Trexler leans forward and stares at the river. "There were discussions concerning the acquisition of more sophisticated weapons. To the best of my knowledge, the organization has never actively sought to obtain this sort of weaponry, and I haven't witnessed delivery or storage of any such weapons."

"Do you know who supplied Deutsche Christen with the light arms?"

Suddenly, Mr. Trexler gets up from his seat and glances toward the museum. Appearing uneasy, his eyes begin twitching nervously, and his head quickly darts from side to side. Noticeably unsettled, he's seemingly worried about the trackers that have been hired by Deutsche Christen.

I tell him, "Sit down on the bench, take a couple of deep breaths, and relax."

After calming down, he replies, "I wasn't privy to information related to any sensitive high-level decisions. You have to understand that as a secondary level board member, I dealt with the day-to-day operations and some organizational plans designated for further action. I had little input regarding the direction of the organization. These high-level discussions and decisions are the responsibility of men like Carl Dietrich."

"One of the notes contained in the envelope you gave me references future disruptions that have been planned. As I recall, the plans encompassed actions throughout the United States. Specifically, what actions will they be employing?"

"A number of coordinated public disruptions will be carried out nationally. Teams of militia will be attacking the infrastructure of the country, creating chaos and instability."

"Can you be more specific?"

"Their plans are to shut down public and private transportation. The main targets will be major automobile thoroughfares, such as Interstates 80 and 74. They'll also be targeting train systems throughout the country. Specifically, they intend on inflicting tremendous damage to the New York subways, plus the California and Florida High Speed lines. I don't know the methods they're going to employ to carry out the plans, but I do know that thousands of militia will be required for the operation. Mr. Carrol, at this point I've pretty much exhausted what I know. I can't provide you with anything more."

"I'm curious as to why you're so willing to provide me with information about the Deutsche Christen plans."

"The answer's complicated. However, after five years of participating in the militia, I became discontent because the organization displayed more interest in building a large military contingent rather than assisting veterans and their families."

While placing my hand under my chin, I lean forward on the bench, and ask, "What occurred that ultimately made you flee from Deutsche Christen?"

"The atmosphere within the organization became uncomfortable. Abuses became more pronounced. Money was being diverted to weapons and military training instead of enhancing our community by embracing career training and family care. After witnessing the dramatic changes of philosophy, I couldn't tolerate the organization's misdirection."

I shake my head in dismay. "From what you're telling me, it appears that the leaders of Deutsche Christen lied, deceiving the well-intentioned members of the organization."

"Definitely!"

Mr. Trexler looks at his watch and panics. "Its 1:00 p.m., Mr. Carrol, and I've spent far too much time here. I've gotta get going. Mr. Dietrich has hired some of the most talented and experienced trackers to capture and kill me, and I don't know how much longer I'll be able to evade them. Possessing important organizational information makes me a threat to their current and future survival. Having been on the run for the past five months, I've already had several very close encounters with the trackers. So far, I've been lucky."

Mr. Trexler sits on the bench and descends into an uncontrollable state of nervousness. His eyes dart from side to side, inspecting the museum grounds for any sign of trouble. His body slides back and forth in his chair. He's breathing heavily, and sweat has gathered on his forehead.

"Jake, are you all right? You appear to be in a state of panic. Try to breathe slowly and naturally."

"I'm sorry, Mr. Carrol. I didn't mean to frighten you."

After Trexler calms down, I ask him if he requires a place to stay for a couple of days, and some cash.

"Thanks for the offers. I can use a couple hundred bucks, but I don't want to compromise your safety by staying at your home. It's much too dangerous."

I reach into my wallet and hand Mr. Trexler some money. I tell him, "Be careful, and contact me if you need anything else."

"Goodbye, Mr. Carrol, and thank you."

While Jake Trexler hurries toward an awaiting ferry, I sit and digest the facts of our conversation. The information he provided, though important, didn't include organizational secrets. He's certainly aware of major facts concerning plans to be implemented by Deutsche Christen, but his overall knowledge isn't what I expected.

Slowly, I get up and begin to walk toward the gate to board a ferry. Its 1:30 and time to head home. Once aboard the ferry, I head to the upper deck and take a seat near the stern. Within a few minutes, we're underway.

After pulling into my driveway, I see Boynton sitting calmly by the front door. Of course, he has the leash in his mouth. When I open the door, he walks over to me and sits down. I put on his leash and walk him across the street. Once we return home, I pick up the phone and dial Linda. The phone rings several times. Finally she answers and agrees to watch Boynton. While we're talking, she tells me she's preparing dinner and asks if we would like to come over. Knowing that she's an excellent cook, I accept. She says, "Everything will be ready within forty-five minutes." I tell her, "We'll be there shortly."

Just as I hang up the phone the doorbell rings. Through the glass I view two well-dressed, middle-aged men. Boynton is already at the front door barking to let me know that we have company. I open the door and ask, "Can I help you?"

Both men display identification showing that they're agents of the Central Intelligence Agency. "Mr. Carrol, I'm Agent Greg Foster, and this is Agent Michael Calabrese. May we come in?"

"Sure." The agents take a seat on the couch next to the front window, while I sit in my usual chair. "What can I do for you gentlemen?"

Agent Calabrese, the younger of the two, is in his early 40's. At six feet tall, he's rather thin. His facial features are ordinary with the exception of distinctly deep dimples on both cheeks. He says, "We understand that you've interviewed Carl Dietrich, the leader of Deutsche Christen."

"Yeah, I did an interview with him several days ago."

"Did he talk about any activities in which his organization may be involved?"

"No, but he did say that his militia has been expanding rapidly. He bragged that his organization now fields well over 1 million militia. He didn't elaborate any further. In fact, he was pretty closed-mouthed regarding any organizational activities. He only spoke of the philosophy of Deutsche Christen and recounted the membership growth."

Speaking with a rather soft but firm voice, Agent Foster responds, "To answer your initial question, Mr. Carrol, we've received information that their organization is acquiring weapons en masse. We're not quite sure of the types of arms being obtained, but sources close to the group indicated they've already accumulated major caches of light weaponry. Our understanding is that these weapons are being stored in camps throughout the United States."

"Based upon information I've received, Deutsche Christen hasn't sought or acquired any sophisticated weaponry or equipment. However, if they plan a military action against the United States, I know heavier and more sophisticated weapons will be required. It will be futile to depend on the light weapons they currently possess. The real question is, where will they secure sophisticated weaponry?"

Agent Calabrese tells me, "In March, there was a major theft at Camp Pendleton. Nearly five hundred stinger missiles were stolen from a weapons depot, over which the Pentagon had jurisdiction. This resulted not only in the theft of the missiles but the loss of three army regulars, who were stabbed to death. Our main suspect is Deutsche Christen. Unfortunately, we have no solid evidence to implicate them. The premises, where the incident occurred, were free of any incriminating physical evidence, including fingerprints or clear photos from the security cameras."

"I wouldn't be surprised if they were involved. Stinger missiles will certainly augment the military power of Deutsche Christen, but it won't bring about the defeat of a major military power. By the way, do either of you know how many camps they currently operate?"

Hesitating slightly, Agent Foster leans forward and says, "We know of 185 above-ground camps, but they've also constructed a number of underground facilities. Regrettably, we don't have an accurate count of those."

"I'm supposed to interview Carl Dietrich this week. I'll attempt to gather more detailed information about their activities. Knowing how guarded and paranoid he is won't make it easy."

"At this point Mr. Carrol, we must be going, but we'll be in touch."

"I'm curious, Agent Foster. Why is the C.I.A. involved in this investigation? I understand your agency only investigates cases concerning overseas national security."

Agent Foster replies, "I'll leave you with this thought. There is a foreign entity connected to the case, but I can't elaborate any further."

"Thanks for your time, Mr. Carrol," Agent Calabrese says. He reaches into his pocket, extracts a card containing his personal contact information, and hands it to me. "Please call me day or night if you obtain any information that may assist our investigation."

"I will. Goodbye, gentlemen. It's been nice meeting you."

After glancing at my watch I begin to panic. Boynton and I should have been at Linda's ten minutes ago. I quickly reach for a bottle of merlot and tuck it under my arm. Then I yell for Boynton. Located just two buildings away, I decide to jog over to her condominium unit. On the way, I attempt to digest the information provided by the agents. Concerning me most is why a foreign government would assist Deutsche Christen. Puzzling as it seems, I can't envision any advantages that would be derived from supporting their militia. What government would be so foolish? They'd be challenging the most powerful military in the world.

We hurry up the steps to Linda's unit. I ring the doorbell and hear her footsteps. When she opens the door, I tell her, "I'm sorry we're late." I explain, "Two C.I.A. agents paid me an unexpected visit and questioned me about Deutsche Christen."

"My God, Sean. The C.I.A. is now involved?"

"Yes, and they seem to be deeply concerned about the group." I hand her the merlot, and we walk inside. Boynton follows her to the kitchen, expecting to receive a treat. He sits next to her while she tells him what a good boy he is and then gives him a dog bone. Linda opens the merlot and pours each of us a glass. We then head into the living room and take a seat on the couch near the fireplace.

While we sip our wine, Linda asks, "What did the C.I.A. agents want?"

"They were looking for additional information about activities of Deutsche Christen."

"Sean, the involvement of the C.I.A. creates a whole new dimension to the activities of Deutsche Christen. Why is the C.I.A. investigating a domestic case?"

"According to them, this is not just a domestic case. There's a foreign connection tied to the activities of Deutsche Christen."

"You know, working for the F.B.I. for over twenty years has taught me to be suspicious about things that don't make sense. The assertion referring to a foreign influence is intriguing, but I don't understand what a foreign government would gain by siding with an enemy of the United States."

"I have my doubts too, Linda, but something about this case scares me."

"Sean, my intuition tells me that Deutsche Christen may be planning widespread disaster for our country. From what you've told me about Carl Dietrich, it sounds like he's hell-bent on destroying the United States and establishing a new form of government. If this is the case, we're in for one hell of a ride—one that could devastate the country and create waves of uncertainty throughout the world. The thought of this is unsettling and makes me very uncomfortable. Having heard so much about this group, I'd really like to forget that they even exist. We have so many positive things in our lives, and we don't need to dwell on the negative. By the way, did you bring an appetite?"

"I'm starving."

"I think that the chicken is ready. Would you grab a couple of plates and set the table?"

We enjoy the roasted chicken while discussing the situation that's unfolding in the Middle East. I say, "The Syrian revolution is causing serious chaos not only throughout Syria, but in Iraq and Afghanistan as well. As a result, the Saudis, Jordanians, and Kuwaitis have become desperate and have begun arming themselves with heavy weaponry."

"From what I understand, Sean, they've even sought to obtain nuclear weapons. In addition, thousands upon thousands of people have been killed as a result of Muslim turmoil. The slaughter has been so widespread. Unfortunately, Christians have been targeted by Islamic extremists and are being exterminated in unimaginable numbers, simply because of their beliefs."

I tell her, "It's unfortunate that the hatred prevalent during the crusades has resurfaced, continuing that fifteenth-century nightmare."

Responding Linda says, "The ideology of the terrorists is more difficult to defeat than their actual military. When you understand that leaders of a group can convince their followers to commit suicide by carrying and detonating bomb packs, then victory is a fleeting prospect."

Just then, my cell phone rings. When I answer, I hear Monica's voice. She tells me, "I received a phone call from Agent Jardine of the F.B.I., informing me that a special ops team has been organized for the purpose of rescuing the children. Their hope is to launch the mission within the next few days. Although I'm excited about the prospects of a successful rescue, I have reservations about the mission's success."

After digesting what she's just told me, I'm puzzled about the decision by the military to organize and implement a rescue mission. I was under the impression that a military rescue wasn't even a consideration. Apprehensive, I wonder how a team and a rescue plan could have been organized so quickly. Understanding the importance of significant preparation in the planning of such a delicate mission, I'm deeply concerned about the welfare of my niece and nephew. My fear, of course, is that Dietrich may exact punishment upon the children if the rescue fails. In spite of my concerns, I tell Monica, "I'll say a few prayers for the success of the mission and the safety of the kids."

"The thought that the children could be home with me in few days is exciting, so I can't give up hope."

"By the way, Monica, how did the authorities locate the camp where the children are being held?"

"According to Agent Jardine, your boss, John Errins, forwarded a note to the F.B.I. advising them of the location of the paramilitary camp as being in Wheeling. The assistant director of the North Pittsburgh F.B.I. field office then authorized the use of helicopters in a fly over operation in northeastern West Virginia to verify the exact location of the camp. When they located it, plans were immediately made for the military rescue."

After hanging up, Linda questions me concerning my conversation. I tell her about the rescue mission and my concerns regarding the likelihood of failure. Exhibiting a look of despair, Linda reaches for my hand to comfort me and says, "The only thing we can do right now is pray."

Intentionally avoiding any further discussion about the rescue, Linda and I continue to talk about the latest news. When dinner is over, I help her clean up and say goodbye to Boynton before I head home. I give Linda a kiss on the cheek, and tell her I'll see her in a couple of days. As I'm walking toward the front door, Linda pleads with me to be careful and not to take any unnecessary chances.

"Don't worry. I'll be more than vigilant."

## CHAPTER 8

# REVISIT

All night, as I tried to sleep, I was plagued with worry about my niece and nephew, and the ordeal they're experiencing. Concerned about the trauma that they may be suffering, I feel emotionally distraught and angry at Dietrich for his unwarranted abduction of the children. Unfortunately, I'm caught in a quagmire, unable to change any of the circumstances concerning the kids' predicament. In addition, I'm deeply worried about the upcoming mission to rescue the children. My confidence in its success is doubtful to say the least.

It's now 7:30. Wayne should be arriving in about an hour. All of my supplies are packed, and I'm prepared for the interview with Carl Dietrich.

Given that I have some time before Wayne arrives, I turn on the TV news. I catch a teaser about the next story, an unusual murder that occurred overnight. The show breaks for a commercial. I impatiently wait to learn more about the story. The anchor returns and begins his report.

"A young man in his early forties was found gruesomely murdered.

He was secured to a chair in a burned-out second-floor apartment on Third Avenue, in the Morrisania section of the Bronx. The man's hands had been nailed to a chair, and his eyes were gouged out. The victim is described as approximately six feet tall and was found wearing a blood-stained hooded jacket. In an effort to discover his identity, the police have been employing all investigative methods available, including forensics and dental impressions, but so far they've been unable to identify him." When closing his report, the anchor recounts one last detail. "To prevent easy identification, the man's fingerprints had been removed and his teeth had been extracted."

My first thought is that the victim could be Jake Trexler. The news report said that he was in his forties and was found wearing a hooded jacket. This partially matches Mr. Trexler's description. Aware that he's been running for his life for the past five months, I wouldn't be surprised if fate hadn't finally caught up with him. After all, he told me it was just a matter of time before the trackers captured and killed him.

I pick up my cell phone to call the NYPD. Hopefully, the information I know about Jake Trexler will assist them in identifying the victim. When I get through, I hear a voice say, "Sergeant O'Malley. May I help you?"

"I'm not completely sure, Sergeant, but I might have some information related to last night's murder in the Bronx."

"Who is this?"

"My name is Sean Carrol."

"Mr. Carrol, hold on for one minute while I connect you to Detective Parisi."

Within a couple of minutes, I hear a hoarse but gruff voice answer. "Detective Parisi."

"Detective, this is Sean Carrol."

"What do you want?"

"I heard about the murder that occurred in the Bronx last night, and I may have some information pertinent to the case."

"Look, Mr. Carrol, I've been up all night investigating this case and need to complete some paperwork. Can you come down to the precinct today?"

"Unfortunately, I'm flying to Kentucky on some important business."

He curtly asks, "Well, what do you have?"

"The man who was murdered may go by the name of Jake Trexler. Is the victim six feet tall and very muscular?"

"Yes, Mr. Carrol."

"Does his face display deep creases, and do his eyelids appear to be sagging slightly?"

"He has deep facial creases. Unfortunately, the fact that he had his eyes gouged out makes it impossible for us to determine whether his eyelids were sagging. Do you remember anything else about the victim, Mr. Carrol?"

"He had a tattoo on his left hand. It featured the words *Semper fi* inscribed over a small American flag."

"I'm glad you called, Mr. Carrol. Do you have any information about what the motive might have been?"

"A right-wing paramilitary group wanted Trexler dead. They're extremely dangerous. Right now, I can't provide any more information, because they have a proverbial gun to my head."

"Mr. Carrol, you've been very helpful, however, I'll need to speak with you as soon as possible concerning other relevant facts of the case. Give me your address and phone number."

After providing the requested information, I say, "I don't know when, or if, I can provide any further information Detective, but I do need you to forget my name for now. You've gotta understand that revealing my identity could be detrimental to some of my family members. Will you promise to keep my name out of the conversation?"

"Yeah, Mr. Carrol, I will."

"Goodbye, Detective."

When I hang up, the limousine pulls into the driveway. I see Wayne step out of the backseat. After opening the door, I greet him.

He grabs my bag, walks it to the limousine, and throws it into the trunk. After we climb into the backseat, I instruct the driver to take us to LaGuardia. While the car is pulling out of the driveway, I tell Wayne about my visit from the two C.I.A. agents. He appears to be a bit perplexed. I tell him, "I'm puzzled as to why a foreign government would band together with Deutsche Christen."

Sighing heavily, he says, "Sean, if a government is bold enough to secretly challenge the United States, then their leaders have a real disrespect for our military and disdain for the politicians who run our government. Besides, what military is powerful enough to challenge the United States?"

"The whole idea scares me, but the fact is that we have no information about who the foreign connection is, and what role they're playing in this rather bizarre affair."

At the airport, we collect our bags and hand our tickets to the sky cap. It's now 9:40 a.m., and our flight is scheduled to depart at 10:30. We hurry through security and quickly walk to our gate. While waiting, I tell Wayne about Mr. Trexler's murder and our discussion at the Immigration Museum. Wayne rolls his eyes and remarks, "This whole series of events is becoming more bizarre and frightening. The sheer viciousness of this group concerns me. What else are they capable of?"

"I really don't know, but they don't appear to have a conscience. If they feel threatened, I'm sure they'll resort to using any available means necessary to retaliate. What I do know is that my niece and nephew must be rescued and brought home safely. They're the only reason I'm playing along with this charade."

It's 10:15 when we begin boarding. After the plane takes off, we lean back in our seats for the hour-and-a-half trip. After arriving at the Greater Cincinnati Airport, we disembark the plane and head toward the entranceway. It's now 12:30. We have thirty minutes before meeting with the representative from Deutsche Christen.

Because of the heavy rain, we remain within the shelter of the entranceway. At 1:00 we push through the large glass doors and walk outside. I immediately spot Mr. Drury holding a black umbrella while standing next to a gray SUV that is parked at the curb. The driver jumps from the vehicle, grabs our bags, and deposits them in the hatchback. Mr. Drury then opens the rear door of the SUV, and he, Wayne, and I climb in. When we do, the driver starts the engine and heads in a northwesterly direction.

Approximately thirty minutes later, we arrive at the bank of what I presume to be the Ohio River. Waiting for us is a large white and red fifty foot long cabin cruiser. We walk toward the boat, climb a small metal ladder, and descend five feet to the deck. Mr. Drury directs me and Wayne to a cabin below deck, where we're tied up and blindfolded.

Within a few minutes, the boat departs from the riverbank. The powerful engine thunders while forcing a path through the surging waves. We're traveling, in what I believe to be a westerly direction. Along the way I wonder about the location of our ultimate destination. Although the trip has taken only an hour, it feels as though we've been traveling for eons. I'm curious about how much more time will pass before we finally arrive at the militia camp. Aside from being long and tedious, the trip has been extremely turbulent due to the powerful waves that batter the hull. Wayne, who's not used to traveling by boat, complains of nausea.

Once we arrive at our destination, his seasickness subsides. Within a few minutes, Dave Drury and a guard enter the cabin and untie the ropes. They guide us to the deck and assist us while we climb the ladder to the dock. After disembarking, we're escorted to the building where the interview will be staged. Mr. Drury opens what sounds like a tent flap that crackles loudly as we enter. Once inside, our blindfolds are removed. While perusing the interior of the building, I notice that a small buffet has been arranged on a rectangular table located in the center of the room. There are a variety of salads, sandwich meats, and rolls, plus an assortment of trappings for dressing the sandwiches. Dave Drury says, "Please have something to eat before the interview takes place." We both decline. Due to the long and tedious trip, we instead elect to pour ourselves some coffee. I continue to look around and notice that the windows of the building have been painted black and wonder what's being hidden from our view.

Once we've set up the lighting equipment and computers, Mr. Dietrich enters the building and greets us. Sensing my detestation for him, he avoids shaking my hand. I organize my questions, access my computer program, and check with Wayne to determine if he's ready. He gives me a thumbs-up. I then turn around to begin the interview and observe Dietrich pacing back and forth in front of the rectangular table. Impatient and nervous, he appears to be a bit on edge. In order to avoid any backlash, I tell myself that I'd better be mindful about the questions I ask.

Before we begin, Dietrich stops pacing and asks me, "Do you recall the parameters of the interview process?"

"Yes, I remember."

When we sit down, I anxiously pose a question. "Has the United States government been an impediment to the Deutsche Christen organization?"

He digests my question for a second and then leans forward in his chair. "They've been an impediment not only to Deutsche Christen, but also to the American people as a whole."

"In what ways have they been an impediment?"

After clasping his hands and placing them under his chin, he says, "The overwhelming regulations they've legislated continue to stymie the creation of jobs, thereby destroying the quality of people's lives. They persist in levying severe tax burdens on the population, further looting money from the hard-working middle class. Instead of investing in our country's security, they continue to create huge social programs by misappropriating funds for these behemoth funnels of waste. In essence, they've created a culture of dependency that has discouraged people from contributing to the growth and welfare of the country."

His description of wasteful government social programs and his preoccupation with military power makes me feel as though I'm listening to the words of a dictator, not a paramilitary leader. I ask, "What foreign government or governments do you believe incorporate the ideals of the perfect government—that is, one with limited regulations and devoid of bloated social programs?"

"That's an easy question, Mr. Carrol. There are two governments that meet that criterion: Russia and China." With glowing praise, he memorializes both Mao Tse-Tung and Stalin, as well as several subsequent leaders of both governments. This characterization shows his personality as not unlike those he is describing: a ruthless, dictatorial sociopath. After his summary, he begins to laugh uncontrollably while banging his hand hard against the table. As a result of his demonstration, food spills over from the table and onto the floor. Ignoring the mess, Dietrich continues laughing. Finally, after a couple of minutes, he stops laughing, regains his composure, and settles into a nearby chair.

I try to digest his behavior. I know I'm dealing with someone who is unpredictable and unstable, but his behavior only serves to reinforce my belief that he's demented.

While reflecting upon what Dietrich has just profiled, I'm aware that history contains well-documented evidence of the genocide committed by Mao and Stalin. Their attempts to systematically exterminate all political and cultural opposition resulted in millions of deaths. Now I believe I finally know the foreign connections to be Russia and China. What I don't know is how these governments correlate with the military plans of Deutsche Christen, and whether they'll support them, especially with equipment and manpower.

Continuing, I cautiously ask him, "Why do you view the Russian and Chinese governments as near perfect examples of balance and strength in governing their people and maintaining respect on the world stage? After all, the leaders of these countries oppress their populations and employ brutal tactics when dealing with dissenters. Gulags are utilized to imprison people, further constraining free speech and squelching growth and productivity. How can you condone the actions of this type of regime?"

"With their central government, they're capable of maintaining firm control over the social and political elements of their society. Without buffers of political push-back, they can institute positive changes to their policies without resistance. As a consequence, their society marches in lockstep with the principles established by their leaders."

Suddenly, the interview reverts to a discussion about the layers of government prevalent within the United States and how inefficient governing is in this so called democratic system. Dietrich attempts to stress the impediments facing any political progress within our system and the lack of expediency that hampers necessary positive change.

Continuing the interview, I raise questions about military strengths and weaknesses of Deutsche Christen and various international alliances throughout the world. The conversation with Dietrich suddenly becomes contentious when I question him about the reasons that Deutsche Christen is amassing huge supplies of weapons and ammunition.

Abruptly, Dietrich ends the interview without answering my question. He stands and starts walking toward the door.

I yell to him, "Now that I've completed the final interview, I'd like to take my niece and nephew home."

He turns, walks toward me, and looks me straight in the eyes and tells me, "They're not ready to leave."

"What do you mean they're not ready to leave? You promised me after the first interview that they would be permitted to return home after I conducted the second one."

"I'm very sorry, Mr. Carrol, but they'll have to remain in our camp a little longer."

"What purpose does it serve to keep them?"

"It serves *my* purpose."

"I took you at your word, Mr. Dietrich, but I guess your word isn't worth very much."

"So I've been told before."

"May I at least see them?"

"I'm afraid they're not at this facility, Mr. Carrol."

Carl Dietrich seems to enjoy tormenting people. I notice his smirk while he conveys the unpleasant news to me about my niece and nephew. He's apparently attempting to make me grovel. By this time, I'm seething with anger. Wishing I could strangle him provides me with an element of emotional relief. Unfortunately, the reality of such an action is impossible under the current circumstances.

When Dietrich leaves the room, Dave Drury blindfolds Wayne and me. He and a guard guide us out of the building and back to the boat. Directing us to one of the cabins below deck, we're tied up once again. The boat begins moving to open water for our trip back to the Greater Cincinnati Airport. Once we reach our destination, the blindfolds are removed, and we're untied. Mr. Drury escorts us to the deck, where we see the gray SUV parked at the end of the dock. Once our bags are loaded, the driver transports us to the airport, and we're dropped off at the main terminal.

Arriving at LaGuardia Airport, we're anxious to get home. We grab our bags and walk to the entranceway of the building to hail a cab. When I walk into my condominium, it's nearly 1:00 a.m. I think about calling my sister, but due to the time, I decide to wait until the morning to call her. Instead, I grab a beer from the fridge, settle on the living room couch, and speculate about the possibility of rescuing the children.

CHAPTER 9

# PLANNING A RESCUE

The next morning after showering, I descend the stairs feeling refreshed. I'd forgotten how a warm shower can make me feel so good. Yesterday's meeting with Carl Dietrich compromised my soul and severely depressed me. He's so morally corrupt, and manifestly capable of contaminating one's entire being. The hatred that I felt for Dietrich yesterday has only intensified.

After pouring a cup of coffee, I take a sip. Just then, the doorbell rings. I can hear Boynton barking, knowing that I'm here. I open the door and see Linda holding his leash while Boynton presses his nose against the glass door. When he catches a glimpse of me, he jumps up on the glass and begins scratching as though crazed. Once I open the door, he rushes in to greet me. I immediately bend down and pet him while he begins crying and licking my face. Linda laughs at the scene of Boynton's extraordinary singular affection.

When I straighten back up, Linda asks, "How did the interview go with Carl Dietrich?"

"It was stressful, just like before. But worst of all, he refused to release my niece and nephew."

"Carl Dietrich is such a bastard. He seems to thoroughly enjoy the pain he inflicts upon others. Considering the circumstances, what alternatives do you have for getting Amanda and Danny back?"

"I'm not quite sure, Linda. The only possibility of a rescue at this point, is the military mission that Agent Jardine informed my sister of. Other than that, I have no alternatives."

"All we can do right now, Sean, is hope and pray that the rescue mission is successful."

'You're right Linda."

"Sean, I've gotta go to the store to pick up some necessities. I'll talk to you later."

"Goodbye, Linda, and thank you."

Once she leaves, I grab my cell phone and dial Monica's number. I was supposed to call her after yesterday's interview, but I was worried about her reaction to the bad news. Besides, it was very late when I returned home. I'm aware that the news I'll share with my sister may crush her emotionally and deepen her depression.

After the phone rings a few times, I hear my brother-in-law's voice. "Hello?"

"Hi, Mike. It's Sean."

"We were hoping to hear from you last night."

"Besides being too late to call, I wasn't emotionally prepared to contact you with bad news. More important, I was very concerned about Monica's state of mind, and I didn't want to distress her any further with the discouraging news about the children. Unfortunately, Carl Dietrich lied to me once again."

"Sean, I don't hold you responsible for the kidnapping, but this whole ordeal is killing Monica. I know that a rescue mission is at hand, but Monica is hesitant to invest all of her hopes in the success of the mission. Right now, she's absolutely beside herself. Her days are spent crying. She sits on the couch all day and most of the night without moving or talking. She scares me. I'm afraid that she'll become seriously ill. Although I prepare meals for her, she pushes the food away. She's already lost over twelve pounds and is becoming weaker and more distant by the day. Her face is drawn, and her complexion has become very pale. I just don't know what to do."

"I'm sorry to hear about Monica's condition. Is there anything I can do to help?"

"I appreciate your offer, Sean, but I can't think of anything more that we can do at this point. I did get a prescription from her doctor to help her calm down. It seems to be working."

"In any event, Mike, the rescue mission to secure the children will hopefully be successful, and they'll return home safe."

"I hope so, Sean, because they're all we have. I don't know that Monica will survive if anything happens to them."

"I know, and I would never forgive myself if that happened. I have to go now, but I'll talk to you soon. Please give Monica a kiss for me."

"I will. Goodbye, Sean."

After hanging up, I rush upstairs to change. Boynton follows me and sits next to the bed while I get ready. Within twenty minutes, I'm on my way to the office. Traffic is a little heavy this morning, but the delay provides me with time to organize my thoughts regarding the article.

When I finally arrive at the office, I spot John Errins heading in my direction. At sixty-four years of age, he looks great. He's been a staple of the *New York International News* organization for over twenty-five years. Sporting short gray hair and wearing his customary black-rimmed glasses, along with his distinctive gray suspenders, he exemplifies the stereotypical newspaper editor, someone who exudes authority and requires respect. He motions for me to come into his office. After closing the door, he points at the couch and asks me to take a seat. "Sean, I don't know what's going on with this Deutsche Christen group, but I have to caution you. An F.B.I. agent by the name of Jardine contacted me. He's not happy about the article you recently wrote concerning Deutsche Christen. He cautioned me that he will not tolerate publication of anymore articles about Deutsche Christen. He told me that he'll shut down our paper if we persist in publishing articles about them."

I lean forward, look directly at John, and tell him, "You and I both know that Dietrich gave me no choice in the matter. If I don't cooperate, he'll harm Danny and Amanda. Did you explain this to Agent Jardine?"

"I did, but he didn't give a damn. He said that you're interfering with an investigation, and that the law will view your actions harshly."

I raise my voice slightly. "What kind of a jerk is this guy? We have two children being held hostage, and he's worried about a newspaper article?"

"Sean, just watch your step. Don't compromise yourself. This Jardine appears to mean business. Just so you know, we're going to publish your next article in spite of Agent Jardine's threat. If he attempts to shut down the paper, we'll make sure that every newspaper across the country carries a story about the insensitivity of the F.B.I. and the threats made by Agent Jardine."

"Thanks for the warning, and especially for your support. I have to get to my office to start writing the article about Deutsche Christen. By the way, John, I believe there's something sinister occurring between Deutsche Christen and two foreign governments. I don't have any specifics, but it appears that something significant is taking place."

"Sean, what are you talking about when you say sinister occurrences involving foreign governments?"

"I'm not completely sure, but these governments may be providing Deutsche Christen with some tangible support."

"What type of support?"

"I don't know yet, but whatever is taking place between these governments and Deutsche Christen could be disastrous for our country."

John looks at me in bewilderment. The frown on his face shows his confusion, something he rarely displays.

While standing in the doorway, I feel a bit frustrated and angry as a result of Jardine's threat. I tell John, "We can talk again later if you'd like. Right now, I really have to get started on the article. See you later."

I work all afternoon and into the night. At 9:15, my cell phone rings. When I pick it up, I hear my brother-in-law's distraught voice. Screaming through the phone, he frantically tells me that the mission to rescue the children was carried out this evening. "Sean, the special ops team was decimated after they became trapped within the perimeter of the entranceway to the camp. They got pinned down by machine gun fire and were then overrun by a massive number of militia. The death toll was very high. According to reports from the military, seventeen troops out of the twenty team members were killed. The three who survived were seriously wounded but luckily managed to escape. It was a blood bath. As a result, Amanda and Danny are still imprisoned within the camp. I'm so frightened and so disheartened about the possibility of rescuing my children."

"My God, Mike, I'm so sorry. The thought that the kids are still at the camp frightens the living hell out of me. Does Monica know about this?"

"Unfortunately, she received the phone call."

"How is she?"

"She's relapsed. After the news about the failure of the mission, all she does is sit on the couch staring blankly at the ceiling. Her body is completely still with her arms lying limp at her side. She's definitely more distressed than she was before."

"I wish there were something that I could do to help her!"

"I've already called the doctor and requested that he stop by to assess her condition. He promised to visit in the morning."

"I hope he can provide some relief, Mike."

After hanging up the phone, I sit back down at my desk and wonder how the children are. I'm sure that Dietrich will find some way of reciprocating for the unwelcome attack on his camp. I only hope that his actions aren't directed at the children. If he hurts them, I swear that I'll kill him. In spite of the distressing information about the rescue, I still have to finish the next article about Deutsche Christen. After working diligently for another hour, I lean back in my chair and put my hands behind my head. The article is finally finished. Knowing my direction before writing allowed me to complete it without being distracted by either emotion or anger. Satisfied with the quality of the article, I smile to myself.

After printing the article, I stand up, and walk to John's office. When I knock on the door, he waves for me to enter. I hand him the article and lean against his desk while he reads it. After handing it back to me, he says, "Sean, the article looks fine. There's no emotion, simply facts. Forward it for printing in tomorrow's paper."

After hurrying back to my office, I e-mail the article to Dietrich and then dial Stan's number. After several rings, he picks up.

"Hi, Stan."

"Sean, how are you?"

"I've seen better days. The reason I'm calling concerns my niece and nephew. If you have some time, I'd like to drive over and talk to you."

"Sounds pretty serious."

"It is. But, I know I can trust your judgment and advice."

"See you later."

As soon as I hang up the office phone, my cell phone rings. When I pick it up, I hear Carl Dietrich's voice. He tells me, "The article is acceptable for publication. Make sure it gets into tomorrow's edition." Before hanging up he threatens, "If anymore attempts are made to rescue the children, then I'll have no choice but to kill them."

Pleading, I ask "Please don't harm the children. It wasn't their decision to launch a rescue." The phone then goes dead. I immediately grab the article and forward it to the front desk specifying that it be printed in tomorrow's edition of the paper. Distressed about Dietrich's phone call and his threat to kill the children, I'm overcome by fear and helplessness concerning the children's imprisonment. I grab my briefcase, run down the front stairs, and head to the parking lot. After unlocking the doors, I climb into the driver's seat, start the engine, and take the thirty-five minute trip to Stan's. When I arrive, I rush to the front door and ring the bell.

Stan answers. "Come on in. I'll get you a beer."

"Do you have anything stronger?"

"I have a bottle of Dewar's. Is that all right?"

"That's fine, Stan. Just mix some club soda with the scotch."

We take our drinks in to the living room and sit on the two lounge chairs located in the front corner overlooking the street. Stan remarks, "You seem pretty uptight. What are you thinking about doing, Sean?"

"I'm not quite sure, but I've gotta find a way to rescue the kids. Unfortunately, the rescue plan developed by the military failed miserably. Most of the team members were killed. Needless to say, Dietrich has threatened to kill Amanda and Danny if another rescue attempt is made. He's a real bastard, and I don't believe he has any intention of releasing them."

"What alternatives do you have?"

I get up from the chair, walk to the front window, and turn toward Stan. "My alternatives are limited to none. At this point, however, I've got to find a solution. The only thing I can possibly do is hire an independent group of mercenaries."

"Sean, you could do that, but they'd be strangers, meaning that their qualifications and trustworthiness would be unknown. In addition, the cost of a mercenary team would most likely be prohibitive. You have to think long and hard about your options. After all, a rash decision could result in disaster, just like the recent attempt to rescue the kids by special ops. Let's sleep on it and revisit the subject tomorrow."

I sigh, knowing that the task of rescuing the children may be insurmountable. "You're right, Stan. I guess my hopes for a quick solution are just wishful thinking. I'm gonna head home and get a good night's sleep. Take care."

"I will. Good night, Sean."

I get in the car and drive home. After pulling into the driveway, I climb the stairs to the front door. I reach into the mailbox and grab the mail. It's mostly junk mail. I'm about to toss everything when I come to the last item. It's a letter from Colonel Gannon, my old special forces commander. I rip open the envelope and begin reading.

> I'm aware of the kidnapping of your niece and nephew. I know Carl Dietrich, having served with him for several years. He was one of the most despised officers in special forces. In fact, we were bitter enemies during our years of service. Nearly twenty years ago, we had an all-out brawl. During the fight, Dietrich pulled a gun and threatened to kill me. Thank God a few officers appeared and disarmed him. Currently, I'm serving at Eglin Air Force Base in Florida, as a special forces commander. If you require anything, please contact me.

His invitation gives me pause. I start to think about reorganizing our special forces team. To prepare for a rescue mission, however, we'd have to retrain under the guidance of someone like the colonel. The real question is, how many of our original team are deceased, disabled, or inaccessible? I have to think long and hard about the feasibility of creating a rescue mission with my old team. The logistics of such a mission will be monumental, without even considering the equipment and weapons requirements.

I continue to ruminate on the plan as I take Boynton for a walk, bring him back home, and feed him. My thoughts are suddenly interrupted by the phone. "Hi, Sean. It's Stan."

"Do you miss me that much?"

"Not really, but I had a thought regarding our conversation tonight. We might want to contact some of our old team to determine how many of them are able to participate in a rescue mission."

"It's ironic you're calling me about this. I just received a letter from Colonel Gannon telling me to contact him if I require anything. It gave me pause to speculate about the viability of reorganizing our old team. Do you believe it's possible to reorganize our special forces team and implement a successful rescue plan?"

"I'm not completely convinced that the mission could be successful, but your first step should be to contact the colonel. Explain the idea to him and ask what he thinks about reuniting our team and creating a rescue plan."

"It's certainly worth exploring. I'll call the colonel in the morning to discuss it. Once I speak to him, I'll call to give you his perspective."

"Great. I'll talk to you tomorrow, Sean."

I hang up the phone and turn on the news while Boynton is asleep on the couch. When a commercial comes on, I walk to the kitchen and pour a glass of merlot. After pouring the wine, I return to the living room and collapse on the couch. The news is full of violence, as usual. There's one disturbing story after another: a drive-by shooting in Bedford Stuyvesant, a holdup in Crown Heights, and a four-alarm fire in White Plains.

Immediately after, the story of Jake Trexler's murder investigation is broadcast. The reporter begins his interview of Detective Parisi by asking about the circumstances surrounding Mr. Trexler's murder. Without hesitation, Detective Parisi recounts the murder by saying, "The unspeakable torture that Trexler endured makes you wonder if the murderers are even human. They employed many sadistic techniques in his torture and murder."

Continuing, the reporter asks, "Can you provide any background about the victim?"

Responding, the detective says, "Mr. Trexler was affiliated with the Deutsche Christen organization, a violent paramilitary group, for over five years. We suspect their involvement. Disenchanted with the organization, Trexler left his position as a board member and disappeared. There's an ongoing investigation, and our investigative team is pulling out all stops to solve the case. Unfortunately, we've been unable to obtain any physical evidence linking the killers. I promise, that those responsible for Trexler's death will be apprehended and prosecuted."

The reporter thanks the detective, ends the interview, and goes to break.

I wonder to myself how the detective believes he can bring these guys to justice. Deutsche Christian has its own little country within a country, not to mention that they're armed to the teeth. In reality, a major military force would be required to deal with them. I think to myself, *Dietrich must be laughing his ass off at such an empty threat.*

## CHAPTER 10

# PUBLIC DISRUPTIONS

The next morning, I gaze through the kitchen window while planning my day. In a few minutes, I'll have to make a phone call to Colonel Gannon. While sipping coffee, I find my thoughts preoccupied with the welfare of Amanda and Danny. Not knowing their plight frightens the hell out of me. I'm worried that they're not being cleaned or fed—or worse, that they're being abused. I feel so helpless about my inability to secure their release. To make matters worse, the flurry of my emotions has drained all my energy, resulting in lethargy.

I grab my cell phone and dial Colonel Gannon. After several rings, the call goes to voice mail. I leave a message, hang up the phone, and walk into my office.

It occurs to me that I haven't spoken to my sister in at least a week. Instead of calling, I sit at my computer and Skype her. Within a couple of minutes, I see my brother-in-law's image. He appears disheveled. He's unshaven, and his hair is unkempt with strands sticking up in every direction. "Mike, how are you and Monica doing?"

"We're doing okay, Sean."

"Is Monica there?"

"Sean, she's lying down. She had a bad day yesterday. Her breathing was strained, and she went into a state of shock, causing her body to shake violently. I was so scared by the episode that I called 911 and her physician. After the EMTs left, the doctor prescribed a sedative to help her sleep. I'm sorry that I didn't call you, but my time was consumed with caring for her most of the day and night. I was so frightened that I didn't leave her side."

"I understand, Mike. There's no need to apologize. Has she been eating anything?"

"Not much, but she's trying."

"Would you have her call me when she has a minute?"

"I'll make sure of it, Sean."

"If you need anything, please let me know."

"Goodbye, Sean, and thank you."

Once I shut down the computer, the house phone rings. I pick up the receiver and can hear the colonel's voice. "Sean, it's Colonel Gannon."

"Hi, Colonel. Thanks for calling me back."

"I got your message, and I'm curious about what's happening with the kids."

"My niece and nephew are still being held by Deutsche Christen. Dietrich's refusing to release them in spite of his promises."

"You know how I feel about him. He's always been a stone-cold liar."

"The reason I called you, Colonel, is that Stan Monahan and I have been debating the feasibility of developing a plan for rescuing my niece and nephew. We want to contact some of the members of our special forces team to determine how many can participate. I'm hoping that you'll consider retraining and assisting us in acquiring the necessary weapons and equipment for the mission."

"Can you provide me with some specifics about this paramilitary group? I need to know information about their troop strength, weaponry, and facilities. In addition, we'll have to study the topography of the area surrounding their camp."

"Colonel, I can provide most of the information that you need. I have a folder that I received from a former board member of Deutsche Christen that provides an abundance of information about the physical makeup of the camp. We can also use Google Earth to check the topography, however, we may have to obtain infrared satellite images from a government satellite to determine the guard positions and general defenses."

"For now, forward me whatever information you've got."

"I'll e-mail it to you sometime this afternoon, Colonel."

"I'm not saying yes, Sean, but I'd like to digest what you've told me and review the information you'll be forwarding. I just need a couple of days to determine the feasibility of success associated with this type of mission. In addition, I'll have to obtain special permission from my base commander, who will need to approve the required training."

"That's fair enough. When you make a decision, give me a call."

"By the way Sean, I heard about the mission to rescue your niece and nephew. The feedback I received indicated that the special ops team wasn't completely prepared. Their training, as I understand, consisted of a single week of planning. Additionally, the tactics they employed didn't anticipate the perimeter defenses of the camp. As a result, they were nearly wiped out before they could even penetrate the main body of the camp."

"Colonel, I suspected that something was amiss with the rescue team's planning. I'm now concerned as to what Dietrich's next step will be. I'm only hoping that the children don't suffer any consequences as a result of the attempted rescue. By the way, do you know who's responsible for planning and organizing the mission? I'd really like to confront him to let him know how he's increased the threat against my niece and nephew."

"I don't know, Sean, but I'll attempt to get that information."

"In any event, I'll talk to you in a few days Colonel. Goodbye."

I take Boynton for a walk, and then return home. As we ascend the front stairs, I can hear the phone ringing. Rushing to open the door, I run inside, pick up the receiver, and hear Linda's distraught voice. She tells me, "All hell is breaking loose throughout the country. Major public and private transportation disruptions are occurring everywhere." Breathing heavily while gasping, she says, "Several railroad breakdowns have taken place on the D.C. Metro line and the New York subways. According to the authorities, the electrical systems have been compromised, and thousands of commuters are stranded, many in the middle of nowhere."

She adds, "Numerous explosions have occurred on major thoroughfares such as Routes 74, 80, 90, and 95 along the East Coast from Connecticut to Florida, and from the central plains west to California and north to Washington. Nearly one hundred people have been injured. As a result, all flights have been grounded nationally, and the airports have been closed until further notice. From what you've told me, Sean, this appears to be the work of Deutsche Christen."

"Definitely! Jake Trexler was emphatic about the violent actions to be initiated by this group. Now I see what they're capable of." I say goodbye to Linda, hang up the phone, and turn on the local news.

The reporter states, "Accounts of disruptions are pouring in from stranded commuters, police, and military sources throughout Chicago, New York, San Francisco, Atlanta, and St. Paul." While describing the massive upheaval, the news anchor appears clearly shaken. Locally, I can hear explosions occurring in nearby Manhattan with random gunfire in the background.

Continuing he says, "An announcement has been made by Congress declaring a national state of emergency. The military and the police have been directed to patrol areas throughout the country with special emphasis on major U.S. cities. In addition, martial law has been declared by all state governors, and a national curfew has been ordered by the president from the hours of 8:00 p.m. to 5:00 a.m. Panicked, heavily armed citizen groups are patrolling their neighborhoods, unaware of the potential threats facing them and their families. This ordeal is creating major chaos throughout the country."

He then describes local conditions. "Fifteen shootings have been reported to the authorities in Harlem, Manhattan, and Queens. Three of the victims have been critically wounded."

I think to myself, *There's no telling the lengths to which Deutsche Christian will go in an effort to disrupt and destroy the lives of American citizens. Creating fear and undermining the very fabric of U.S. governmental authority is a powerful weapon, one that could lead to complete anarchy.*

When looking through the front window, I notice several military vehicles passing by while patrolling the streets. The soldiers in the vehicles are armed with rifles and machine guns. It appears to be a very tense situation. I guess one could call it a powder keg: just one mistake, and everything will explode. In the midst of this chaos, I believe the members of Deutsche Christen are hoping for an overall breakdown of government authority. This would create the perfect opportunity for them to implement governmental change.

The explosive nature of these events is causing people to overreact. A couple of blocks away, I can hear gunfire. Screams permeate the air. The authorities are employing bullhorns to warn residents to remain in their homes for their own safety. Utter confusion has taken hold causing skirmishes between local residents and military patrols. In the background of the skirmishes, numerous military choppers are firing tear gas in an attempt to disperse rioters. Based upon what's occurring, I wonder whether civil commotion may be the ultimate result of the fear-mongering being promoted by the militia.

In view of what's occurring, I head up to my bedroom and open the sliding door to the clothes closet. I reach into my briefcase and extract a Beretta 84 Cheetah pistol. From the top shelf of the closet, I grab an ammo case and then walk over to the bed. While sitting on the edge of the bed, I place the case on my lap and remove a box of bullets. I load the magazine clip, head downstairs to the living room, and then walk into the kitchen. After opening the lower closet door next to the sink, I place the gun and ammo case in one of the kitchen pots. Storing them here will provide me with easy access and ensure a safe hiding place for the weapon.

The news is still on, with reports of continuing violence. According to the reporter, "Injuries have risen to over three hundred, and the death toll is now at ten."

I dial Linda's number; she immediately answers. "Linda, it's, Sean. Based upon what's occurring, it might be a good idea for you to stay here tonight. So many major disruptions are occurring that I'm concerned for your safety."

"I'll come over for a little while and then decide whether I should stay."

"Because of what's happening, I'm not sure that it's safe for you to walk over here alone. I'll meet you at your place and escort you. Maybe you should pack a change of clothes. Before I leave here, I'll prepare the guest bedroom in case you decide to stay."

"Sean, give me forty-five minutes to straighten up and get dressed. See you shortly."

## CHAPTER 11

# PREPARATION

After we return to my home, I get Linda settled in. I take her tote bag to the guest room and then head downstairs. When I get to the landing, I notice Boynton licking her face. His tail is wagging so fast that the living room lamp is in danger of being knocked off the end table. Linda takes a seat on the couch, and I head to the kitchen to pour us each a cup of coffee. Upon returning to the living room, I hand her a cup and take a seat next to her. Of course our discussion focuses on today's disruptions.

As I begin mentioning Deutsche Christen and describing their purpose for creating national chaos, the phone rings. I pick up the receiver and hear Colonel Gannon's voice. "Sean?"

"Yes, Colonel?"

"I assume that you've heard about the disruptions that are occurring throughout the country?"

"Yes, sir, I sure have. These disturbances are definitely the work of Deutsche Christen."

"How are you so positive?"

"Recently, I had a clandestine meeting with a man by the name of Jake Trexler. Because he'd previously been a board member of Deutsche Christen, he had privileged information about the group. He warned me about the militia's plans to attack and destroy multiple facilities throughout the United States. Some of the actions the organization was to carry out are what we are witnessing now: the disruption of transportation systems and the destruction of major thoroughfares throughout the country. There may be more events to come, but I can't be sure."

"Sean, I've been thinking about our discussion of the other day. Based upon not only the abduction but also today's events, we should develop a plan to rescue your niece and nephew. The base commander has okayed our mission. He's aware of your family circumstances and is providing us with extensive training facilities to ensure the success of the rescue. Next week, I'll be free for a few days and would like to visit with you and Stan. Together we'll take the necessary steps to create a plan that will ensure the success of the mission."

"When can you fly up to New York?"

"I'll catch a flight a week from this Monday and arrive at McGuire Air Force Base sometime around 11:00 a.m. After we finish our conversation, I'll reserve a seat on one of the C17A Globemaster transport jets."

"Do you need me to pick you up at the base?"

"That's not necessary. I'll just rent a car from the rental firm located next door to the base."

"When do you have to return?"

"I can only stay until Thursday, because there's a mandatory meeting of all base commanders on Friday. Those three days should provide us ample time to develop a plan for the mission."

"By the way, Colonel, you're welcome to stay in the guest room here at my condominium. You'll have a comfortable king-size bed and plenty of room for your personal belongings."

"That sounds great. It sure beats my current base accommodations. I look forward to seeing you and Stan. Goodbye, Sean. See you next week."

When I hang up the phone, Linda points a threatening finger at me and questions me about my conversation with the colonel. I tell her, "He's making a trip to New York to talk with Stan and me about developing a rescue plan." From her demeanor, I detect concern.

After throwing her hands in the air and waving her arms, she displays exasperation about the possibility of the rescue. She asks, "Why do you need to undertake such a dangerous mission?"

I raise my voice. "No one has been able to free the children, and I don't believe anyone will even attempt to. This leaves the entire matter in my hands. If anything happens to Amanda and Danny, I won't be able to forgive myself, especially if I don't make a concerted effort to rescue them."

"What about the welfare of your special forces buddies and their families? Don't you think that they should be considered?"

"Linda, you have to understand. We're brothers. What happens to one happens to all. We swore our allegiance to each other when our unit was initially organized. If something were to happen to one of my team members, I'd be obligated to assist him."

"I'm just so worried. You haven't served in the military in over twenty years, not to mention the fact that you've gotten older."

"If this is the only chance we have to save the kids, then I have to try, no matter what the odds are."

She begins to cry.

I tell her, "Unquestionably, the mission will be dangerous. Understanding the militia's defenses, and our ability to operate covertly will determine the success or failure of the rescue."

After I assure her that our training and plans will support the success of the mission and the safety of our team, she reluctantly accepts my explanation. I believe she understands my need to rescue the children and the futility of her objection. I reach for her hand, caressing it between my palms. She kisses my cheek and then embraces me, squeezing tightly while resting her head on my shoulder. "You know, Sean, I've always cared for you—more than you may ever know. If anything ever happens to you, I'll be devastated."

"Nothing is going to happen to me. We're going to take all of the necessary steps to refresh our military skills and develop a comprehensive plan for the rescue. In addition, all precautions will be taken to ensure the safety of our team and the children."

"I understand. However, you've gotta know I'll be a nervous wreck, wondering where you are and what you're facing during the mission."

"Linda, you realize I have no other options. What matters most is the welfare of those two children. After all, they've been forced into a dangerous situation—something they didn't create. At this point, I hope that you and I can agree to disagree. Please understand, and trust in me."

After comforting Linda, I make what I hope will be a quick phone call to Stan. "Hi, Stan. It's Sean."

"What's up?"

"I just want to let you know that Colonel Gannon will be traveling to New York. He wants to talk with both of us about planning a mission to rescue Amanda and Danny. He'll be arriving a week from this Monday and staying until Thursday. Are you able to carve out a few days next week so that we can develop a plan for the mission?"

"No problem. I'll see you next Monday. In the meantime, I'll make arrangements to take a few days off from work."

I hang up the phone and decide to make dinner. While Linda prepares the salad, I grill burgers outside. After everything is prepared, we sit at the kitchen island and eat while discussing the disruptions caused by Deutsche Christen, and the negative effects they may have not only on the city, but the country. Linda turns on the kitchen television and tunes in the news to get a sense about tensions and violence taking place in the city.

The reporter states, "Shootings and riots continue throughout the five boroughs, stretching police resources to the brink. Overall, more than ten people have lost their lives, and over one hundred and twenty are injured. Several residential complexes were set on fire, destroying nearly three hundred apartment units. In spite of the intervention of National Guard units to quell the mayhem, violence continues."

We finish our meal and clean up while sipping our wine. After putting away the dishes, Linda wanders into the living room, picks up the remote control, and turns on the news. Obviously concerned about the disruptions, she says, "I'm going to watch the news and decide whether I should go home or stay."

The news reporter says, "Many disruptions have subsided, but there are still large pockets of unrest throughout the city."

Concerned about the dangers of the ongoing disruptions, Linda decides to stay. Hopefully, tomorrow will bring some peace and calm to the area.

## CHAPTER 12

# BACK TOGETHER

I descend to the living room landing and bend down to pet Boynton. Looking around, I don't see Linda and wonder where she is. It's now 9:15 a.m. I'd better call her at home to ensure that she's okay. When I call, Linda immediately answers the phone. I say hello and ask, "Why didn't you wake me when you left?"

"I didn't want to disturb you. You were in such a deep sleep. Knowing how much stress you've been under lately, I didn't want to interrupt your rest."

"When I awoke, I was concerned about you, worried that something may have happened."

"I'm fine, Sean. There's nothing to worry about."

"I'll talk to you later, Linda."

After hanging up the phone, I make a pot of coffee and feed Boynton. I gaze through the living room window and observe the dark gray sky stretching well beyond my view. Regrettably, the sky and the accompanying rain display no sign of dissipating, promising an all-day event.

I grab my jacket, hook Boynton's leash, and jog across the street to the open lot. I unhook his leash and watch as he runs into the open field, seeking refuge behind a hedgerow. Within a few minutes, he charges back, thoroughly soaked from the rain.

After drying and petting him, I head into the kitchen and pour a cup of coffee. I then walk into the living room and flip on radio news. Under discussion are the public transportation and highway disruptions that recently occurred. A panel of three people a senator, a congressman, and a general are engaged in a heated exchange that is being moderated by the news anchor. The anchorman asks the panel, "Who was responsible for the recent attacks within the country?"

The general immediately responds, "The disruptions were caused by an organization by the name of Deutsche Christen. This group is a violent militia that is attempting to undermine the U.S. government."

The senator interrupts. "They aren't an undermining factor at all, but rather a local militia group made up of ex-military."

Irate at the senator's assertion, the general references a C.I.A. report. "The unification of numerous paramilitary organizations throughout the country has been verified. They have developed a standing army of over 1.1 million and are creating camps throughout the United States, meant to counterbalance the U.S. military. Senator, based upon this report, how can you dispute the intent of this group and refer to them as a local militia?"

The panel members begin shouting over one another in a desperate attempt to be heard. Unfortunately, all of the clamor is distorting the message. I think, *My God, someone has to reel these people in, because they're making absolutely no sense.* Needless to say, they're wasting the listeners' time. Disillusioned, I turn off the radio and pour another cup of coffee.

It's now 10:00. Stan will be arriving in two hours, so I decide to walk into the living room and grab the envelope that Jake Trexler provided. I know how invaluable it will be when planning our mission. Most important among the documents are the topography maps, especially since we'll determine our tactics based upon the makeup of the surrounding terrain.

After grabbing paper and pencils, I place the documents on the dining room table so that we'll be ready to begin planning once Stan and the colonel arrive. Just then, the phone rings. When I answer, a voice asks, "Is this Mr. Carrol?"

"Yes."

"This is Dean Balstral. I was speaking to Colonel Gannon regarding your plans to undertake a rescue mission to free your niece and nephew."

"Mr. Balstral, we don't have any plans as of yet. By the way, who are you and why are you calling me?"

"I'm about to get to that. Colonel Gannon is a very good friend of mine. He informed me that you'll be needing some military hardware. Being a weapons merchant, I'll be able to provide whatever you require. Due to the circumstances surrounding your mission, I'll make sure that you receive the most sophisticated weapons available at a nominal cost."

"That's very generous of you, Mr. Balstral. Don't take this the wrong way, but I've never met you, so quite frankly don't know whether I can trust you."

"When the colonel arrives, you can question him about me. We've been friends for over twenty-five years. All of our dealings have been above board, and we've never betrayed each other."

"I'll talk to him when he arrives. How can we get in touch with you, Mr. Balstral?"

"No need. In three days I'll call you. Goodbye, Mr. Carrol."

I'm disconcerted about the call and don't understand why Colonel Gannon is conveying information about our future mission to a stranger. If Carl Dietrich becomes aware of our plan, there'll be hell to pay. In addition, the children are still imprisoned at the Wheeling camp. Their welfare could be in serious jeopardy.

It's 12:00 when the doorbell rings. I rush to answer. Boynton sits while I move to open the front door. Recognizing Stan, he becomes very excited and jumps up on the glass, trying to reach him. After I open the door, he waits for Stan to enter. Once he's inside, Boynton jumps up on his chest and begins licking his face. He pets Boynton and then heads into the kitchen.

After Stan takes a seat at the kitchen island, I grab a cup, fill it with coffee, and hand it to him. Stan sips the coffee and asks, "Have you heard anything about the kids?"

"There hasn't been any news concerning them for over a week. I did, however, speak to my brother-in-law the other day. He told me that Monica is having a difficult time. She's being sedated by her doctor in order to calm her."

"That damn Dietrich should be shoved off of a mountaintop. He's a real bastard."

"All I know is that I need to get the kids back and make sure that my sister is okay."

He nods. "You're absolutely right."

Just then the doorbell rings. I open the door to see the colonel in full military dress blues. After shaking his hand, I reach for the small duffel bag that's resting on the door saddle of the entranceway. Based upon my memory of the colonel, I'm amazed that he hasn't changed much. Standing at six feet one inch tall, with short cropped blond and gray hair and a thin muscular physique, he's the poster child for our modern-day military. When he enters, the colonel greets Boynton first and then waves to Stan.

"Let me take your bag Colonel. I'll bring it up to the room. Everything is ready for you. Do you want to freshen up a little? I know it's been a long morning for you."

In a calm, gravelly voice, he says, "Just direct me to the bathroom."

"It's up the stairs and to your left."

When the colonel comes back downstairs, he finds us in the kitchen. I offer him a cup of coffee. "No thanks, Sean. I've had more than my share today. Maybe we should just get to work."

"That's fine, Colonel, but I have a question for you. I received a phone call from a man by the name of Dean Balstral. He was inquiring about our mission and what weapons hardware we'll require for the rescue. Who is this guy?"

"I've known Dean for over twenty-five years. He's provided me with some very valuable information about the military capabilities of some of our enemies. During Desert Storm for instance, he knew exactly what firepower the Iraqis had prior to our invasion. He was even aware that the Iraqi MiGs had been buried in the desert outside of Baghdad."

"That's fine, but to be frank with you, I was very upset and worried after he called. My main concern is the welfare of my niece and nephew. If word of a potential rescue mission were ever to be revealed to Dietrich, there's no telling what he'd do to the children."

The colonel nods. "I understand, Sean. Don't worry—Dean is a trusted friend. He won't betray our confidence."

"Not knowing, Dean Balstral, I can't comment on his character, but I trust you and respect your judgment."

We begin to talk about the feasibility of success of the rescue. Not knowing anything about the defenses of the camp, much less the number of militia, we brainstorm about what means should be employed to obtain this information. Going in blind will result in sure fire failure. Planning, as we've been trained to do, is the only way in which we can operate.

A major challenge we face is determining a means of acquiring the layout of the Wheeling camp. After discussing several possibilities, we finally agree that Colonel Gannon will contact General Henry Stanton, a longtime friend. The general is third in command at the National Reconnaissance Office (NRO) of the Pentagon in Arlington, Virginia. The NRO is responsible for the design, construction, and operation of all of the U.S. government's spy satellites. In addition, this department is critical to providing imagery, measurements, and intelligence to other government agencies.

In cooperation with the NRO, we'll be able to employ satellites to obtain exact information about roads, structures, and movement of military equipment within the camp. More important, we'll be able to secure specifics about the quality of security along the periphery of the camp and the immediate area within. This is critical, because our planning will be focused on the number of guards posted in and around the camp, and the weapons they have at their disposal. The varying distances between each guard post will also help us pinpoint the most vulnerable zones for entry and attack.

We work diligently for nearly three days to develop a plan. By Thursday, we've created a prototype that will permit us entry to the camp, allow us to complete our mission, and ensure the safe return of the children. Critical to the mission is the insertion of our team into the camp and our movement within. We determine that our team will split into two units, inspecting the interior grounds from east to west. The idea is to work our way to the center of the camp while searching each structure for any sign of the children. Completing our mission without detection is our main challenge.

On Thursday morning, Colonel Gannon rises at 5:00. After a

one-hour drive back to McGuire Air Force Base, he'll secure a flight to Eglin AFB. Before he departs, we have a cup of coffee and some breakfast. Our conversation focuses on the training we'll undergo. We've determined that a solid month of intensive special forces fitness and weapons training will be required. This is the minimum time needed to condition the team, recertify us as weapons experts, perfect our knowledge and training for, and implementation of the rescue plan. I know that my family will be impatient for the rescue, however, the mission's success is most important. Needless to say, I'm uncomfortable about the time delay, but I need to ensure the safe rescue of the children.

When we finish breakfast, the phone rings. I pick up the receiver and recognize Dean Balstral's voice. "Good morning, Mr. Carrol."

"Good morning, Mr. Balstral."

"Is the colonel still there?"

"Yes, he's right here." I turn to the colonel. "Dean Balstral is on the line."

Colonel Gannon takes the phone and puts it on speaker. "Good morning, Dean."

"Colonel, did you develop the plans for the rescue mission?"

"We did, but the mission can't be carried out for at least a month."

"Have you explained to Mr. Carrol who I am?"

"Yes, but I believe your call to him was a bit premature and a little insensitive."

"Sorry, Colonel. I thought he might want some reassurance that there are people out here who are concerned about his niece and nephew, and who are willing to help."

"Next time, be a little more empathetic."

"I'll make sure of it."

The colonel hangs up the phone and sips the last of his coffee. He extends his hand to me and says, "I'll be in touch within the next couple of days."

I walk him to the front door and thank him for his assistance. I tell him, "Having your support means a lot to me. The next few steps will be critical to the success of our mission."

"They definitely will, Sean."

I watch as the colonel pulls his rental car out of the driveway and heads back to McGuire AFB. I'm grateful to have his support, and I hope and pray that our mission is successful.

## CHAPTER 13

# THE TEAM REUNITES

A few days later, on Saturday afternoon, the colonel calls. "Hi, Sean. I'm calling to let you know that the arrangements have been made for the training program."

"That's great news, Colonel."

"Have you and Stan contacted the team?"

"We've been in touch with everyone. The entire team, with the exception of Ray Wharton, has agreed to participate in the mission. Unfortunately, Ray had a stroke last year and is now confined to a wheelchair. When I spoke to him, he was upset that he couldn't participate in some way. Ray explained that he has no feeling on the left side of his body, and I noticed that his speech was slurred."

"That's awful. Ray's a great guy and an outstanding soldier. We'll really miss him. At least you have sixteen of your team available to participate. In addition, I have two outstanding candidates from my special forces team here at Eglin who have volunteered. This force will be adequate to accomplish what we need. The training program is set to begin next Thursday and will continue for the entire month of June. As we discussed, fitness and weapons training will be our main focus. Everything will be done in coordination with our mission plan."

"Thanks for the information and your help, Colonel."

"I'll contact Dean Balstral to acquire the necessary equipment and weapons. I'll make sure that everything is in place by next Thursday."

"Great Colonel. In the meantime, I'm going to visit my sister in New Jersey to let her know about our plan. I'm concerned about her mental and physical state, but I believe that my visit may give her some hope that the children will be home soon."

"I pray that she's okay, Sean."

"Thanks, Colonel."

I then call Stan and leave a message, asking that he call me. When I hang up, Boynton begins barking for me to let him in. He's panting heavily. When I open the door, he rushes to his water bowl and nearly inhales its entire content.

I decide to call the members of my team to advise them of the arrangements for training. After an hour, I've spoken to or left messages for everyone.

About thirty minutes later, Stan calls. I tell him about the training schedule.

Great Sean, "I can't wait to see everyone." We then make arrangements to go to the airport together early Thursday morning.

After hanging up the phone, I take out a steak for dinner. I turn on the outdoor grill and then make a salad while the steak cooks. Upon realizing I haven't seen Linda for at least a week, I call her and ask if she'd like to come over for dinner. Unfortunately, she tells me that she's meeting with a friend for a shopping trip at the local mall. She promises that she'll call me tomorrow. I'm disappointed, but I know I'll see her soon.

While I grill the steak, I begin making plans in my head. I'll need to ask Linda to watch Boynton while I'm away, and I'll have to contact John Errins to arrange for a leave of absence from the paper. After dinner, I'll call John to make the arrangements. When I speak to Linda tomorrow, I'll ask her to watch Boynton.

Once dinner is ready, I take my plate into the living room and turn on the news. Judging from the news reports, it seems like the only good thing that occurred today was that the Yankees beat the Red Sox in Fenway Park by a score of ten to two.

The next news story piques my interest. The reporter states, "Explosions along the Appalachian and Ohio railway in West Virginia have caused the derailment of an SD90 engine and several tank cars. Two of the tankers were carrying chlorine gas. As a result of the explosion, the tankers were ripped open, allowing the gas to escape and threaten the safety of several nearby residential subdivisions. The authorities believe the incident to be of a suspicious origin."

While thinking about the circumstances of the incident, I wonder if Deutsche Christen isn't somehow involved. After all, the explosion happened right in their backyard. Thank God only a few residents were affected and that the fumes didn't overtake any more people. The gas is deadly and could have suffocated everyone within the proximity of the leak. If the authorities hadn't interceded, a major catastrophe could have occurred.

## CHAPTER 14

# UNIFICATION

When Thursday finally arrives, I'm so jumpy that I spill my morning coffee all over the countertop. I grab some paper towels to sop it up, and I take a few deep breaths in an attempt to calm myself. It's now 5:00, and Stan should be arriving shortly. I can feel the pounding of my heart. I'm both nervous and excited. After all, it's been years since I've done any special forces training, let alone gone on a life-or-death mission. What if it doesn't go well? What if we fail? How will I face my sister? How will I face myself? I push these thoughts out of my head. I've got to stay positive. Any success of this mission will be largely dependent upon maintaining confidence.

At 5:15 the limousine pulls into the driveway. I grab my bags, jump into the backseat, and greet Stan. We arrive at Kennedy and get through security by 6:30. Our flight is scheduled to leave at 7:00.

After landing, Stan and I secure our bags. We immediately head to the entranceway and flag down a car to transport us to Eglin Air Force Base. The trip takes ten minutes. When we arrive at the base a marine

*Conflux*

sergeant and a corporal approach our car. The sergeant leans in the driver's side window, requests our names, and checks the manifest to verify our authorization to be admitted into the base. After confirming our identity, he orders the corporal to drive us to our quarters.

The corporal drives us to the Poquito Bayou housing development. We travel a few blocks to Chinquapia Drive and then pull into the driveway of a two-story duplex. Our driver informs us that our quarters are on the right. We exit the car and walk over to the front porch where I take in the neighborhood. Rows of identical houses, like matchboxes, are plopped on unimpressive square patches of lawn. Every house is the same dull gray color. I think to myself how a simple paint job and some minor landscaping would improve the drab appearance of the neighborhood.

I ask the driver, "Have any other team members arrived yet?"

"Yes, two of your team arrived last night. They're staying at one of the housing units not far from here."

After claiming the two rear bedrooms, Stan and I begin unpacking. When we finish, the doorbell rings. I rush to open the door and am surprised to see Colonel Gannon and Bo Carton standing at the entranceway. Bo rushes in and grabs me, wrapping his huge arms around my body and crushing me in a bear hug. He's a very powerful black man, standing at six feet five inches and weighing nearly 250 pounds. I notice that he still has that infectious smile that lights up a room whenever he enters. After recovering from Bo's enthusiastic greeting, I reach to shake the colonel's hand. Just then, Stan walks from the bedroom, greets the colonel, and embraces Bo in a man hug, saying, "It's great to see you, buddy. Too many years have passed since we've been together."

"You're right, brother."

We all take a seat in the living room and begin reminiscing about the team and our experiences together. I ask Bo, "Do you remember the night we were attacked by a large contingent of Taliban fighters near Kholm, in Afghanistan?"

Bo nods. "Yeah, that was one hell of a scary night. I recall that the Taliban relentlessly pounded our position. It felt as though the heavens were collapsing all around us."

I say, "We're lucky to have survived. Unfortunately, we lost Sam Weaver."

Stan responds, "We're lucky not to have lost our entire team. Given the huge numbers of Taliban fighters involved in the battle, this could have been a bloodbath for us."

Our conversation drifts to family issues and ordeals experienced over the years. Bo lost his son to a drive-by shooting. In spite of his trauma, he organized a boxing club and gymnastics team at the local YMCA. In cooperation with several other adults, including two high school coaches, they were able to train and nurture young boys—and more important, keep them off of the streets and away from the gangs.

I tell him, "I couldn't imagine losing a child. However, you created something positive out of a tragedy, Bo. Most people would have curled up in a dark emotional corner, avoiding any further contact or involvement with life. You've got the type of stuff heroes are made of."

"I'm really not a hero, but our program has been very successful. As a result of our efforts, several other nearby towns have begun similar programs. Ours was the thought of one man, however, its success is the result of many individuals who have brought their talents and ideas together to help our young people."

When we finish our conversation, the colonel informs us that our training gear and uniforms are in the garage. Each backpack is marked with one of our names. He states, "Your training will begin tomorrow at 6:00 a.m."

It's mid-afternoon when Charlie Davis and Duane Weathers arrive. I shake their hands but can hardly believe how Charlie has aged. He features a short gray beard, deep creases in his face, and a receded hairline that makes him appear almost bald. Although I'm concerned about his appearance, I know of Charlie's determination from our earlier training, so I'm confident he'll be just fine. He was one of the best marksmen in special forces, having won two all-forces shooting contests.

Duane, on the other hand, looks great. He's maintained his muscular six foot three inch, 220-pound frame. He's the perfect image of fitness and health. His skills at hand-to-hand combat were formidable, matching those of the best fighters on all special forces teams.

Stan and I assist them by carrying their suitcases to the remaining two upstairs bedrooms. After they're settled in, we all decide to take a walk around the complex to seek out more of our team. We head next door and find four team members settling in. After exchanging greetings with everyone, we return to our quarters and organize the remainder of our belongings.

At 3:00, I hear a loud knock at the door. I open it and see Colonel Gannon. "Hi, Colonel. I'm a little shocked that you're wearing civilian clothes. I've always seen you in a military uniform."

"Every once in a while, I let down my hair and relax. That's why I'm here. I've come to invite the entire team to a barbecue at the officers' club. A celebration on your last night of freedom seems in order. I rounded up a couple of vehicles to transport everyone. Can you gather the team and meet out front?"

"Absolutely, Colonel."

When we arrive at the officers' club, there's a large crowd of people entering. We rush inside for the reunion. Although our gathering is a somber occasion, it's still great that we're together. When we enter, I *see* a large table located in the far left corner of the hall. We hurry to claim our seats, anxious to exchange information concerning the last twenty years of our collective lives.

Most of our team has been employed by the government, however, several began start-up businesses, while others entered the workforce as employees of large corporate operations.

While Stan and I are talking, someone taps me on the shoulder. When I turn, two young special forces officers salute and then greet us. One introduces himself as Lieutenant Grant Hisan, and the other is Lieutenant Joe Harvey. Stan and I stand to shake their hands. Lieutenant Hisan informs me, "Lieutenant Harvey and I will be participating in the rescue mission for your niece and nephew."

"I want to thank both of you. My family and I greatly appreciate your sacrifice."

Lieutenant Harvey responds, "We're happy to help in any way we possibly can, especially on a mission like this." I thank them again. They salute, shake our hands, and walk away.

When 11:00 p.m. rolls around, we begin boarding the vehicles in order to get back to the housing facilities. All of us know that 5:00 a.m. will arrive soon enough, and we have to be ready for our training by 6:00. Understanding that the first few of days of training will be intense, we must make sure that we adhere to an early bedtime ritual.

The next morning, we begin our training with calisthenics, long-distance running, wall climbing, and weapons fire. This first day of training is sobering to most of us. Feeling the severe pain, I find my memory transported back to our initial special forces basic training. I was younger then. No matter, the pain seems to be just as intense. Leg cramps, shortness of breath, and muscle pain resulting from repetitive exercises such as push-ups, chin-ups, and jogging have caused several of my team members to nearly collapse. Thank God for modern-day painkillers such as Advil and Tylenol. Without them, our journey would be almost impossible. The training is intensive and harsh, and it saps all of my strength and stretches my muscles well beyond their limits. Needless to say, collapsing into my bed is the guidepost of my day.

Despite our ages, a week later we're all adapting while tolerating the pain and stress. Our stamina is also increasing, with strength and agility improving daily. Knowing the importance of our mission, everyone performs beyond expectations, dedicated to our ultimate goal.

Concerned about my sister, I make a phone call to her. "She immediately picks up the receiver. "Hello?"

"Monica, it's Sean. How are you?"

"I'm a bit tired, but I feel much better."

"We're completing our third week of training. It won't be long before we undertake our mission."

"Sean, I'm excited but frightened about the potential consequences of the mission. I'm worried for the children, but your welfare is critical to me as well. In view of the failure of the initial military rescue, the prospects of a successful rescue mission seems almost too good to be true. I keep picturing the children at home with us, but I don't feel confident in the mission's success."

"Monica, try to be positive. We'll be successful. Don't you worry."

"I'll try, Sean."

"By the way, Monica, I find it strange that I haven't received any e-mails or texts from Mr. White concerning another interview. By now, I should have received some form of notification from him. At this point,

I wonder what Dietrich's motivation is, and why he finds it necessary to continue the imprisonment of the kids."

"There could be any number of reasons why, but it seems he always has an angle for his behavior."

"I guess you're right, but I'll continue to check my phone messages and e-mails. Right now, I've gotta go, Monica. Say hi to Mike for me."

Now that the other soldiers and I have completed our third week of training, the colonel informs us that we'll be spending our last week rehearsing for the rescue. He tells us, "We received the satellite images from the National Reconnaissance Office. They provide detailed military information about exterior and interior security for the Wheeling camp. Several vulnerable areas on the perimeter of the camp will allow for easier access when attempting entry."

I say to the colonel, "The perimeter of the camp appears to grant us easy access. Are there any difficulties within other areas?"

"Assessment of the interior of the camp reveals impediments that may hinder our progress. Specifically, a series of barbed-wire fences, along with staggered rows of gun turrets and machine gun nests are positioned within the overgrowth of the camp periphery. The irregular positioning of the weapons posts will make it difficult for our team to avoid enemy fire. We'll have to carefully plan the speed of our entry and determine how best to overtake the various installations."

Having created a physical model of the periphery of the Wheeling camp, we practice maneuvers for nighttime entry. Utilizing night vision goggles, we coordinate precise entry, search, and exit plans. By practicing our tactics over and over, we become a well-oiled machine capable of unified movement.

Colonel Gannon is allowing the team two days of rest and relaxation before we meet at the Greater Cincinnati Airport. We'll gather there and be flown by a CH-47 Chinook helicopter that has been optimized for reduced noise. We'll land just two miles west of the Wheeling camp. Accompanying us will be an Apache attack helicopter, which has been deployed to ensure the safety of the team and the success of the uncertain mission.

With the end of June approaching, we're required to morph from training to active coordination of our entry plans. Thanks to our intense training, physical preparation, and arms proficiency, we're ready for our mission. In addition, we've all been recertified as weapons experts by special forces training officers. Now we must undertake the mission.

# CHAPTER 15

# MISSION

After landing at the Greater Cincinnati Airport, I disembark the American Airlines passenger jet and head straight to gate 28 at the end of concourse B, where we've been granted special permission to use a small landing area for our mission. The choice of a public airport as our source point, will enable us to camouflage our mission. Our enemies won't suspect that our military operation will emanate from a public locale. Here the team gathers to board the waiting Chinook helicopter. Once on board, we'll change into our battle fatigues. Based upon our assignments, our weapons and equipment have already been sorted for each member of the team.

Each of us will holster an MK23 handgun with a suppressor. Four M240 Bravo fully automatic light machine guns, and ten FN Scar17 CQCs with grenade launchers have been distributed, along with wire cutters, an abundance of ammunition, and five .338 Recon sniper rifles. The mission will be taking place after dark, so we'll all carry night vision goggles.

As 1900 hours approaches, we begin our countdown to takeoff. At 1915 hours we are on our way. The accompanying AH-64 Apache Longbow helicopter is equipped with the most sophisticated weapons and radar systems available. Newly fitted, the Apache employs the Hydra rocket system plus two thirty-millimeter chain guns, providing us with an added layer of security.

We begin to organize our equipment and review our plans during the one-hour flight. Colonel Gannon tells us, "Sean and Stan will be on point to take out the guards who protect the western camp perimeter. Lieutenant Hisan and I will handle things on the eastern end. The remainder of the team will gather on the beach and wait for us to return. After completing the first phase of the mission, we'll implement our plan for penetrating the camp security."

When we land in the open field, located approximately two miles west of our target, the rear cargo bay door opens. We hurry to gather our equipment and weapons. After organizing everything, we extract two SOC-R river boats equipped with two M240B machine guns each. Powered by two Mercury Opti-Max JP engines, these boats can almost fly. In addition, they're operation is nearly silent.

After we load our equipment, we carry the boats to the shore of the Ohio River, located approximately eight hundred feet away. The thick overgrowth surrounding us provides much-needed camouflage, however, it slows our progress to the river bank. In spite of the terrain, the thin shoreline with its hard, rocky surface serves as the perfect pad for launching our boats. We lower them, climb in, and secure our assigned equipment and weapons.

It's now 2030 hours and we're ready. The engines are started while we push off from shore. Silently, we travel down river, maintaining focus on our destination while clasping our weapons in case of any unexpected encounters. Our landing target is one thousand yards west of the camp. After shutting down the engines, we coast into the riverbank, where Rich Mendez and Bo Carton jump from the boats and grab the ropes to guide them to shore. The remainder of the team then climbs out, lifts the boats, and carries them into the brush.

After camouflaging the boats in the thick overgrowth, we head east toward the Wheeling camp. When we approach the camp's perimeter, Stan and I move south through the mud paddies and heavy grassy overgrowth in order to dispose of the first guard, located five hundred feet away at the western corner of the camp. In turn, Colonel Gannon and Lieutenant Hisan head southeast in order to eliminate a second guard, positioned at the eastern corner of the camp near the riverbank.

While moving slowly toward the first guard's position, Stan circles behind the guard in order to surprise him. When he's within striking distance, Stan charges and forces his arm around the guard's neck. The guard gasps and then collapses after his larynx has been crushed. We deposit his body in the grassy overgrowth just within the camp perimeter and then hurry back to the edge of the river bank. Kneeling in a circle with the others, we await the return of Colonel Gannon and Lieutenant Hisan. Within a couple of minutes, they rush toward us.

We continue kneeling and review our tactics. Our plan is to split into two teams of seven each. Harrison and Davis will remain behind at the edge of the riverbank to protect our rear flank. They're each armed with a grenade launcher and a machine gun. Our immediate challenge will be to clear out the gun turrets and machine gun nests located along the interior perimeter of the camp. Once these defenses are cleared, Colonel Gannon will lead his team east and then south while my team travels west and then south. After taking our positions, we'll slowly move toward the center of the camp, creating a pincer maneuver. Hopefully, our tactics will result in a quick rescue of the children.

Bo Carton and I separate from our team and quietly move toward the first machine gun nest, located just within the perimeter of the camp. Colonel Gannon and Lieutenant Hisan move east in order to eliminate a machine gun nest located in the deep brush of the entryway. Holding fast, the remainder of the team hugs the camp periphery, awaiting our signal to advance. We slowly approach the machine gun nest and notice that it's empty. Relieved, we move on to our next target.

After penetrating deeper into the camp, we spot a gun turret. Two guards are standing atop the platform with their backs to our position, unable to see us. One of them is smoking a cigarette while the other is animatedly motioning with his hands and talking. Bo and I slowly move toward the turret, mindful of maintaining silence. When I unholster my gun, Bo throws his knife, hitting one of the guards squarely in the back, causing him to fall to the ground. I quickly fire my pistol, striking the other guard who crashes against the base of the gun turret and slowly slides onto the concrete platform. Rapidly, but carefully, we approach them to ensure that they're dead. Bo notices movement from one of the guards. Immediately, he points his pistol and fires, killing the man.

Continuing, we pass another empty machine gun nest. Thank God for this unanticipated good fortune. Having completed this first phase of the mission, we move slowly toward the center position of the two teams. I signal with a flashlight for the teams to follow. We assemble and kneel in a circle, awaiting Colonel Gannon and Lieutenant Hisan.

When they finally arrive, we listen intently while the colonel provides instructions. "We must stick to our plan. One team is to move in an easterly direction while the other team moves west. We will inspect each building from the perimeter to the center of the camp until we locate the children. Once we locate and rescue them, the entire team will be notified via cell phone text to gather on the river bank just north of the camp." We give each other a thumbs-up and head off.

When we approach some cottages on the southwest side of the camp, we encounter two armed guards standing at the northeast corner of a warehouse building. Stan and Gary Price circle behind the building from the west and emerge at the southeast corner. Both hold pistols aimed squarely at the guards. Startled, the guards begin to run. Stan and Gary open fire, striking one of the guards, who instantly falls to the ground. The other continues running. Stan and Gary fire several more rounds, riddling the second guard's body with bullets. He goes down. Stan immediately takes quick, light steps over to the guards. He approaches the guard who fell first and checks his vital signs. The man's eyes suddenly open wide. Before Stan can react, the guard grabs his arm and attempts to flip him. Stan falls to the ground and struggles with him. Caught by surprise, Gary takes aim but sees that Stan and the guard are tangled. If Gary takes a shot, he'll risk killing Stan with friendly fire. Stan wrestles one arm free and pulls his knife from the sheath. He stabs the guard in the chest until the man goes limp.

After inspecting the remaining cottages, we withdraw from the area, disappointed that we've been unable to find the children. We continue moving eastward, carefully inspecting each building that we encounter, but with no success. Just then, I notice a dimly lit, one-story, ranch-like structure in the distance. We cautiously converge on the building and edge toward the side screen door. Glancing inside, I glimpse the silhouette of two people. Their dark, motionless images are reflected in a shadow onto a nearby interior wall.

I order Stan, "Follow me inside, but first make sure that the rest of the team forms a line around the exterior of the building to watch for any militia." We carefully open the screen door and enter the kitchen. Just then, I hear noise in the room ahead of us. The silhouette disappears, and the quiet screeching of someone's panicked voice is heard. After rushing into the room, I witness my niece and nephew crying while standing in the corner of the living room. One of the militia is holding a gun to Amanda's head.

I tell him, "There's no need to hurt the children. Just let them go, and we'll back off." Suddenly, gunfire erupts shattering the front window. As he falls back into a sitting position against the wall, I watch as blood spurts from the side of the gunman's head. I rush and grab the kids, hugging them tightly. Amanda is shaking uncontrollably, aware that she could have been killed. Assessing their condition, I notice that both are wearing clean clothes, but their hair is tangled in knots, and their foreheads and cheeks are caked with dirt. Showing no outward sign of abuse, they are safe, for which I'm very thankful.

I quickly grab a rag from my backpack, douse it with water from my canteen, and wipe the blood from Amanda's cheeks and neck. We then hurry from the scene, working our way toward the center of the camp where we hear a voice bellowing from a southeasterly direction. Stopping, I instruct the team. "Remain here, notify Colonel Gannon that the children are safe, and watch for any unusual activity."

Cautiously, I move in the direction of the voice, anxious to view the scene and verify a clear path for our escape. The man, who is speaking to a large crowd of people, is pontificating about the role of the current government and why it should be displaced. After listening for a couple of minutes, I begin to hurry back to the team. Suddenly, someone strikes me from behind.

After falling to the ground, I turn and glimpse the image of a tall, thin figure and immediately recognize Dave Drury's face. Holding a knife in his right hand, he charges at me. I quickly get up. When he gets close, I grab the front of his shirt, fall back against the ground, and flip him. He lands on his back with a thud. Getting up, I face him. Once again, he charges at me while flashing the knife. With a jump kick to his chest, I knock him to the ground. After pulling himself up, he tosses dirt into my face, blinding me. While I struggle to reclaim my vision, he lands two punches to my head, knocking me to the ground. Again, I rush to get up. Drury charges while waving his knife. He stabs me in the left arm, and I fold over, holding my arm. Instantly, my shirt is doused in blood. When he reaches with the knife again, I grab his hand and twist it into his body, breaking his wrist. He screams in pain.

Turning toward the crowd, I notice that the militia members are charging us. Just then, I receive a cell phone call from Colonel Gannon, advising that his team is retreating to the river bank. I hurry back and instruct everyone to withdraw to the river. I pick up Amanda and begin running. Stan carries Danny. In our rush to escape, we hear shots being fired at us from behind. Three guards are in pursuit. Bentley turns and fires the grenade launcher, killing all three. We continue running, knowing full well that the entire camp is now aware of our presence and in heavy pursuit of our team.

When arriving at the river bank, I see the other team waiting. Colonel Gannon tells me, "We now have to get ourselves moving."

Suddenly, we hear what appears to be a large contingency of

paramilitary. With boots pounding from the south and shots being fired from the nearby woods, they are attempting to cut off our escape route.

Quickly, we move west along the river bank and rush to reach our destination. Just then, the sound of thundering boat engines erupts from behind us. When we finally arrive at our destination, I grab Amanda and Danny and hug them tight. They are both frightened, and Amanda is crying. I lift them into the boat. Quickly boarding, I hug the kids once again, and tell them, "Lie down on the deck." After everyone boards, we push off and head toward open water. Immediately behind us are six cabin cruisers in heavy pursuit of our team. Closing in, they begin firing machine guns. We return fire with the M240B's that are mounted on the rear of our boats. Stan turns with his grenade launcher in hand and fires, hitting one of the lead boats, causing a tremendous explosion. Hearing more machine gun fire from behind, I observe as Charlie Davis falls to the deck after being struck by a bullet. The medic immediately rushes over to tend to him. Unfortunately, the wound proves to be fatal. After looking up at me with a forlorn expression, the medic sorrowfully bows his head.

The pursuing boats continue to follow. When we get closer to our pickup point, the Apache helicopter rises above the trees and takes aim at the enemy boats. After it fires several rocket rounds, three of the boats are hit and immediately explode. Realizing the futility of continuing their pursuit, the remaining two boats turn and flee down river. When they disappear, we coast into the river bank and jump to shore. Charlie's body is covered with canvas and gently laid on the boat deck. The team then picks up the boats and carries them back to the waiting Chinook helicopter. After entering the cargo bay, we lower the boats and carefully remove Charlie's body. We place him on the floor and take our seats on the wall benches. A somber mood consumes the entire team. Dejected, we all bow our heads. A couple of our team weep uncontrollably while we digest the loss of our team member and friend. Previously, we'd only lost four of our team, all during the Iraq and Afghanistan wars. This loss, as before, deeply impacts each of us. We mourn, realizing we have lost not only a team member but also a brother.

The medic hurries over to inspect the knife wound to my arm. Grabbing a knife, he quickly cuts open my sleeve and exposes the gash. Bo Carton hands him the first aid kit. As the medic douses my wound with disinfectant, I wince in pain. It almost feels worse than getting stabbed in the first place. While bandaging my arm, he tells me, "Sean, make sure that you keep this clean. Once you return home, contact your physician for further treatment. You don't want an infection."

"Jeez, you sound like my mother."

"Just do it, wise ass."

When the helicopter lands at the Greater Cincinnati Airport, we all change into our civilian clothes. Before disembarking, everyone shakes hands and says goodbye. I thank my team members for their help and tell them, "If you ever need anything, I'll always be there for you."

I grab Danny's and Amanda's hands and begin walking down the helicopter ramp. While we're walking, I can see Charlie's body being carried to a waiting ambulance. I let go of the children's hands and respectfully salute Charlie. The remainder of the team likewise salutes while we observe the ambulance slowly pull away. One member of our team rushes toward the ambulance, screaming for the EMTs to stop. He hands an American flag to them and requests that it be draped over Charlie's body. Glancing at the children, I'm very thankful that they've regained their freedom, but the cost to Charlie's family is unimaginable.

After catching an early morning flight back to New York, Stan, the children, and I are happy to have completed the mission. Unfortunately, Stan and I lost one of our team members. It'll now be up to Colonel Gannon to contact Charlie's family and give them the sad news. Of course, the entire team will attend the funeral in Cleveland, where Charlie lived.

When disembarking, we head outside to hail a cab to my sister's home in New Jersey. Anxious about the family reunion, I can't wait to witness the excitement when the kids see their parents.

Entering North Arlington, I see the Cape Cod–style homes standing in rows along the streets like soldiers at attention during a military parade. When we turn onto Allen Drive, the street where my family lives, I dial Monica and hear her voice.

"Hello?"

"Monica, it's Sean."

"Where are you?"

"Look out your front window."

I hear her scream, and then I see her and Mike rushing through the front door and running toward the cab. Amanda and Danny jump from the cab and rush to their parents, screaming as they approach. Hugging and kissing the children wildly, my sister and brother-in-law are overjoyed to have the kids back. What a torturous experience the family has undergone over the past couple of months. Now, the children are back home safe, free from the confinement and danger of the paramilitary camp.

Having greeted the children, Monica and Mike walk over to Stan and me and hug us. I see tears running down Monica's cheeks. When I hug her, I can feel how thin she is, having lost so much weight as a result of the stress and worry stemming from the kids' abduction. Black circles have formed under her eyes because of her lack of rest. Grateful, the two of them invite Stan and me for lunch. I tell them, "We'll take a rain check. Right now, you need time to reacquaint yourselves with the children."

By this time, several of the neighbors have come over to greet Amanda and Danny, and hug my sister and brother-in-law. Excited and thankful, everyone smiles and talks, happy that the children are home safe.

Stan and I walk over to Monica and Mike and say our goodbyes. I tell them that I'll call in a couple of days to arrange for a proper celebration. After kissing and hugging Amanda and Danny, Stan and I climb into the cab and head home.

When I walk through the front door, I throw my belongings on the living room floor and pour a glass of merlot. I fall back into the soft, plush cushions of the couch. Thankful that the children are safe I smile, realizing that the rescue could have been a disaster. In spite of the loss of Charlie, I believe the mission to be a success.

## CHAPTER 16

# RAGE FROM THE MILITIA

Three days after our mission, July 6, is the day of Charlie's funeral. Having ridden from Cleveland Hopkins International Airport to 24 Meister Road, I exit the taxi and slowly walk up the steps to the two-story beige colonial. After knocking on the door, I hear the footsteps of someone quickly approaching. When the door opens, I see the face of an unfamiliar woman. She introduces herself as June Wieler, Elizabeth Davis's sister.

I enter, and ask her if Elizabeth is available. Mrs. Wieler requests that I take a seat on the living room couch, while she excuses herself and heads up the stairs to tell Elizabeth that she has a guest. Patiently waiting, I stand and begin glancing at the many framed family photographs scattered throughout the living room. Seeing Charlie's picture everywhere causes simultaneous guilt and sorrow. This emergence of emotion produces an intense disheartening feeling. He made the ultimate sacrifice while rescuing two children he didn't even know.

When I turn from the fireplace mantel, Elizabeth is standing in front of me. She extends her arms and grabs my hands. Her face is drawn, and her eyes are red from crying. While hugging me, she says, "Sean, I don't blame you for our loss. Charlie was a fine man and was dedicated to his strong beliefs and principles. Because of him and the rest of the team, you were able to rescue two innocent children."

"Elizabeth, I'm so sorry for your loss. Charlie was a special person who believed in people. He'll be sorely missed. If I could trade places with him, I'd do it without hesitation."

"I know you and Charlie were military buddies, and he had great respect for you. He didn't feel that way about many people."

"Thanks for that Elizabeth."

"I hate to rush you, but it's time to go. The limousine will be here at any moment. Why don't you ride with us to the church and cemetery?"

"Thank you, I will."

In spite of the beautiful weather, the funeral was a somber affair for everyone present. The team was especially moved by the many people who testified to Charlie's character and generosity. Knowing him, we can all appreciate and understand the uniqueness of such a wonderful human being. What a terrible loss it is for his family and friends.

After the funeral, everyone meets at Charlie's house for the repast. When I walk into the backyard, I see several folding tables set buffet style, featuring an abundance of luncheon meats, cooked salmon, roast beef, ham, salads, and an assortment of dressings for sandwiches. There are over two hundred people in attendance, including Colonel Gannon and our entire special forces team.

While I'm standing under the canvas tent near the back of the house, Colonel Gannon walks over and tells me, "I received a message from one of my officers stating that when Carl Dietrich returned from overseas, he went ballistic after hearing about the rescue. The officer, who is related to a member of Deutsche Christen, claimed he witnessed the entire episode." Realizing that not only were the children rescued, but also that eighteen of his militia had been killed, Dietrich began throwing chairs and flipping tables. He even attacked two of his commanders, breaking the nose of one and the jaw of the other. The colonel tells me, "Be careful Sean. Dietrich will do anything to avenge our attack."

"Don't worry—I'll be vigilant. Just to let you know, my sister, my brother-in-law, and their children have been temporarily relocated by the F.B.I. to an out of state location for their safety. I'm afraid that Dietrich will attempt to kidnap the children again, so I don't want to leave anything to chance."

After three hours at the repast, I have to leave. It's nearly 4:00 and my flight is scheduled to depart at 5:35. After saying good-bye to the team, I search for Elizabeth, and find her seated on the living room couch next to the fireplace. She's having a conversation with her sister. Interrupting, I apologize by telling her, "I have to catch a flight back to New York." I kiss her on the forehead and tell her that I'll be in touch soon. Noticing a tear running down her left cheek, I wipe it away with my handkerchief. Then I head through the front door to a waiting taxi.

After arriving at LaGuardia, I exit the plane and hurry to the front gate in order to secure a cab. It's now 7:00 p.m. When pulling up to my condominium, I decide to collect Boynton and then walk back home. In his excitement, he's jumping and pulling with the energy of a meerkat. It's very heartwarming to know that he missed me, even though I've only been gone for less than a day.

When we walk through the front door, Boynton charges toward the kitchen. Sitting in front of the cabinet where his treats are housed, he waits patiently until I open a package and extract a rawhide bone. Immediately, he takes the bone and runs into the living room, where he'll be kept occupied chewing for an hour.

I head into the living room and turn on the TV. Reporting, the news anchor states,

> "Several military skirmishes have occurred in West Virginia during the early afternoon. A large contingency of militia attempted to seize the small village of Cameron, West Virginia. As a result, the National Guard was called in to quell the violence. The town of nearly nine hundred and fifty residents located south of Wheeling, was overrun by several hundred militia from Deutsche Christian. Heavily armed, the group attempted to occupy the town.

Residents were held at gunpoint and forced to turn over valuables such as jewelry, cash, and collectibles. Along with this, rifles, pistols, and a plethora of ammunition was confiscated. Once the National Guard arrived, a massive battle ensued. There was rampant gunfire and explosions everywhere. The militia attempted to encircle and trap the guardsmen but were subdued once tanks from the National Guard arrived. Fifty militia were killed or wounded, and thirty were captured. The remainder escaped north toward Wheeling. Realizing the militia's military capabilities, the police and National Guard elected not to pursue them. Instead, they chose to set up a contingent of two hundred troops and a dozen tanks to patrol and protect the small community."

From all appearances, the Deutsche Christian organization is getting bolder while testing the response and tactics of the U.S. military.

Reflecting on the news report and my conversation with Colonel Gannon, I realize that something strikes me as odd. While at Charlie's funeral, the colonel mentioned that Carl Dietrich had just returned from overseas. Why would he have gone overseas, and where did he go? The implications of his trip clearly support the reports of interference and support from foreign governments. A conspiracy may be developing, and

I'm worried about the long-term consequences of Dietrich's association with a foreign entity.

During the early morning, I'm jarred from my sleep by Boynton's growling. I calm him and roll over. The clock displays the time as 2:00. Slowing getting up, I slip my pants on, grab the .45 snub-nose pistol from under my mattress, and head to the stairway landing. Hearing nothing, I cautiously walk downstairs to inspect the living room and kitchen. Boynton has come down and is growling while he faces the front door. Peering through the front window, I see the shadow of a man on the other side of the door, off to the right. Backing up, Boynton and I fade into the shadowy refuge near the corner closet. Just then, I hear the sound of a key being inserted into the front door. Slowly, the door opens, and an intruder quickly enters. He heads toward the stairs. When he passes us, I strike him in the back of the head with the butt of my gun. He begins to fall, but I catch him just before he hits the floor. Suspecting that he may have accomplices, I don't want to alert them.

Within a couple of seconds, two other men enter the living room. Boynton charges and attacks them. Immediately, I rush from the corner, strike one of the intruders with the gun handle, and wrestle him to the floor. He knocks the gun from my hand and punches me. In response, I get to my knees and grab the metal candlestick from the end table next to the couch and strike the man on the side of his head. Just then, Boynton grabs the other man's wrist and attempts to force him down. The man pulls a gun from his jacket and points it at Boynton. Seeing this, I quickly get up, charge the man, and knock the gun from his hand. When I do, he strikes me with something very hard and heavy, knocking me to the floor. Boynton grabs his leg and jumps to bite his throat. Just then, the man strikes Boynton in the head, causing him to yelp loudly and collapse on the floor.

Jumping up, I charge and punch the man. He falls back but then rushes at me. When he does, I glimpse the face of Dave Drury. Quickly, I grab his arm and flip him through the glass top of the coffee table. The other intruder quickly gets up and rushes through the front door, disappearing. When Drury gets up, I see his forehead bleeding profusely. The lobe of his right ear has been completely severed. He comes at me with his knife extended. When he tries to stab me, I slide behind him and force my arm around his throat, squeezing hard and suffocating him. When I let go, his lifeless body falls to the floor.

Immediately, I rush to Boynton and lift his head. He's breathing heavily but appears to be okay. With the porch light shining on his face, I can see a contusion over his left eye. Running into the kitchen, I turn on the lights, grab the first aid kit, and return to the living room.

After treating Boynton, I place a blanket on the kitchen floor, pick him up, and then lay him down. I then grab my cell phone and make a call to the police. Within fifteen minutes two squad cars arrive along with a team of EMTs. The police make a quick examination of the premises. Drury is declared dead, and the other intruder is lifted to a gurney, strapped down, and wheeled to the ambulance. While removing the intruder, one of the

EMTs advises me that the man has sustained a fractured skull and a large contusion to the back of his head.

One of the police officers asks me if I'm okay, and I give a thumbs-up. He then directs me to take a seat in the kitchen and begins questioning me. "Mr. Carrol, can you describe what happened and tell me who's responsible for the break-in?" After I tell him about Deutsche Christen, the abduction, and the rescue, he releases a heavy sigh. "I didn't see any signs of forced entry. Do you know how they gained access?"

"I can only say that I heard a key being inserted in the front door, but I don't know how the intruders would have secured a key."

He continues questioning me. After a couple of hours, he says, "I think that we've covered everything we need to for now. We may require some additional information, but we'll contact you if necessary."

When the police complete their investigation, another EMT crew arrives and removes Drury's body. When they leave, I begin cleaning up the living room debris. Glass shards and strips of broken glass are strewn everywhere. One of the coffee table legs has been shattered, resulting in dry splinters of broken wood. When I walk toward the front door, I stoop to pick up some pieces of glass. Just as I bend down, I notice my front door key lying within a small mound of wood shards resting near the edge of the couch. The key is the one that I had buried under the small fir tree to the left of my condominium unit. I recognize it by the green color of the stem. The only ones privy to the location of the key are Linda Mancuso and me. The odds of someone guessing that a key had been buried, much less knowing its location, are slim to none. While caressing the key, I speculate about the possibility of Linda's disloyalty, but doubt creeps in. I wonder if Dietrich somehow forced her cooperation by making a threat to her and her family's welfare. The prospect that Linda has compromised our friendship suddenly causes me to erupt in anger. I grab a dining room chair, throw it against the living room wall, and stand stoically while it crashes through the exposed Sheet rock. Aware of our long-term friendship, I'll have to assure myself that any conclusion I arrive at must be indisputable.

It's now 6:00 a.m. Boynton is lying on his blanket, whimpering in pain from his head injury. I walk over and pet him while at the same time inspecting his head wound. I then make a pot of coffee and sit at the kitchen island, wondering what Dietrich's next move will be.

## CHAPTER 17

# TREXLER'S DEMISE

After taking a short afternoon nap on the couch, I roll over only to experience Boynton bathing my face with his tongue. I quickly examine the cut on his head to discover that a scab is already forming. His left eye is slightly closed, but he seems to be in fine spirits.

Grabbing my clothes from the base of the couch, I dress, wash my face, and make some coffee. While the coffeepot perks, Boynton and I walk to the open lot across the street. In spite of his injuries, he's full of energy. He begins running in wide circles around the field, until finally succumbing to exhaustion and collapsing in the low grass just ahead of me.

After we return home, Boynton heads to the kitchen. He sits directly in front of the refrigerator and peers at me. Knowing the refrigerator contains a small treasure trove of leftover hamburgers, he's determined to harass me until I finally give in. Opening the refrigerator, I peer out of the corner of my right eye only to observe Boynton performing a dance on the kitchen floor. He's acting out knowing that he's gotten his way. After filling his bowl, I place it on the floor and watch while he devours its contents.

Just as I turn to pour myself a cup of coffee, I hear the doorbell ring. Boynton rushes to the front door while I peer through the front living room window and see the figure of a rather disheveled middle-aged man. Resembling the character of Inspector Columbo, he's wearing the trademark beige trench coat. Standing at five feet eight inches, he's makes for a rather unimposing figure and displays a severe nervousness by hurriedly pacing back and forth on the front landing. When I open the door, he flashes his badge and in a deep, raspy voice says, "I'm detective Parisi. Are you Mr. Carrol?"

"Yes. What can I do for you, Detective?"

"I wanna discuss the circumstances surrounding the murder of Jake Trexler."

When he enters, I gesture for him to take a seat on the couch. "Would you care for a cup of coffee?"

"That'd be great, Mr. Carrol."

I put a pot of coffee on and return to the living room only to observe Boynton lying on his back while Detective Parisi runs the palm of his hand over Boynton's belly. "I can see you like animals, Detective."

"Yeah, for my entire life I've lived with cats and dogs. My father was an animal lover. Guess it's genetic."

"It sounds like the coffee is ready. How do you like yours?"

"With two lumps and a little milk."

I return from the kitchen, hand him the coffee and ask, "What did you want to discuss about Jake Trexler?"

"You know that his death was quite gruesome. Our investigation is currently at a dead-end, because we haven't been able to extract any physical evidence from the scene. The guys who murdered Trexler were pros. They made sure that the entire crime scene was wiped clean. They left no fingerprints, blood, or other physical evidence."

"I'm not surprised Detective. Mr. Trexler told me that the Deutsche Christens had hired the best trackers available. He was pretty nervous when I last saw him. He said that the trackers had been following him for months, and that he narrowly escaped capture on a few occasions."

"Mr. Carrol, we did find something strange before the autopsy was performed. Sewn into Mr. Trexler's jogging pants was a one-inch by two-inch piece of paper. The following three sets of numbers were written down."

Parisi shows a photograph of the paper, which displays the following numbers:

46 by 38, 59 by 30

29 by 57, 90 by 4

39 by 96, 75 by 16

"Detective, these numbers are latitude and longitude coordinates. I've seen more coordinates in my military career than I care to admit. I wouldn't mistake these configurations. We have to determine the corresponding locations of the coordinates—and more important, their significance. Let me get my map."

After standing up, I walk over to the living room closet and reach for my map. Wrapped up somewhat like a scroll, it's rolled and secured with a large brown rubber band. After sliding the rubber band off, I unroll the map. Detective Parisi follows me while I head into the dining room. He opens the map, places it on dining room table, and then holds it down. I begin to match the coordinates to the corresponding locations.

"The first set of numbers is latitude 46 degrees 38 minutes north, longitude 59 degrees 30 minutes west. The coordinates correlate with the Gulf of St. Lawrence. I wonder why this area is important. This isn't a location—it's simply a body of water. Detective, read me the next set of numbers."

"They're 29 by 57, and 90 by 4."

"These correspond with New Orleans." Hoping to make a connection among the three locations, I need to decipher the final one. "Give me the last numbers."

He says, "It's 39 by 96, and 75 by 16."

"These correlate with Philadelphia. Detective, I'm not sure what we have here. What common elements link these three locations?"

He scratches his head and says, "The only common thread is water."

"Water?"

"Look at the map. The waterway is the only common element."

"But I don't know what's significant about water. ... Wait a minute. These could be the routes being used to smuggle weapons to the Deutsche Christian camps. Mr. Trexler told me about large caches of weapons that had been smuggled on cargo ships and barges throughout the United States."

"What types of weapons were they smuggling, Mr. Carrol?"

"Jake Trexler told me that only small arms had been brought to and stored at the camps."

"Did they obtain any large weapons like tanks, artillery, or missiles?"

"I don't know. Jake Trexler told me that he was unaware of any attempts by Deutsche Christen to secure sophisticated weapons or heavy equipment. Here again, he claimed to be a second-tier board member, not privy to high-level decisions such as major weapons purchases. My suspicion, however, suggests that Deutsche Christen is making inroads with other governments to obtain sophisticated weaponry. Logic dictates that they'll require this type of hardware should they challenge the U.S. government."

Shaking his head from side to side, Detective Parisi manifests his deep frustration concerning not only the Trexler case, but the series of events being orchestrated by Deutsche Christen. With a succinct comment he says, "I hope your wrong Mr. Carrol."

Throwing my hands in the air I reply, "I do too, Detective, but I don't think so."

"I want to thank you, Mr. Carrol. You've been extremely helpful. As far as the coordinates are concerned, I'm not quite sure what I'm gonna do with this information, but I know that the military will be interested."

Cautioning him I say, "Detective, be very careful about what you say and do. Be especially wary concerning who you speak to about this information. Deutsche Christen is a very dangerous organization with friends everywhere. They will stop at nothing to preserve their secrets."

"I'm nervous about the potential danger that I'm facing, but I've gotta trust somebody, if I'm gonna solve this case. Once again, thanks Mr. Carrol and have a good day."

"Goodbye, Detective."

# CHAPTER 18

# VENGEANCE

Two days later, I'm enjoying a cup of coffee while sitting at the kitchen island. Its 10:00 a.m. when my phone rings. Picking up the receiver, I can hear John Errin's voice. "Hi, Sean."

"Hello, John. What's up?"

"Sean, my secretary received a rather disturbing call from Carl Dietrich."

"What the hell did he want?"

"He threatened to blow up the newspaper building if we didn't turn you over to him and his organization. We've evacuated the building and notified the authorities. They've guaranteed twenty-four hour surveillance of the premises for the next few weeks."

"John, you know that he's seeking revenge for the special forces attack on his camp. A few days ago, he sent a few of his goons to my house in an attempt to avenge the attack. They broke in and tried to kill me. Fortunately, I killed one of his right-hand men and severely injured another. His desire for retribution will now take center stage as he tries to get even. I'm sorry that you're in the middle of this mess, and that I'm jeopardizing the welfare of the paper."

"Don't be sorry, Sean. We went into this assignment with our eyes wide open. I want you to be aware of the threat so that you don't get caught off guard; be vigilant and try not to take any unnecessary chances. These people are dangerous, and they apparently will do anything to avenge your attack on their camp and the killing of their confederates."

"Thanks for the heads-up, John."

After hanging up the phone, I walk outside to get my briefcase. Having forgotten to bring it in last night, I need to locate some notes I had written about Deutsche Christen. When descending the stairs, I catch sight of my car, and my blood runs cold. Scrawled across the hood in red paint is the word "killer." Deep scratches across the trunk spell out, "You're next." I look around, searching for anyone suspicious. The street's empty. I carefully open the passenger's side door and extract my brief case. Aware that Deutsche Christen possesses a large cache of C-4 explosives, I'm very wary. Knowing that I'm a target of Dietrich and his organization, I'm concerned that a bomb may have been planted.

Wondering if I should check the undercarriage or phone the police first, my curiosity wins out. I place my briefcase on the ground and stoop to investigate. Quickly searching the undercarriage, I notice a flashing red light attached to a small square box positioned below the driver's seat and slightly toward the rear. I stand, grab the briefcase, and hurry up the stairs to my condominium. When inside, I reach for my cell phone and dial 911.

A dispatcher answers and requests my name. I tell him and then anxiously inform him that it's an emergency.

"What's the emergency?" he asks.

"A bomb has been planted on the undercarriage of my car."

He instructs me to hold on while he contacts the Bomb Disposal Unit. While waiting, I can feel my stomach churning. The tension I feel from the threat of an explosion is intense. Within two minutes the dispatcher switches me to the receptionist at the B.D.U. "Mr. Carrol, I understand that a bomb has been planted on the undercarriage of your car."

"Yes. I just discovered it."

"Please give me your address and phone number."

I provide him with the information. He then instructs me, "Stay clear of the vehicle and make sure no one else approaches." Assuring me that they will dispose of the bomb, he advises that their units will arrive at my location within ten minutes.

After hanging up the phone, I rush to the front door and make sure that no one approaches the car. Five minutes later, a series of police vehicles arrive and cordon off the street. I open the door and walk toward the police unit located just to the right of my home. A police lieutenant asks if the targeted vehicle is mine, to which I respond, "Yes."

At this point, he tells me, "You'll have to evacuate the area and stay away from the car."

Pleading, I tell him, "My dog is inside the condominium. I can't leave him there."

I accompany him while he rushes to rescue Boynton. He then ushers both of us to the B.D.U. vehicle located just across the street. From here, I see two officers suiting up to investigate the explosive device. By this time, the area has been completely cordoned off, and people in the surrounding homes have been evacuated. The two officers stoop down next to the vehicle with an infrared camera to view the vehicle's undercarriage. Slowly guiding the camera, they assess the device. Within fifteen minutes they return to their vehicle. I can hear them discussing the situation.

A few minutes later an officer walks over to speak with me. He says, "We need to remove your vehicle and detonate the bomb in a remote area near our headquarters. The bomb is too powerful to ignite here. It contains six pounds of C-4 plastic explosives and is placed on the vehicle's undercarriage in such a way that it will be impossible to remove without destroying half of the homes on the street." He goes on to tell me, "A flatbed truck has been dispatched to remove the car."

Continuing, he asks, "Mr. Carrol, do you know who planted the bomb?"

"Although I'm not positive, I believe that an organization by the name of Deutsche Christen is responsible. They've hired a couple of trackers to kill me. These guys have already murdered a man by the name of Jake Trexler. In fact, Detective Parisi of the N.Y.P.D. has been investigating Trexler's murder for quite some time." Based upon this incident, I think to myself, *I've really got to be vigilant about my surroundings; otherwise, I could become a victim like Jake Trexler.*

Shortly thereafter, the flatbed truck arrives. The driver and the police confer about the safest procedure for loading and transporting the car. They're apparently concerned that any unnecessary jarring of the vehicle could cause detonation. After their discussion, the driver slowly and methodically loads the car onto the flatbed and carefully hooks heavy cables to the chassis. In order to prevent too much movement of the vehicle while being transported, the driver, under the watchful eyes of the B.D.U. officers, hitches additional chains from the car chassis to the bed of the truck. The entire process takes thirty-five minutes.

An entourage of police vehicles escorts the flatbed. When the caravan begins to drive away, I grab Boynton, turn, and head toward my condominium. While climbing the stairs, I can hear my phone ringing. I rush to open the door and pick up the receiver. An unrecognizable voice asks, "Mr. Carrol?"

"Yes?"

"You're in serious danger."

"I already know that."

"Do you remember Jake Trexler?"

"Yeah, I certainly do."

"Well, the same two trackers who killed him have been hired to make you their next target. Not only were they trained in espionage as C.I.A. field agents, but also they served as Green Berets in special ops. Just be careful, Mr. Carrol. These guys mean business. They lack a conscience and won't give up until you're dead." Nervously he says, "Someone is coming. I've gotta go." The line goes dead.

A moment later, the doorbell rings. From the kitchen I can see Linda Mancuso patiently waiting at the front door. I immediately flash back to the break-in at my condominium still unsure of Linda's true involvement and her real motives toward me. I walk slowly to the door, open it, and invite her in. Appearing somewhat nervous, her left eye is twitching, and her body is swaying slightly. Instead of looking directly at me, she's peering down at the wooden floor of the living room. Unsure of why she has come over, I invite her to sit down. She folds her hands together and asks, "Where's Boynton?"

"He's napping on the back patio. All of today's excitement must have knocked him out."

"Sean, I came over to tell you that some family issues have arisen that require my attention."

"Are they serious?"

"Not too serious, but important enough to demand that I travel to Utah. My sister has had a minor heart attack. She needs someone to assist with her business affairs."

"I'm sorry to hear about your sister. If there is anything I can do to help, Linda, just let me know."

"Sean, would you check my condominium now and then while I'm away?"

"That's not a problem."

"By the way, do you know what all the commotion was about this morning? The police evacuated me and several of my neighbors, but they wouldn't explain why."

"Yeah, I discovered a bomb planted on the undercarriage of my car, and I contacted the police."

"What's going on?" Linda asks.

"From all appearances, the Deutsche Christens have upped their ante and are now employing every means at their disposal to kill me."

Looking up at me with an angry expression, she says, "Carl Dietrich is such a monster. Based upon his past military record in Iraq, he should have been hung for the atrocious murders of so many innocent people. If he had been, you wouldn't be confronted with the danger you're facing now."

I wonder how Linda knows about his actions in Iraq. This isn't something readily known, but she appears to be well aware of Dietrich's background. In my mind, I continue to question her real allegiance. I feel emotionally torn and saddened about our uncertain friendship, but I still can't jump to conclusions. I need to determine the facts.

I answer, "You're right. For now, though, have a safe trip and don't worry about a thing. I hope your sister recovers."

Linda kisses me on the cheek and then heads out.

## CHAPTER 19

# MISSING

Four days have elapsed since Linda left to visit her sister in Utah. She hasn't called or e-mailed. This isn't like her. She's very organized and circumspect, thanks to her many years working for the F.B.I. I hope she hasn't encountered any trouble.

Although I'm not panicked yet, I think it might be a good idea if I contact her sister. I don't have a phone number or an e-mail address, though. I decide to head to Linda's condominium to look around and see what I can find.

With her door key in hand, I walk over to her unit. I let myself in, head to the kitchen, and begin rifling through the drawers in search of an address book. While looking around, I can't help but notice the many framed pictures that populate Linda's condominium. Over the years she's taken so many beautiful photographs featuring monuments, waterfalls, natural disasters, and mountain skylines. Since high school, photography has been her first love.

Finding no sign of a phone book or other registers, I walk into the living room and head directly to the small hazel wood phone table located in the corner near the front closet. Opening the top drawer, I immediately spot a black leather phone book. Impatiently, I begin turning the pages searching for her sister's name. Within a few seconds, I find an entry for Carrie Fleischer. Her address is shown as Utah, like I remembered. I dial the number listed. The phone rings several times before I finally hear a woman's voice. "Hello?"

"Carrie?"

"Yes?"

"This is Sean Carrol, Linda's friend."

"Oh, hi, Sean. Is there something wrong?"

"I don't know, Carrie. Linda told me she was going to visit you."

"That's strange. She never mentioned anything about taking a trip out here."

"Carrie, I don't know what's happening with Linda, but there's something odd about her behavior. She left here four days ago, allegedly traveling to help you. According to Linda, she was visiting you because of your recent heart attack."

"Heart attack? I'm as healthy as a horse."

"This is so strange. When did you last speak to her?"

"The last time I spoke to Linda was about two weeks ago. I must say this is bizarre. I wonder why she would go to such lengths to fabricate a story like this."

"Just sit tight, Carrie. I'll try to reach her by cell phone. I've got a suspicion about her motive for creating the story, but I'm not entirely sure of her reason. Let me know if you hear from her."

"I will."

"Good-bye Carrie."

I immediately dial Linda's cell phone number. It rings multiple times, but she doesn't answer. I wonder where she is and what she could possibly be up to. Perusing the contents of the phone table, I locate a small pad of unmarked paper located in the upper left corner on the table's surface, hidden under a pile of envelopes. Underneath the phone table is a waste paper basket. After pulling it out, I reach in and find several sheets of paper. Glancing at them, I notice a list and the imprint of some notes. Maybe the imprints will provide some clues about her plans.

I extract a pencil from the drawer, turn it sideways, and shade the paper. This is an old trick I learned while investigating some earlier cases as a wet-behind-the-ears reporter. Once shaded, the imprint clearly displays several initials, including DC and OH. Directly at the base of the page is the name Carl. I wonder what the hell is going on. Immediately, I flash back to the break-in at my home. The key I found after the incident gave me pause to question Linda's loyalty. Now her guilt seems almost assured, but there's still the possibility that she's a victim of circumstances, whatever those may be. Having been friends with her for forty years, I'll have to give her the benefit of the doubt.

Suddenly, it occurs to me that her cell phone contains a GPS tracking device. To access the unit and secure the location of the phone, I'll require police assistance. I decide to contact Detective Parisi. I dial his number. The phone rings a few times before he answers.

"Parisi," he responds in his usual gruff voice.

"Detective, this is Sean Carrol."

"What can I do for you, Mr. Carrol?"

"I need your assistance to access a GPS unit for a cell phone."

"Why do ya need to access this GPS unit?"

"I believe the person who owns the phone may be in trouble."

"What kinda trouble?"

"I'm not sure, but it involves Deutsche Christian."

"Say no more. Come on down to the precinct. We'll see what we can do."

Before driving to the precinct, I check on Boynton to make sure that he has enough water for the afternoon. Having tended to him, I grab my car keys and rush through the front door to the rental car. Because my car was destroyed by the detonation of a bomb, I persuaded the manager at the local Diamond Rental office to drop a car off at my home. This was a lifesaver.

The precinct is only twenty minutes away. As I speed through traffic, Linda's image floods my thoughts. I'm concerned about the danger she may be in. She's been so much a part of my life that, I'd be heartbroken if anything happened to her. Still, I don't understand what her tie is to Dietrich.

After arriving at the police station, I park in the guest lot located just behind the precinct. I vault from my car, rush inside the building, and head directly to Detective Parisi's office by taking the elevator to the third floor.

When I exit the elevator, I approach a small, windowless office located just outside of a large meeting room. I see Detective Parisi seated behind an old beat-up metal desk. When I enter, the detective is completing what appears to be an incident report. Upon seeing me, he immediately requests the cell phone number that I need traced. He asks, "Whose number are we tracing, and why do you need to track the location?"

After sitting down, I inform him, "The cell phone number belongs to a very special woman I've known since childhood." I continue telling him, "She may be caught up in some trouble with Deutsche Christen." I then provide him with the cell phone number. After picking up the desk phone, he requests that someone immediately come to his office with a GPS tracking device. Within ten minutes, an officer arrives clutching a small handheld unit. The officer enters the number and awaits a response. "Aha, I have it," he says. The officer informs us that the device has tracked the signal to Martin's Ferry located four miles west of Wheeling, West Virginia.

Leaning over the desk, I stare at Detective Parisi and say, "I appreciate your help, and I hope that I can rely on you to assist me again should circumstances require."

"Of course, I'll help you. Just answer me one question. What's the woman's link to this group?"

"I wish I knew. Unfortunately, she never confided in me about the true circumstances of the trip she was taking. I'm beside myself, worrying that she might be in danger."

"I'm here if you need me, Mr. Carrol." Detective Parisi shakes my hand and tells me to call him should I require anything else.

I leave the precinct and rush to my vehicle. When exiting the parking lot, I notice that my mind begins to wander. Thoughts begin swirling in my head. Images of my niece and nephew, interviews with Carl Dietrich, and concerns about Linda are jumbled in a small corner of my mind. Assailing my sanity, these thoughts are inhibiting my ability to focus. My car begins swerving. I cross the center line, nearly hitting an oncoming vehicle. I think to myself, *If I don't control my thoughts, there's a possibility I could cause an automobile accident.* Truly, my mind is operating on overload. The sheer volume of problems and stress incurred over the past couple of months is finally catching up with me. I decide to pull over to the shoulder of the road to clear my head and refocus. I can feel my head beginning to throb and the tenseness in my shoulders and neck peaking. I arch my back against the driver's seat and close my eyes. Within a few minutes the throbbing subsides and clarity begins to return. I suddenly feel rejuvenated and calmer.

Just then, my cell phone rings. After answering, I hear a subdued voice ask, "Sean?"

Immediately, I recognize Linda's voice. "Where are you?"

"Sean, please help me."

"What's wrong?"

"Nothing, I'm just tired," she says. "Can you pick me up at La Guardia?" She then tells me, "I'm calling from a cell phone that I borrowed from a flight attendant, because I misplaced mine."

"What flight are you on?"

"I'm flying American Airlines from Cincinnati. I'll be arriving at terminal B, gate number three, in about twenty minutes."

"Cincinnati? I thought you went to Salt Lake City. What's going on Linda?"

"Let's not discuss this now, Sean."

"Okay, but I'm gonna need some answers. Are you all right?"

"Like I said, I'm just a little bit tired. Otherwise, everything is fine."

Sensing trouble, I immediately put the transmission in gear and merge into traffic. The airport is only fifteen minutes away; I should arrive just as Linda's flight is landing. On the way, I wonder what's happened to her, and I'm suspicious of her motive for calling me. Although apprehensive, I'm reluctant to believe she would draw me into a trap. She sounded so dejected. I just hope she's all right.

When I arrive at La Guardia, I rush inside to meet Linda. In the terminal, I scan the flight information display system for the arriving flights. Her plane has just touched down. It'll be a few minutes before she'll be able to disembark. Nearly fifteen minutes later, I recognize Linda ambling down the concourse. She's clutching a cane and limping. I quickly walk to her, grab her left arm, and rest it on my shoulder. She seems very sullen and is clearly in severe pain. I guide her to a bench a few feet away and slowly ease her onto the seat. Knowing Linda, I find it very strange that she's wearing sunglasses and has covered her head with a scarf. This is definitely out of character for her. While reaching for her hand, I notice several bruises below the right pinky finger. The center knuckles on her right hand are also bruised, displaying a dark purple hue. It appears as though she punched something very hard. "What happened, Linda? How did you sustain these injuries?"

Linda drops her head and begins crying. In a low voice she says, "Sean, I'm so sorry."

"What are you sorry for?"

"For betraying you."

"How did you betray me?"

"I foolishly helped Dietrich gain access to your condominium."

"What made you do that?"

"He and two of his cohorts cornered me while I was walking to my car one morning. They forced me back into my condominium and put a gun to my head. Dietrich told me that he needed access to your computer to extract all the information you had pertaining to Deutsche Christen. To ensure my cooperation, he told me, if you don't help me, I'll have to kill Sean Carrol. Concerned about your welfare and safety, I cooperated by providing the location of the door key."

"Where would he have gotten the idea that I kept any data about his organization?"

"He's a very suspicious person, to the point of paranoia. There's no telling where he got the idea."

"What type of information did he think I had?"

She says, "He believed that some of your information contained facts about certain activities that would legally incriminate him and his organization."

"I still don't fully understand why you would trust Dietrich, especially knowing what he's capable of."

"Let's talk about this later, Sean. Right now, I just want to get home and relax."

I lift up her sunglasses, and observe a large contusion over her right eye. The lid is almost closed from the swelling, and a scab has formed above her eyebrow.

Knowing that she won't be able to walk the considerable distance to the car, I find a flight attendant and implore him to obtain a wheelchair. He waves in acknowledgment while running across the concourse. Within five minutes he returns with a wheelchair. We slowly get Linda to her feet and guide her into the chair. I give the attendant twenty dollars and thank him for his help.

Linda and I then head to the baggage area to retrieve her luggage. At the carousel she points to a brown and beige overnight case that is circling toward us. I grab her bag and carefully hand it to her. We then head to the car. The attendant who assisted me earlier rushes over and insists on accompanying us. When we reach the car, he helps me carefully move Linda from the wheelchair and onto the passenger seat.

When he departs, I tell Linda I'm going to take her to the emergency room. Angrily she tells me, "I don't need medical assistance; just take me home." Reluctantly, I pull out from the parking lot and head back to my place.

The thirty minute drive home seems to take forever, because I'm anxious to get Linda settled in. I'm very worried about her condition. When we finally arrive, I help her out of the car and head into my condominium. Once she's settled on the living room couch, I begin heating up the teapot. A cup of tea is just what the doctor ordered.

While Linda sips her tea, I sit in the living room chair, mulling over the viciousness of Dietrich and his organization. They're acting barbarically in addressing any resistance to their ambition for government control. The question is, what actions will they take now to ensure their success?

CHAPTER 20

# SHAME

When I awake the next morning, I'm surprised that Boynton isn't licking my face. This is unusual, but I believe our house guest may have something to do with it. After getting dressed, I walk down the hall toward the stairway. While passing the guest bedroom, I catch sight of Boynton. He's attentively watching over Linda while she sleeps. When I pass, Boynton gets up and follows me downstairs.

After entering the kitchen, I prepare the coffee pot and turn on the burner. I then put out food and water for Boynton. He meanders in, wanders over to the water bowl, and begins drinking. He doesn't appear to be very interested in eating this morning, but I'll leave the bowl of food out just in case he gets hungry later.

Shortly afterward, Linda slowly limps through the kitchen doorway. She appears a little steadier than yesterday, but she's definitely not ready for a marathon. Rushing over to assist her onto a stool, I'm very careful not to touch the bruises on her hands. They still exhibit a deep purple hue, and her knuckles are noticeably swollen. Having made her comfortable, I pour her a cup of coffee and place it on the counter in front of her. She reaches for the cup but grimaces in pain when she attempts to lift it. I reach over to hold the cup for her, but she pushes my hand away. "Sorry, Linda. I just wanted to help."

"I didn't mean anything by that, Sean."

"Not a problem. Would you care for some breakfast?"

"A piece of white toast with some butter will be fine."

"Coming right up."

While she's sitting at the center island, I ask her what happened in Cincinnati. She looks at me but doesn't answer. I press her for an answer and stare at her with mild rage. Knowing that she betrayed me to Carl Dietrich is infuriating, but realizing the trauma she endured at his hands softens my anger.

Finally, she responds. "Dietrich threatened to kill me, my family, and my friends if I didn't cooperate with him. He wanted more information about your plans, and details you had concerning Deutsche Christen. After I refused to answer, he exploded in anger. His temper erupted into a maniacal rage. Being the monster he is, he beat and violated me over a three-day period. After four days, he instructed his guards to have me cleaned up and driven to the airport. Thank God for the compassion of one of the guards. If he hadn't helped me, I don't know if I would have gotten home."

"My God, Linda. You certainly took a chance by meeting with

Dietrich. You could have been killed! What I don't understand is why you went there in the first place."

"Carl Dietrich has had a hold over me for years. About five years ago, my husband, who was a C.I.A. agent at the time, got caught up in a burglary. Somehow, Dietrich set him up. Don was told that a smuggling ring had plans to steal weapons from a factory located in Richmond, Virginia. The weapons were high-level explosives and Javelin antitank missiles."

"And your husband was taking this on by himself?"

"Believing he could trust Carl Dietrich, and hoping to gain some notoriety, Don broke into the factory. He didn't realize that he was playing right into Dietrich's hands. The real thieves were Carl Dietrich and a handful of his associates. When Don realized his mistake, it was too late. By then, he was neck-deep in the scheme. Unbeknown to Don, Dietrich had already filmed him while he illegally cut through the fence and disarmed the alarm systems. About fifty missiles were stolen, along with C-4 explosives. From that time on, both Don and I were trapped."

"Did Dietrich shake your husband down and try to extract any more favors from him?"

"No, but shortly thereafter, Don, retired. Our marriage soon disintegrated. The relationship between us became so strained that he filed for divorce without mentioning a word to me. The overwhelming embarrassment and shame of the incident had caused the fracture in our marriage. Subsequently, he moved to Florida, and I haven't heard from him since. That was five years ago, as I said."

"I'm so sorry, Linda. I wasn't aware of your husband's problem."

"That's okay, Sean. It's something I'm extremely ashamed of. It isn't a subject I routinely talk about."

"Something that appears very strange to me is Dietrich's association with Deutsche Christen while he was an officer in special forces. It leads me to believe that Dietrich's escape from the Catawba treatment center was enabled by Deutsche Christen."

"Based upon what I know, Sean, he has only one allegiance and that's to Carl Dietrich. He'll use and abuse anyone in order to satisfy his own needs."

"How did your husband know Dietrich?"

"Don was in special forces during the second Iraq war. While in a training seminar in D.C. during 2007, he met Dietrich. They became fast friends, and my husband trusted him. Unfortunately, Dietrich didn't view the relationship as anything other than a business arrangement, a convenience, and something he could collect on later. Don was a pawn. Unfortunately, the outcome was devastating to both my husband and me. Not only did our marriage disintegrate, but also Don had an emotional breakdown. He lost faith in everyone around him and retreated within himself."

"Believe me, Linda. I don't know how or when, but someday, I'm gonna get my hands on Dietrich and make him pay for all of his transgressions against us."

CHAPTER **21**

# FOREIGNERS AT THE DOOR

It's Saturday, a week later, and I've nearly completed my weekend piece about the effects of politics on U.S. military power. Commenting on the recent military budget cuts, I point out that certain decisions made by Congress have seriously affected not only the size of our force strength but also our weapons development programs. Nearly $750 million in military spending has been stripped from the recently passed federal budget, causing panic among the joint-chiefs-of-staff. Considering the cuts made in the prior two years, the joint chiefs are scurrying to reassess and revise the current budget. The prior cuts mandated the elimination of several new programs and the firing of thousands of active-duty military personnel. The current budget cuts will further hamper our defense capabilities, exposing our country to severe external and internal danger. Considering the serious military threats confronting us at every turn, I question the foolhardiness of the Washington politicos. Their actions are simply insane.

Since it's a beautiful day, I decide to take a walk to Sammy's, a luncheonette located a couple of miles from home. Though it's a small place by current standards, it seats nearly fifty people. They serve flavorful comfort food such as chicken stew, corn beef hash, and a variety of steak dishes. By walking to Sammy's, I'll force myself to get some exercise, grab a bite to eat, and finish my article.

It's 2:45 when I arrive. Entering, I notice that most of the tables are empty. I say hello to Gus, the owner, while he's standing behind the counter at the entranceway. After taking a seat at a table against the rear wall, I order a light lunch of salad, soup, and a chicken salad sandwich. Then I begin working on my article. Nearly half an hour later I drop my pen, lean back against the chair, and stare at the front entrance. When I do, the reflection of the sunlight gleams through the front glass doors, nearly blinding me. Just then, I'm startled by the figure of a man who is unexpectedly standing next to me. Although the glare from the front door inhibits my vision, I notice that he's dressed in military fatigues and is wearing a dark green beret. He asks, "Are you Mr. Carrol?"

"Yes. Can I help you?"

"May I sit down?"

I wave my hand, gesturing that he take a seat. After sitting down, he introduces himself as Doug Clark and says, "Mr. Carrol, I'm aware that you've done a couple of interviews with Carl Dietrich. I also understand that you're one of the few outsiders who are familiar with their intent to destroy the U.S. government. Having read your recent articles about Deutsche Christen, I'm convinced that you alone possess the ability and tenacity to unravel their secrets and expose their plans to illegitimately assume power within the United States."

"Please continue, Mr. Clark."

"As a government field intelligence operative, I've infiltrated the organization. Several of my military buddies hold important positions within the group. They've guided me through the maze of political layers within Deutsche Christen and have provided me with some valuable information concerning the groups acquisition of weapons and the direction in which the organization is headed. It just so happens that I've received some critical information regarding a major weapons shipment scheduled to take place within the next couple of days."

"Before you begin, how did you find me here?"

"I simply shadowed you while you walked."

"I'm confused as to why you're contacting me. Shouldn't you be conveying this information to the military or the C.I.A.?"

"I've gotta be careful about who I provide this information to, because many people within the government are sympathetic to the cause of Deutsche Christen. Due to your extensive investigative reporting background and your reputation, I believe you're the only one capable of obtaining critical information about the activities of Deutsche Christen."

Continuing he says, "The militia is building up its military power by obtaining sophisticated weapons. They're on a war footing with no sign of halting their advance. What I've learned about their impending actions simply reinforces their determination to upend and replace the U.S. government."

"Mr. Clark, their campaign to destroy everything that I hold sacred frightens the hell out of me. Just to let you know, this push isn't about the philosophy of the members of Deutsche Christen, it's really about the ego maniacal mindset of one man, Carl Dietrich. He views himself as the next Che Quevara, the late Latin American revolutionary. Like him, Dietrich is a socio-path with no filters to control his lust for power. He'll say and do anything to advance his cause."

"Knowing Dietrich, I'm well aware of his background and his ambitions to create a military regime. Having already accumulated a massive cache of weapons, he continues to augment his stockpile. In fact, in two days a weapons shipment is scheduled to take place. The SS *Catanga*, a commercial transport ship sailing under the flag of Panama, will be traveling north from the mouth of the Mississippi at New Orleans. I don't know the stopover points for delivery, but I am aware that weapons will be delivered somewhere in the Midwest."

"How did you obtain this information, and is it credible?"

"As I mentioned, I'm a very good friend of some high-ranking board members of Deutsche Christen who have become disillusioned with the organization. I served with them in the Marine Corp. during Desert Storm. We've been close friends for nearly twenty-five years. Their positions allow them access to very sensitive information concerning plans of the organization. There's no question about the validity of this information."

"What types of weapons are being shipped?"

"I don't know specifics, however, the weaponry are, as I understand, extremely sophisticated. According to my sources, the weapons are registered as backhoes imported from China."

"Is there anything else that you can tell me?"

"At this point, I've told you pretty much everything that I'm aware of. If you decide to investigate the shipment, be very careful. Guarded by hundreds of highly trained and well-armed members of the militia, you'll be in danger every step of the way. I hope you decide to investigate the weapons shipment. In any event, good luck with whatever you decide to do. Goodbye, Mr. Carrol."

Shaking my head, I wonder what the significance of this particular shipment is. I grab my cell phone and call John Errins. I tell him about my encounter with Mr. Clark and outline some of the details he informed me of. "John, if accurate, this could make for one hell of a story."

"Is the information credible, Sean?"

"I'm not 100 percent sure, but my gut tells me the information is reliable. The guy appears to be trustworthy, and the story seems very plausible. He maintains that he's good friends with several of the Deutsche Christen hierarchy, having served with them during Desert Storm."

"Sean, I'm concerned about the danger associated with this assignment. This could be deadly if the militia catches you spying on their operation. The members of Deutsche Christen will do anything to preserve their secrecy. The members of Deutsche Christen have no conscience when it comes to murder. You could be seriously compromising your safety and those who join you."

"John, I understand all of that, but you've gotta realize that someone has to expose this threat. Even though dangerous, I really have no choice."

"Okay, you've got the assignment. Just make sure you take Wayne to obtain photographic evidence but most important be vigilant. In the meantime, I'll make some transportation arrangements for you while you're in New Orleans."

"Thanks, John. I'll see you in a few days."

It's a Tuesday evening, and I'm on my way to Kennedy Airport where I'll meet Wayne for the flight to New Orleans. Our plan is to arrive at our hotel the night before the cargo ship is scheduled to reach the mouth of the Mississippi. This way, we'll be well rested and assured of intercepting the ship before it sails upriver.

When I arrive at Kennedy, Wayne is standing near the curb, just in front of the terminal entranceway. The weather is severely uncomfortable with the temperature at 98 degrees and the humidity at nearly 100 percent. When I exit the taxi, the heat from the asphalt driveway nearly smothers my breathing while I struggle to slowly slide from the backseat. Wayne and I hurry to the gate to board our flight. After touching down at New Orleans International Airport, we secure a cab and drive to the Hilton Hotel located on Canal Street. From here, we're just a few blocks from the Mississippi River.

The next morning, we grab a quick bite to eat and then check out.

After hurrying through the hotel entranceway, we hail a cab and ride a few blocks, arriving near the Mississippi just beyond the Audubon Aquarium. The rancid odor of nearby rotting fish, and the smell of salty air serve to quickly awaken my olfactory senses. I pay the cabbie and assist Wayne with his equipment. A few hundred feet away, we spot the *Orleans Fancy*, the fishing boat that's been chartered for us. Approximately sixty feet long, the boat has a hull that is narrow and sleek. The engines are already running with a quiet roar, becoming louder as we approach. Hurrying, we board and introduce ourselves to the captain, whose name is Wilbur Foreaux. A small man at five feet five inches and maybe two hundred pounds, he speaks with a heavy Creole accent. In spite of his accent, I'm able to clearly understand him.

After storing our gear below, we return to the deck and await the arrival of the cargo ship. Captain Foreaux orders two crew members to weigh anchor while his first mate steers the boat to open water. Slowly moving, we stop just east of mid-river so as not to block river traffic.

Within twenty minutes, we catch sight of the SS *Catanga* sailing upriver past our position. While observing the ship, I can't help but notice the deep rust marks on the exterior hull. The severely faded gray paint and sporadic touches of white stains further blemish its appearance. We continue to watch as the ship passes, and then wait a few minutes before following. I observe, as several ships and small boats of varying sizes glide past. When the SS Catanga is nearly out of sight, the captain orders two-thirds speed ahead. Within fifteen minutes, we catch sight of the ship but lay back so as not to reveal our position. Coasting near the river bank, we watch intently as the cargo ship negotiates its way up the Mississippi past Memphis, heading north to Cairo, Illinois. At the conflux of the Mississippi and Ohio Rivers, the ship makes a stopover, allowing for its cargo to be unloaded onto an awaiting barge.

Using binoculars, I watch intently from a small inlet located on a diagonal, across from the docks. Conspicuously absent, the dock workers have been replaced by approximately two hundred surrogates dressed in military camouflage. Some are carrying machine guns and rifles in case of any encounters with the U.S. military. Hastening to unload the cargo ship, they cover each wooden crate with heavy canvas, and then load, strap, and harness the containers before lowering everything onto an awaiting barge. The cargo is bolted in place and chained to the deck. The entire process takes nearly three hours. Wondering what types of weapons are being unloaded, I'm extremely curious because of the sheer size of the containers. Still, I'm apprehensive about the success of our assignment and frightened by the presence of armed militia. Should we be detected, my safety and that of the entire crew could be compromised. In the meantime, Wayne has photographed the entire event, cataloging all phases of the unloading and loading process.

After the transfer is completed, a notch tug is hitched to the barge. In accordance with maritime procedures, a manifest must be reviewed by the harbormaster's representative. Subsequently, a bill of lading is to be signed, acknowledging the transfer of title of the shipment. Within a half hour, the tug and barge are on their way, heading down the Ohio.

We continue to shadow the ship, making sure not to follow too closely. Although our trip is risky, the calm river waters and clear sunny weather allow for a more pleasant journey, helping to emotionally camouflage our concerns. Within two days, the tug and barge amble past Paducah, Kentucky, and continue hugging the tree-lined shore along the winding river bend, until finally arriving at a large steel dock located thirteen miles south of Paducah on the Illinois side of the river.

Seeking refuge, we slide into a small alcove and drop anchor. Immediately, Wayne and I hurry down the ladder to a small isthmus of land with sparse rows of trees and low-lying bushes. Once again, Wayne photographs the unloading process while I peer through the overgrowth with binoculars, watching as land crews hustle to prepare the dock for unloading the equipment. I count nearly fifty workers who have been hired to complete the task. When the barge is anchored, the crews begin to uncover and unfasten the equipment. After a temporary bridge is erected, we watch as many of the workers hastily retreat from the barge, while a small crew mount the equipment and quickly drive to land. The identity of the equipment has been intentionally concealed, by disguising the shipment of military tanks as backhoes.

When the tanks reach land, they are driven down an old dirt road and quickly swallowed up by the overgrowth of trees and brush. Twenty-five tanks have disembarked, leaving an equal number on the awaiting barge.

Darkness soon descends. The vessels begin their journey to the next destination. While shadowing them, we diligently continue to distance ourselves so as not to compromise our safety. When the vessels float past Newburgh, they pull slightly left toward the Indiana riverbank. Approximately eighteen miles south of Newburgh, the barge docks at a floating steel platform. The size of the platform is enormous, measuring at least 400 feet long and 350 feet wide. It can easily accommodate the unloading of the equipment. Once again, the tanks are uncovered and unfastened. Crew members quickly drive them to the riverbank, where they are then loaded onto flatbed trucks, covered, and transported away.

While observing the unloading process, I see the exterior trim lights of our boat suddenly begin flickering, exposing our location. The captain shouts, "Shut down the lights immediately, and restart the engines." Realizing that the light sensors hadn't been deactivated, the captain knows that they've triggered the system. As a result, our position has been compromised, and we're in danger. Suddenly, horns from the SS *Catanga* begin blaring—a signal that we've been discovered. Within a couple of minutes, we can see two large inboard cabin cruisers rushing downriver while firing machine guns at our position. Scrambling to escape the oncoming threat, Captain Foreaux turns the boat around and forces open the throttle to flank speed, hoping to distance us from the pursuing vessels. In the meantime, the first officer radios the coast guard station in Michigan City. Due to the distance from our position, it will take several hours before assistance can reach us. Advising the dispatcher about the weapons shipment, he provides him with name of the ship, and its current location. Hopefully, the military will pursue and capture the ship.

While fleeing, we continue increasing the distance between us and our pursuers. In the turmoil of our escape, multiple rounds of machine gun fire are heard. I can hear the bullets from the machine guns skimming along the surface water like flat rocks being tossed from the nearby shore. Panicked, we grab all the weapons we can find and take positions along the deck. If the militia attacks, at least we'll have a fighting chance to escape. A few minutes later, we notice that the pursuing boats have retreated, and are heading back toward the SS *Catanga*.

Suddenly, our boat slows to half speed. Rushing to determine the problem, the captain lifts the door of the engine compartment, turns on his flashlight, and reaches inside. Yelling for his first mate, the captain says, "Get a large flathead screwdriver and some heavy-duty tape." I rush to assist him, only to discover that one of the main oil pressure lines has been severed by a bullet from one of the machine guns. The line is leaking profusely. Captain Foreaux yells, "Shut down the engines until we make repairs." After toiling for a half hour, the captain makes the necessary repairs, replenishes the oil, and orders that the engines be restarted. When we begin moving, everyone releases a loud sigh of relief.

In spite of the success of our assignment, I'm aware that our lives could have been easily forfeited. We now need to get our documentation to the *New York International News* and expose the prevailing threats presented by Deutsche Christen.

Just then, my cell phone rings. I pick it up and hear Colonel Gannon's voice. "Hello, Sean."

"Hi, Colonel. What's happening?"

"I just received a call from General Stanton. He advised me that he received a security bulletin today verifying that our defense satellites have recorded suspicious shipments of heavy military equipment. The bulletin refers to cargoes that have emanated from China and Russia. He informed me that pictures of the cargo ships and river vessels clearly display sophisticated military equipment being transferred to barges along the Delaware, Columbia, and Ohio Rivers. On the coasts of Washington and California, satellites also captured visuals of several cargo ships that were docked while military equipment including tanks, heavy artillery, and surface-to-air missiles were being unloaded. The general notified the joint-chiefs-of-staff about the reports. In the meantime, the White House is being briefed and cautioned about the urgency of the situation."

"Oh, my God, this likely means that the final steps are underway to arm Deutsche Christen."

"I think you're right Sean."

"Colonel, I can't say much on my cell, but I've just witnessed a shipment of tanks being delivered to Deutsche Christen. When I see you, I'll provide you with specifics about the deliveries. You've gotta know that this proliferation of weapons shipments definitely indicates that Deutsche Christen has cut short the time frame for military action. Our very survival will now be contingent upon halting future deliveries."

"Sean, based upon what's occurring, the general has asked if there is some way that we can reorganize our special forces team and infiltrate some of the militia camps. He's appointed me to head up a special task force for the purpose of infiltrating enemy militia camps and attacking them at vulnerable locations. I'd like you to join my unit. We need to quickly assess the weapons strength of Deutsche Christen and provide the general with details about the inventory. I've also told the general that we'll require additional satellite images displaying the defensive capabilities of each camp to be infiltrated."

"Let me know when the mission is scheduled, Colonel. I'll definitely participate."

# CHAPTER 22

# THREAT AND BETRAYAL

It's a clear, warm, August day. I grab an iced tea and decide to turn on the national news while Boynton climbs onto the couch and lies next to me. The reporter is describing an incident in Iraq involving an attack by the Iranian Guard. He reports, "A force of about one hundred guardsmen attacked a small military convoy of Kurds near Fallujah. A firefight ensued killing twelve members of the convoy."

Suddenly, a special report flashes on the screen. From his van on the scene in Philadelphia, a reporter and his news crew are shadowing a ship along the Delaware River, where an international incident is unfolding. He states, "A Russian cargo ship slated to deliver consumer products such as vodka and caviar is now suspected of carrying military weapons. Traveling north on the Delaware River, the ship has nearly reached the conflux of the Schuylkill and is approaching southwest Philadelphia." Without warning, I hear the ear-piercing sound of sirens that disrupts the tranquility of the mid-afternoon setting.

"Overhead," the reporter says, "I see two coast guard cutter helicopters circling the ship. Using a megaphone, they are delivering a message demanding that the vessel stop and allow troops to board and inspect."

While I watch, the camera slides slightly to the left, capturing the scene of a Sentinel-class coast guard cutter pulling to the stern of the ship, with its .50-caliber machine guns at the ready. Just then, I see two coast guard boats pull to either side of the ship while gunfire flares. The crew of the Russian ship is firing nonstop at the boats. Out of nowhere, I hear cannon fire. A massive explosion erupts above the ship as one of the helicopters is hit, causing it to spin out of control and burst into thousands of embers that descend onto the river and the nearby shore. I watch as the coast guard vessels open fire on the ship. The Russian vessel, however, appears to be impervious to the firepower of the coast guard cutter's weapons. From what I can see, the ship is top-heavy. It appears that the hull of the vessel has been reinforced with thick steel plates to absorb heavy weapons fire.

With the action suspended, the reporter cuts to a commercial break. I fall back into the soft cushions of the couch, stunned at what I'm witnessing. Events are spinning out of control with the Russians and Chinese having been emboldened by the lack of U.S. military response. The permissive silence of the United States has encouraged the Chinese and Russians to take liberties that are unacceptable. Where this will lead is anyone's guess.

Returning to the scene along the Delaware, the reporter says, "I've just received word from a representative of the coast guard that the surviving helicopter retreated to secure assistance."

Shortly thereafter, I watch as the USS *Cole*, a guided-missile destroyer, is spotted steaming up the Delaware. Stopping his vehicle, the reporter accesses his laptop to determine information about the ship. Returning he says, "The USS *Cole* emanates from Norfolk, but it's been dispatched to patrol the northeast coast. Luckily today, the ship is patrolling the New Jersey coast near Cape May."

Suddenly, the camera veers off and focuses on the developing incident. Once the camera hones in on the scene, I can see the USS *Cole* approaching the Russian ship as the coast guard vessels recede from their positions. In spite of pursuit by the destroyer, the cargo ship defiantly continues unimpeded north on the Delaware. When the U.S. destroyer moves in, I hear weapons fire from the cargo ship. As a warning, the destroyer responds by firing a .25 mm chain gun at the vessel. Ignoring the response from the USS Cole, the Russian crew continues their aggressive behavior.

To halt any further attacks and prevent potential injuries to innocent bystanders, a cruise missile is activated. After locking on to the Russian ship, the missile is fired and immediately strikes the side of the ship's hull causing a tremendous explosion, one that rocks the Philadelphia area with a seismic tremor.

I see buildings adjacent to the shore swaying, while some piers along the river's edge crumble. The shocking scene displays the hull of the Russian ship split in half, as though precisely sliced by a surgeon's scalpel. I can see remains of the ship and cargo scattered in sparse collections from bank to bank along the Delaware. Among the debris, I view a few charred and dismembered bodies floating. While I watch, coast guard vessels descend on the scene and remove the bodies of the Russian crew.

The cameraman focuses on the helicopter rescue, where two injured Russian sailors are being hoisted to the fuselage to be transported to a local Philadelphia hospital. There, they'll be treated and then interrogated about information pertinent to their mission.

I watch as river debris and the ship's hull are cleared by cranes and river barges that have been dispatched to the scene. Once everything is removed, commercial traffic will again be permitted access to the docks.

In the meantime, Colonel Gannon calls me and says, "Sean, I've organized some of our team for the mission to infiltrate the Deutsche Christen camps. Our goal will be to determine the firepower of the paramilitary. General Stanton wants us to create an inventory of the types of armaments stored within the camps. This information will enable the joint-chiefs-of-staff to assess the potency of the paramilitary. Due to the gravity of the situation, however, the general has requested that everyone report to Eglin Air Force Base by tomorrow morning. In the meantime, I'll develop plans for the mission."

"See you tomorrow, Colonel."

It's now 3:30 p.m. I pack my equipment and call Linda to ask her to watch Boynton. I haven't talked to her since last week, when she was leaving for Denver where she hoped to photograph the city skyline and some of the rural areas located outside of the city. She answers the phone. "Hello?"

"Hi, Linda. It's Sean."

"How are you? I haven't talked to you in a couple of weeks."

"I've missed you so much Linda, but with all the craziness going on, my time has just evaporated. We'll have to make a point of getting together next week."

"I can't wait."

"Linda, I'm heading out of town for a few days. I wonder if you can watch Boynton."

"I don't have any plans for next week, so that's not a problem. I can pick him up in a few minutes."

"Where are you headed to, Sean?"

"I can't talk about the specifics, but it involves a short military mission."

"Is it dangerous?"

"You know there's always an element of danger with any military mission."

Linda, when you come over why don't you stay for a while? I've got a couple of beautiful steaks I can grill."

"That sounds great Sean."

After dinner we clean the dishes and have a cup of coffee. It's nearly 9:00 when Linda gets ready to leave. I grab Boynton's leash and hook it to his collar. Before Linda leaves, I kiss her and tell her that I should be back within a couple of days. She cautions me to be careful. After Linda waves goodbye, she and Boynton head out the door.

The next morning, I awaken early, drive to Lakehurst, and catch a flight to Eglin. After touching down, I immediately disembark and secure a ride in a waiting Jeep. Hurrying to Colonel Gannon's office, I rush up the stairs and walk the hallway. It's 8:30, when I enter. I salute the colonel and reach to shake his hand.

He tells me, "General Stanton received a phone call from James Halsberg, the secretary of defense. The secretary ordered him to expend all efforts necessary to obstruct the delivery of weapons shipments from China and Russia. He also ordered that all active-duty and National Guard units be called up, because he's assigning them to flood the national waterways and major coastal areas. In conjunction with the coast guard and the navy, thousands of troops will be employed to board vessels suspected of transporting illegal weapons."

Continuing, the colonel says, "According to the general, he and his staff have been overwhelmed with numerous military communiqués while attempting to substantiate the flow of heavy weapons into the United States. They've barely been able to manage deployment of our troops and weaponry. General Stanton has also advised me that numerous weapons shipments have been intercepted, but many avoided detection and have presumably found their way to the paramilitary camps."

In the midst of this national turmoil, I'm excited to have rejoined our special forces team in time for the infiltration mission. We've organized our team and are ready to board a cargo jet. I check my watch and see that it's now 1400 hours, just three hours before our initial infiltration mission into the Deutsche Christen camps. When the plane takes to the air, Colonel

Gannon calls the teams together, telling us, "We have a five hour window to finalize the infiltration mission. The purpose, once again, is to inventory the weapons arsenal of Deutsche Christen with special emphasis on heavy artillery, tanks, and surface-to-air missiles. Stealth and speed are the key words for this operation, but we must be vigilant each step of the way."

Under the auspices of a private military flight emanating from Newark International Airport, we'll be landing at Philadelphia International Airport. This will enable us to secretly transfer to a military helicopter more suited for our mission. When our plane lands, we disembark and hurry to a small clandestine area near terminal F. Here, we appear as an inconspicuous group of troops on leave for holiday. We board a waiting CH-47 Chinook helicopter located just five hundred feet from our plane. After boarding, we drop our equipment on the floor near the benches. Colonel Gannon announces the time and orders us to synchronize our watches.

When we arrive at Wheeling, the Chinook lands. Five of us disembark and begin heading east toward the camp, while the remaining ten team members travel to their destinations. A military radio is left at the scene. It will be utilized to contact the flight crew of the Chinook once we've completed our mission.

Our destination is a mile away. We must be on guard to anticipate the unexpected. Approaching the perimeter of the camp, Stan and I cautiously walk through a field of heavy, marsh-like overgrowth. In spite of the wet and muddy ground cover, we quickly manage to reach our target and position ourselves. We view two guards stationed six hundred feet from our position. Guarding the northwestern perimeter of the camp, they appear preoccupied in conversation. It's now 1715 hours. The moon is hidden by heavy cloud cover, providing us with much-needed camouflage. Everything is cast in a greenish glow through my night vision goggles. We slowly approach the guards. When we are about thirty feet from their position, we increase our pace and overwhelm them. Stan grabs the arm of one of the guards. Twisting, he snaps the neck of the first guard, while I pull my knife from the sheath and stab the second guard. Taking them by their feet, we drag their bodies into the brush.

While heading back to the river bank to rejoin our team, we encounter three militia walking toward us from the east. With the night vision goggles, I'm able to determine that they're armed with machine guns. Stan and I slip the pistols from our holsters and carefully aim at the approaching militia. Our pistols are fitted with suppressors and will be nearly silent when fired. When the three militia are within forty feet of our position, we fire multiple rounds. After the men fall to the ground, we quickly but cautiously approach to determine their condition. One attempts to crawl away. Before he can escape, Stan fires two rounds from his pistol, killing him. After disposing of their bodies we rush back to our team.

We all kneel in a circle and quickly discuss our plan. Moving south, we cautiously and quietly negotiate our way. At the tree-lined perimeter of the camp, I hold out my arms to stop the others from proceeding any further. The woods are eerily quiet this evening, free of sounds from katydids and crickets. This is very unusual.

Ordering my team to remain where they are, I slowly move deeper inside the perimeter of the camp. Furtively moving through the overgrowth and woods, I hear voices quietly sounding orders while they rustle within the brush. Judging from the sound of their movement, I figure there must be at least two dozen militia. Turning, I head back to my team and signal for them to withdraw to the landing site. While we rush from the area gunfire erupts. Stan turns and tosses a grenade squarely in the middle of the area from where the gunfire is emanating. A tremendous explosion occurs, followed by screams that pervade the air. Just ahead, we're met with overwhelming firepower from the militia. It appears that hundreds of paramilitary forces are flooding the scene from the riverbank and the nearby woods. Further on to our right, we encounter a trio of militia who begin firing at us. Our team drops to the ground and fires at the group, killing all three.

We jump up and once again begin running. Before reaching the landing site, I hear machine gun fire from behind. Stan stumbles and then falls to the ground, screaming, "I've been hit!"

Reaching out, I pull him to his feet. "Hold on, Stan, I need to get my right shoulder under your left arm. This way we'll be able to speed up our pace." We struggle to escape the rush of the pursuing militia. Finally after arriving at the landing site, we dive for cover in the brush.

Able to feel the moisture of Stan's shirt, I worry that he could bleed to death before we're able to secure medical treatment. Knowing that I could lose my best friend scares the hell out of me. Removing my knife from the sheath, I tell Stan, "I'll roll you over on your stomach so that I can cut open the back of your shirt to examine the wound." Hiding behind the thick overgrowth, I turn on my flashlight and check the wound. I can see that he's been hit in the upper back just below his right shoulder. Gently rolling him over on his back, I discover that the bullet has exited through his chest cavity, but I can't determine whether any internal injuries have been sustained. "Hold tight, Stan, while I grab the first aid kit from inside my backpack." After cleaning and disinfecting the wound, I bandage it as well as I can. Unfortunately, the bleeding continues unabated. In the meantime, we can hear the sound of militia rustling through the nearby overgrowth. My senses tell me that they're near the riverbank, about three hundred feet from our position.

While I tend to Stan, Bo radios the helicopter crew to advise them of our situation, while our other two team members guard the perimeter of the landing site. After signing off, he tells me, "The other two teams encountered a similar fate. Unfortunately, Team 2, designated for the Marietta camp, was annihilated.

I tell Bo, "They must have known we were coming. The question is, how'd they find out?"

I can hear the crickets and katydids chirping from the woods. This may signal the withdrawal of the militia. I ask Bo to stay with Stan while I head toward the river to see if any militia are lingering. Cautiously, I move closer to the river bank to assure myself that no stragglers remain. After inspecting the area, I see no signs of militia. Satisfied, I return to the landing site and await the Chinook. At 1930 hours we sight the helicopter. Once it lands, Bo and I lift Stan to his feet and support him while we rush to the cargo bay. Due to the loss of blood he's very weak. On board, Bo and I gently place Stan on a bench and cover him with blankets in order to maintain his body heat.

I salute the colonel and tell him, "Stan was hit by machine gun fire. He's in serious condition. The sooner we secure medical treatment, the better."

"Sean, the pilot has already radioed ahead. EMT units will be there upon our arrival."

Along the bench I see the surviving team. Two of their members sustained flesh wounds, but nothing serious. When the cargo bay door closes, we settle in. The helicopter then takes to the air. I continue monitoring Stan's condition, worried about his continuing loss of blood. Removing some of the bandages, I replace them with fresh ones and then with a clean cloth in hand, I wipe the blood from his chest and stomach.

Soon we arrive at Philadelphia International Airport where three ambulances are waiting. The emergency medical technicians rush up the platform to the cargo bay and lift Stan and the other two injured troops onto gurneys. Before pulling away, I climb into the ambulance to accompany my friend to the hospital.

At the Hospital of the University of Pennsylvania, Stan is rushed into an operating room. By this time, he's unconscious and is hooked up to an oxygen tank. Seeing the mad rush of medical personnel, I become anxious.

I ask myself, what if Stan doesn't make it? I quietly say a prayer asking that my friend survive. Then I grab my cell phone.

While I dial Betty, fear grips my emotions. I realize that Stan may not pull through. Disconcerted, I wonder what I'm going to say to her.

"Hello?"

"Hi, Betty. It's Sean." From the sound of my voice, she knows that I'm calling with bad news. She begins to cry. "Betty, please don't cry. Get a hold of yourself. Stan was wounded when we were escaping from the militia. He was shot in the back, near the right shoulder blade. I'm not sure of his condition yet, but I'm gonna continue to question the medical staff about his status."

"Sean, I'm going to buy a ticket for a flight. What hospital is Stan in?"

"He's in the Hospital of the University of Pennsylvania."

"I'll pack a few necessities and see you in a couple of hours."

After hanging up, I head back to the waiting room to check on Stan's condition. There's a hurried flow of emergency personnel going to and coming from the operating room. I walk toward the swinging doors. While waiting to speak with a medical attendant, I begin to lose my patience. I hurry to the nurse's station and ask a nurse, "Can you tell me Mr. Monahan's condition?"

Responding she says, "I'll check with one of the operating room nurses and get right back to you." She walks toward the operating room and pushes through the swinging doors.

While I'm waiting for her to return, the loudspeaker announces a code blue. Panicked, I rush toward the swinging doors and peer through the small square window, hoping to get a glimpse of what' taking place. Medical personnel are scurrying about, in a near panic. They're rushing medical equipment into the operating room. Apparently, Stan's condition is deteriorating. Just then, the nurse comes back through the swinging doors and informs me, "Mr. Monahan is in distress. His breathing is labored, and he's experiencing convulsions. The surgical team is doing everything possible to save him."

"Oh my God!"

I feel my heart sink, worried that Stan isn't going to make it. I take a seat on the floor and rest my back against the wall located in the waiting area not far from the operating room doors.

Nearly three hours later Betty enters the waiting room. Her face is drawn, and her eyes are red from crying. She comes over to me and asks, "How's Stan's condition?"

I get up, gently take her arm, and guide her to a small couch located in the right corner of the waiting room. I tell her, "A while ago, the nurse told me that Stan was in distress. It's been over two hours since I spoke to her, so we'll have to wait for one of the nurses or the doctor to update us on his condition." Betty begins crying and uttering something unintelligible. I hold her tight, telling her, "Stan's in God's hands. I know he'll be all right."

Soon after, the doctor exits the operating room and heads to Betty and me. His blood-stained gown attests to the medical battle he's just waged to preserve Stan's life. He introduces himself. "I'm Doctor Cantel.

Mr. Monahan's condition is presently stable but serious. We'll be able to better assess his medical situation within the next twenty-four hours. As you know, he received a wound from a bullet that penetrated under the right shoulder area. Before the bullet exited through the chest, however, it pierced the right wall of the lung and perforated the lower right lobe of the bronchus. Due to the damage to the bronchus lobe, his breathing was severely inhibited. He nearly succumbed to his wound twice during the operation. Thank God he's strong; otherwise, he wouldn't have survived. He's currently resting in the intensive care unit, where he'll be monitored twenty-four hours daily."

"What are the chances of survival, and when will we know?" I ask.

"We have a forty-eight-hour window. If he survives that time frame, his chance of pulling through will be almost assured."

Betty asks, "When will we be able to see him?"

"You can see him for a few minutes now, but then you'll have to leave so that the nursing staff can attend to him."

We both thank the doctor and decide to sleep in the waiting room after we visit Stan. This way we'll be here should anything happen.

CHAPTER 23

# MOUNTING CRISIS

Three days later, while I watch the morning news, the anchor reports that the mounting military crisis involving China and Russia is stretching our resources to the brink. He relates, "Numerous military actions have been implemented not only to protect our country's waterways but also to shore up the porous border areas between the United States and Mexico."

After completion of the news report, the broadcast switches to a reporter who is standing outside of the Pentagon. He states, "Reports have been pouring into the National Reconnaissance Office, warning that military advisers from China have been smuggled into the United States. The satellite data presented clearly displays hundreds of Chinese military dispersing to areas throughout the U.S. Several hundred arrests have been made, but many Chinese military have avoided capture."

Continuing, he states, "Several protests have since been lodged by the government of the Republic of China, condemning these arrests and demanding the release of their citizens. Ignoring these protests, agents of the C.I.A. and F.B.I. have been intensively interrogating those arrested. Promised asylum, many detainees have provided valuable information about the intention of the Chinese and Russian governments. Some of the higher ranking Chinese officers have even furnished details about new weapons technologies being developed by their military."

At the climax of the news program, I decide to drive to the newspaper and begin writing the article about the recent bombings of two mosques located in Jersey City. It's 2:00 p.m. when I arrive at the newspaper. After exiting my car, I begin heading to my office. Suddenly, I'm stopped by a police officer who requests my personal identification. He's part of the detail temporarily assigned to protect the premises from an attack by Deutsche Christen. After providing identification, I hurry up the stairs to my office and start organizing notes and police reports that I received from a detective friend.

Ten minutes later, John Errins knocks on my office door and enters. "Sean, I have another assignment for you, but you'll have to understand the political nature of the story before beginning any investigation."

"I'm already working on the article concerning the mosque bombings, John."

"Don't worry, Sean, I'll have someone else complete that article. The news story I'm referring to is significant and requires a seasoned investigator such as yourself."

John tells me, "A United Nations pronouncement has been adopted by Congress to censure the Republic of China and the Russian Federation for their violation of U.S. territorial integrity. As a result, an emergency session of the United Nations Security Council has been announced. Over the objections of the Chinese and Russian governments, the U.N. secretary general has rejected their demand for abrogation of the meeting and has, based upon the credibility of all evidence provided, supported the U.S. ambassador."

"John, I heard about the arrest of a number of Chinese military who illegally entered the United States. Does the U.N. meeting address this issue?"

"Yes, but there are a number of additional violations that will be discussed."

"How did you get this information?"

"It was provided to me by a U.N. official I've known for quite a long time. He's been a solid source of information to me for nearly twenty years."

"What's the agenda for the meeting?"

"In the Security Council chamber, the United States ambassador will have the opportunity to present her case. The notification to the U.N. concerning violations of U.S. sovereignty and territorial integrity by the Republic of China and the Russian Federation will be presented to the fifteen member council. While parties to the dispute, however, the Russian Federation, the Republic of China, and the United States must abstain from voting. Sean, it will therefore be the responsibility of the remaining twelve member nations to vote and take appropriate action. In order to pass the resolution, nine yea votes will be required for censure."

"When is the meeting scheduled to take place, John?"

"It's scheduled for this Thursday."

"I'll have to do some research and make the appropriate arrangements for my attendance."

By Wednesday, I've received clearance to attend the upcoming meeting of the Security Council. On Thursday morning, I drive to the United Nations building and am escorted by an usher to a press seat located in front of the horseshoe shaped chamber table in the Security Council meeting room. When the session begins, the council president calls Ms. Hanley, the U.S. ambassador, to address the council members. At forty-five years of age, Ms. Hanley has served in numerous government positions since graduating from Yale at the age of twenty-one. Standing at a slender five feet seven inches, she's pleasantly attractive but not stunning. She exhibits an air of confidence and an authoritative demeanor. After rising, she slowly and deliberately walks to the dais. Supported by a large array of electronic equipment, her presentation promises to be informative and impactful.

While addressing the members of the Security Council, she states, "I wish to thank all members of the council for allowing me to present our case regarding the violations of U.S. territorial integrity." Continuing, she says, "On the screen, you will see satellite images of dock workers unloading military equipment illegally shipped to coastal and inter-coastal areas of the United States. Some of the equipment is clearly marked with Chinese and Russian insignias."

I carefully listen while Ms. Hanley presents visual evidence of the alleged violations. The ambassador continues by delivering a stinging rebuke concerning the Chinese and Russian aggression. I watch as the members of the council listen intently to the violations she enumerates, beginning with the exportation of weapons to Deutsche Christen. She says, "Knowingly, and without regard to our sovereignty, both nations committed these violations that clearly represent an invasion and act of war." Enraged, she continues, "I challenge both China and Russia to dispute these accounts of their violations."

Although invited to address the council regarding the allegations, the ambassadors from both the Republic of China and the Russian Federation decline.

In spite of the evidence presented, the resolution for sanctioning China and Russia is rejected. Jordan, the wildcard, voted in opposition to the United States, thereby precluding any action by the Security Council against either country.

Outlining his position, the Jordanian ambassador casts doubt on the credibility of the information presented by the U.S. ambassador and her staff. Alleging that the evidence has somehow been falsified, the Jordanian ambassador questions the U.S. motive for taking action in the Security Council. I think to myself, *How any of the members can dispute the validity of this overwhelming mountain of evidence is beyond belief.* I'm convinced that political motivation is at the heart of the U.N. decision, and that this action is specifically intended to embarrass the United States. As expected, the other two nay votes were cast by Argentina and Chile. Unfortunately, instead of preventing a crisis, the United Nations, I believe, has tacitly encouraged ongoing hostilities.

Obviously infuriated by the vote of the Security Council, I watch as Ambassador Hanley rushes out of the building. Before she climbs into the awaiting limousine, I approach her. When she sees me she reaches to shake my hand, "Sean, it's been a long time since I've seen you."

"I know, Ambassador. You've come a long way since then."

Responding, she says, "Sean, I'm in a rush. The secretary of state is anxiously waiting for me to let her know the outcome of the U.N. vote."

"Ambassador, I'd like an interview with you for a news report. Can we make arrangements to meet sometime next week?"

"Sean, if you can, why don't you come to D.C. with me now? We can talk along the way."

I nod. "I don't have any appointments or other pressing issues. I'll be more than happy to accompany you."

We climb into the limousine and head to La Guardia. After arriving, we catch a charter flight to Reagan National Airport in D.C. While in flight, Ambassador Hanley urgently dials the White House from her cell phone and is immediately connected to Martha Carrighan, the assistant to the secretary of state. "Hello, Martha. It's Ambassador Hanley. Will you please connect me to Secretary Castle at once? It's urgent."

"Ambassador, Secretary Castle is in a meeting, but I'll try connecting you."

Just then, I hear the secretary's voice. Hanley says, "Hello, Madame Secretary. I'm sorry to interrupt your meeting, but the Security Council has rejected our proposed resolution sanctioning the Russian Federation and the Republic of China."

I can hear the secretary's voice screaming into the phone. "What? I thought we had an airtight case."

"I thought so too. Unfortunately, the Security Council members were unwilling to accept our evidence, and instead questioned the credibility of our information."

When the ambassador shuts off the phone, she tells me, "Secretary Castle is quite upset about the ruling from the Security Council. She told me that the secretary has to make some urgent phone calls to the secretary of defense, several members of Congress, and certain Pentagon officials regarding the impact of today's U.N. vote. She's ordered me to come directly to the White House after landing. A meeting is being arranged to address not only today's vote, but also our current status within the United Nations."

"What do you mean, Ambassador?"

"Sean, you don't have to address me as 'Ambassador.' We've known each other far too long. Just call me by my first name." Continuing she tells me, "For several years, our administration has been considering secession from the United Nations. With all of the recent tumult within the organization, including discrimination toward the U.S. delegation, harassment of our staff, and the ever-rising radical elements within the U.N., the case for secession has become more intense."

"How will secession impact our relationship with our allies and friends within the organization?"

"I don't really believe our relationship with those countries will be affected."

We continue discussing the difficulties involving several members of the United Nations and the ineffectiveness of the organization. Once we arrive at Reagan National Airport, we rush to a waiting limousine and further discuss the U.N. decision and the ramifications for the country.

After arriving at the White House, we head directly to the Roosevelt Room, where a meeting has been arranged with the secretaries of state and defense, several cabinet members, and two congressmen. Seated at the far end of the table when we walk in, the secretary of state stands when she sees us. Immediately, she walks over to greet us. The ambassador introduces me to Secretary Castle, who informs me, "This is an informal meeting. You're welcome to stay, Sean, but please keep the proceedings to yourself." While we shake hands, the secretary whispers to the ambassador, "Sheila, we must take strong action to admonish the U.N. representatives for this clear injustice and affront to our country."

Secretary Castle begins the meeting. She outlines her dissatisfaction with the United Nations and angrily communicates her outrage over the result of today's vote by the members of the Security Council. Charging them with discrimination and animosity toward the United States, she says, "I propose a withdrawal of the United States from the U.N., in conjunction with defunding the organization. This is a bold move, but it is one that I now know has been considered by numerous parties during the past several years." She pauses. "After all, we provide approximately 22 percent of the funding required to run the U.N. In the case of China and Russia, they provide barely 8 percent of the budget. We must thoroughly discuss this issue and determine whether withdrawal from the U.N. is the appropriate action, or if another alternative should be employed."

Beginning with Secretary of Defense James Halsberg, questions are raised about the benefits of membership in the United Nations. Citing a number of examples, the secretary makes the case for withdrawal. "The abysmal voting record of the Security Council alone provides enough justification for withdrawal. In addition, the lack of substantive action after the invasion of Nepal by China, and the North Korean missile launch against South Korea, are additional reasons for severing our ties with the United Nations. There is a clear undertone of animosity exhibited by many members toward the United States, and the U.N. has simply shirked its responsibility in properly settling conflicts."

Congressman Neely of Utah, currently serving as chairman of the House Armed Services Committee, has long been an outspoken critic of the United Nations, vehemently denouncing the U.N. as irrelevant in the current world environment. He states, "I support Secretary Halsberg's argument in favor of withdrawal. Further, I denounce the U.S. government for providing billions upon billions of dollars in support of such an ineffectual and corrupt organization."

I listen intently to the arguments presented and attempt to digest the current environment prevalent within the United Nations. Aware of the administration's discontent with the organization, I hadn't understood the depths of dysphoria that pervaded our government.

Angered by the illustrations of the congressman and the secretary of defense, Senator Benjamin, the chairman of the House Ways and Means Committee, erupts in a tirade against withdrawing from the United Nations. Citing several positive reasons to remain in the U.N., he states, "The intervention of U.N. troops in Rwanda in 1997 for the purpose of preventing genocide, and in Somalia in 1993 to preserve a ceasefire, and again in Afghanistan in 2002 to establish a sustainable peace throughout the country justifies continuing our membership within the organization."

He argues, "Without the presence of the U.N. peacekeeping troops, a bloodbath would have arisen in each one of these countries. Let us also not forget the many United Nations missions to provide food for impoverished nations and medical aid for disease outbreaks. Why, in the last decade alone, the United Nations has been instrumental in reducing HIV infections by 20 percent worldwide. Do you call these successes ineffective?"

Furious, Ambassador Hanley vaults from her seat. Staring directly at Senator Benjamin, she responds, "With all due respect, Senator, you have no idea of the daily indignities my staff and I must endure from representatives of numerous outlaw nations within the U.N. Due to the policies of our current administration, the United States has become a laughing stock. Constant harassment and outright mocking comments from these delegates, regarding our directives and policies, are continually being hurled at us. We're forced to absorb the indignities of discrimination and loathing animosity. The hostility exhibited toward our staff has created an unworkable environment for all of us."

Continuing she states, "You speak of U.N. successes. Our mission to the United Nations has been stymied when presenting issues and ideas on health, poverty, and terrorism. Representatives from other countries have exhibited antipathy toward our mission by obstructing our petitions and, in effect, isolating us. I ask you, Senator, how does the United States make progress within the United Nations when this atmosphere exists?"

Somewhat embarrassed, the senator responds, "Ambassador, I didn't realize the severity of the circumstances and the environment prevalent within the U.N. This definitely justifies the rationale for our country to consider discontinuing participation as a member. However, we must still explore other avenues to deal with the environment prevalent at the U.N. In spite of these circumstances, we should keep an open mind."

Startled at the senator's comments, Secretary Castle rises and inquires, "Does anyone else have an opinion about the participation of the United States in the United Nations?" She also asks, "Are there any other appropriate alternatives that should be considered?" Hearing no response, she requests that an open vote for withdrawal be cast. She states,

"The result of this vote will determine the actions to be taken concerning the United States' participation in the U.N. If the motion is passed, then a signed declaration will be forwarded to Congress notifying them of the committee's recommendation to withdraw from the United Nations. Having no power, the committee can only recommend solutions, not implement them."

The secretary then calls for a show of hands. The vote is tallied. By a margin of six yea votes to one nay, the recommendation to withdraw from the U.N. is approved. Secretary Castle advises everyone that she will draft the declaration and have it forwarded to each committee participant for their signature. The declaration will then be delivered to Congress. If approved, formal action will be taken.

Subsequent to the meeting, Secretary of Defense Halsberg requests that Secretary Castle and Ambassador Hanley remain to discuss a pressing matter.

Hearing this, I get up and step into the hallway where I wait for Ambassador Hanley. Noticing that the door is slightly ajar, I move closer and hear Secretary Halsberg speaking about a secret meeting that he had with Ambassador Hinto of Japan yesterday. I hear him say, "The ambassador visited my office and advised me that his government has obtained sensitive political and military information concerning the Chinese-Russian relationship."

Continuing, Secretary Halsberg states, "The two countries have formed a mutual defense pact ensuring that if one party is attacked, the other will come to its aid. In conjunction with this, they've instituted regular maneuvers encompassing more than one million troops. These exercises are currently taking place in the Indian Ocean, extending as far north as the Bay of Bengal and involving the countries of India, Myanmar, Thailand, and Indonesia. Threatening this rim of countries will, I'm sure, cause a military eruption."

Shocked at the news, Secretary Castle asks, "Is this information accurate, and how did the Japanese acquire the details?"

Secretary Halsberg relates, "The information was obtained from a Chinese colonel who was caught in a homosexual tryst with a staff member of the Japanese Embassy. After extorting the colonel, the Japanese were able to obtain particulars about the Chinese-Russian partnership. Knowing that he would be imprisoned if his relationship with the staff member were to be revealed, the colonel cooperated fully with the Japanese officials."

Overwhelmed, the ambassador says, "My God Jim, this relationship is a major threat worldwide. The destructive prospects of this partnership is frightening."

Secretary Halsberg tells them, "Just so you know, I've passed this information along to the White House and the joint-chiefs-of-staff. Knowing the volatility of this alliance, the joint chiefs must create a counterweight to this Chinese – Russian threat."

After concluding their discussion, the ambassador says goodbye to Secretary Halsberg and Castle and exits. I greet her, and we hurry down the hall and depart the White House.

# CHAPTER 24

# SEARCHING FOR THE TRAITOR

It's 10:00 a.m. when I arrive back at the hospital in Philadelphia. It's been seven days since Stan was admitted for emergency surgery. Thank God that he survived the effects of the bullet wound. Last week, it was touch-and-go; we weren't sure if Stan would pull through. He had so many unpredictable episodes of irregular breathing, caused by a buildup of fluid in his lungs, that we were convinced he was dying. Luckily, he's a fighter who never surrenders.

Betty and I stand at the edge of his hospital bed. Stan's awake, but he's still weak from the trauma of the wound and the operation. He has trouble speaking, so his only means of communication is to write short notes on the mini pad I purchased from the hospital gift store.

The doctor enters and tells us, "Stan will be transported by helicopter to a downtown heliport in Manhattan today, and then he'll be driven by ambulance to Mount Sinai Hospital, where he'll remain for approximately ten days. There he'll be carefully monitored for any complications that may arise. Infection is our greatest concern. Once he's discharged, he'll walk with the aid of a cane. During the next couple of months he'll have outpatient physical therapy sessions for at least four days a week during the first month, and then two days a week thereafter for another month."

It's now 11:00 and almost time for the nursing team to prepare Stan for the flight to New York. Betty will accompany him in the helicopter, and I'll meet her at Mount Sinai Hospital sometime tomorrow afternoon.

When the nursing team arrives to prep Stan for the flight, I say my goodbyes. Betty leans over, kisses me on the cheek, and says, "Sean, thank you for all of your support and especially your friendship."

Responding, I say, "Everything will be okay." I then leave the room and head to the rental car for the long ride home. The trip will take two and a half hours from Philadelphia, but the solitude may help me to uncover the traitor who compromised the infiltration mission of our teams. In my mind, one of two people betrayed us. If Dean Balstral is the guilty party, then I know his reasoning is purely mercenary. On the other hand, if Linda turns out to be the traitor, then our years of friendship will be dissolved. What a tragedy. Once I determine the guilty party though, retribution will be allotted.

Pulling into the driveway, I grab my bag and rush up the stairs and into my condominium. I desperately need a shower. Once I'm finished, I'll retrieve Boynton from Linda's place. I've missed him so much and can't wait to see him. When I arrive at Linda's and ring the bell, Boynton charges toward the doorway. He then sits, waiting patiently for Linda to open the door. When she does, I bend down to pet him while he begins licking my face.

Linda asks, "Would you care for a cup of coffee?"

"May I have a bottle of cold water instead? I'm pretty thirsty from rushing around this morning." We sit at the center island in her kitchen and talk about Stan and the other members of my special forces teams who were ambushed during the mission. I had spoken to Linda several times during the week, advising her of Stan's condition and informing her of the ambush. She appears very concerned about the loss of my team members and speculates as to how Deutsche Christen learned about the mission. Listening to her words and sensing her concern reassures me that she may be innocent of the betrayal.

"Sean, who else besides the team members knew about the infiltration mission?"

"The only other people who had knowledge of the mission were Dean Balstral, the base commander, and you. Before accusing anyone, however, I'll have to verify some information."

"When you find this person, what do you intend to do?"

"I'm not sure yet Linda. Whoever it is will be in for some serious consequences. After all, several of my buddies have died or been injured because of this traitor. I'm determined to settle the score."

After Linda and I talk for about a half hour, I decide to head home. I thank Linda for the water and kiss her. When I stand to leave, Boynton rushes over to me with his leash. He's anxious to be in familiar surroundings. I hook the leash to his collar and start for home. Before heading to the condominium, we stop at the open field. Boynton runs around for a few minutes and then rushes back to me. I'm hungry and tired, so I'm glad Boynton is so eager to get home. When we enter the condo, Boynton rushes to his water bowl while I grab my cell phone. My hope is to reach Colonel Gannon and request his assistance in determining who the traitor may be. The phone rings several times with no answer. I leave a voice mail message asking that the colonel call me. I then head to the kitchen and prepare a pot of coffee. Just then the phone rings. When I answer, a man's voice begins laughing loudly. I ask, "who's calling?"

"Carl Dietrich," he responds. "How did your teams enjoy their visit to our camps?"

"Your lighthearted reference to the injuries and deaths you've caused simply reinforces the fact that you're an insane and sadistic bastard."

"Never, *ever* call me insane. When I see you again, I'll kill you!"

"I can't wait for you to try."

"Rubbing more salt into the wound, Dietrich says, "Mr. Carrol, you're welcome to visit my camps whenever you're looking for trouble."

I slam the phone down, begin cursing, and picture myself holding a gun to Dietrich's head while pulling the trigger. I think to myself, if only I could. After heading back into the kitchen I grab a cup of coffee. I'm so angry recounting the insensitivity of Dietrich's taunting and threatening comments that I throw my coffee cup against the wall, causing a flood of coffee to splatter on the wall and cascade down onto the kitchen floor. Because of the fact that he and his militia viciously murdered and injured some of my team, I'm determined to get revenge. Just then the phone rings again. I pick it up and recognize Colonel Gannon's voice.

"Hi, Sean."

"Good morning, Colonel."

"I received your message this morning. What's happening?"

"Colonel, I know you're aware that someone betrayed our mission. I've been attempting to discern who that individual might be. Can you tell me besides the team members, Dean Balstral, the base commander, and Linda Mancuso, who had knowledge of the mission?"

"Nobody else knew about the mission."

"Based upon what I know of those with knowledge of our mission, Dean Balstral concerns me the most. As a weapons dealer, he could have been enticed by promises of a large weapons contract."

"Sean, you don't really think he had anything to do with the betrayal, do you?"

"We have to be objective about the possibilities, Colonel. I realize that you've known him for twenty-five years, but money does strange things to people."

"What about your friend Linda? She had knowledge of the mission."

"Yes she did, but I've been unable to determine her guilt. I'm gonna continue questioning and probing her about the mission with the intent of determining her involvement, if any."

"Well, what do you think we should do, Sean?"

"I'd like to meet with Balstral and hear for myself what he has to say about his possible involvement in the betrayal of our team. I want to hear his denial. I'll meet you at the base in Florida, and then we can confront him."

"Sean, I'm going to call Dean right now and ask him to meet us the day after tomorrow. I'll call you back shortly."

"Great, Colonel."

About thirty minutes later the phone rings. When I pick it up, I hear Colonel Gannon's voice. "Sean, I called Dean but wasn't able to reach him. I'll try again later and call you after I speak with him."

"Goodbye, Colonel. I'll talk to you later. Right now, I have to head over to the hospital to see Stan."

"Tell Stan that I asked about him, and that I hope he's feeling better."

"Will do, Colonel."

I think to myself, *I wonder what action I should take once I determine the traitor.* In any case, I'll have to control my anger and keep things in perspective so that my retaliation isn't too harsh.

CHAPTER 25

# MESSAGE TO THE UNITED NATIONS

Having just arrived in Washington, D.C. for my newspaper assignment, I hurry up the stairs of the Capitol Building to observe the congressional vote for the U.S. withdrawal from the U.N. Before reaching the senate gallery, I bump into an old acquaintance, Dan Wyles, a reporter from the *New York Times*.

"Hi, Sean."

"Hello, Dan. How are you?"

"I'm great, Sean, never been better. I haven't seen you since Debbie's funeral."

"Yeah. That was three years ago."

"My God, how time flies."

"What's been taking place in Congress today, Dan?"

"The House of Representatives passed a bill an hour ago mandating defunding of and withdrawal from the United Nations. Currently, the

Senate is taking up the House's bill and will likely come to a resolution sometime later this afternoon."

"I guess we're in for a long day."

"I think you're right, Sean."

"Dan, it's been great seeing you. I've gotta head up to the gallery to observe the proceedings. Take care."

When I arrive in the gallery of the senate chamber it's packed. People are jammed in from wall to wall. I manage to squeeze into a small space located near the front of the gallery from where I can observe the proceedings. Senate members are in the throes of finalizing the revisions to the House's bill. The Senate majority leader has just called for a vote. Taking their seats the members begin the voting process. Amazing as it may seem, Democrats and Republicans are coalescing in their approval of the legislation. A small number of senators, however, are arguing against the bill, wishing instead for the United States to remain a member of the United Nations. If the legislative bodies pass the bill, it will be forwarded to the president for his signature. Once it's signed, the U.S. ambassador to the United Nations will immediately call for an emergency session of the U.N. General Assembly. A formal pronouncement of the withdrawal will then be delivered directly to the secretary general of the U.N. This legislation, if approved, will have wide-ranging repercussions within the United Nations and will also cause worldwide economic and military turmoil unlike anything we've ever experienced.

Before the actual withdrawal, however, the United States must close the U.S. mission to the U.N., withdraw from all government delegations, and give notice of withdrawal from accession to the U.N. Charter and Statute of the International Court of Justice. These tasks, I'm sure, will be performed with the utmost urgency.

In the midst of the voting, the Senate majority leader interrupts to announce that skirmishes have erupted between the National Guard and the paramilitary in the states of Oregon, Minnesota, and Ohio. He says, "As a result of the skirmishes, numerous American and paramilitary troops have been killed or wounded. Meanwhile, the fighting continues." He requests, "Everyone bow your heads in observance of a moment of silence to honor our fallen and injured troops."

As predicted, the Senate passes the bill for withdrawal from the U.N. late Tuesday afternoon. Immediately thereafter, the bill is referred to the president for his review and signature.

At 3:35 p.m., I begin walking to the cafeteria to get a cup of coffee. The day's been a long one, and I need a pick-me-up. On the way, I bump into Ambassador Hanley. "Hi, Sheila. How are you?"

"I'm a bit frazzled. I've just come from a meeting in the West Wing with the president and several of his cabinet members. The president refused to sign the bill for withdrawal from the United Nations."

"My God, doesn't that man have any backbone? Sheila, I'm heading downstairs for a cup of coffee. You seem as though you could use a cup. Why don't you join me?"

"Sounds like a great idea."

After entering the cafeteria, we head to a quiet unoccupied area in the rear of the room. Here, we can talk freely without any eavesdropping or interruptions. While the ambassador takes a seat, I walk to the counter, grab two cups of coffee, and return to the table.

When I sit down, I ask Sheila, "What occurred at the meeting today?"

"The meeting got underway at about 3:00, with John Morgan, the White House Chief of Staff, moderating the discussion. Predictably, President Burleigh was vacillating about signing the bill, wary of the potential negative political impact. He views the U.N. as an instrument for furthering his agenda and believes withdrawal from the organization will constrain any hope of implementing climate change regulations, decolonization mandates, or nonproliferation of nuclear weapons treaties. Having served as an adviser to him when he was an Illinois senator, I'm aware that he's always demonstrated inflexibility, cowardice, and a dearth of political foresight. Acutely aware of his intransigence and fear when confronting major U.S. or international issues, President Burleigh's ambivalence remains a hallmark of his administration."

"Knowing you, I wonder how you tolerated such a shallow leader who's incapable of making decisions on important policy issues."

"I guess you can say, It was my way of climbing the ladder."

"Did anything else occur at the meeting?"

"In spite of advice from John Morgan and the other advisers, the president turned a deaf ear, claiming that if the bill passes it will create international havoc. Admonishing the president, Mr. Morgan warned him.

Public opinion overwhelmingly favors withdrawal from the U.N. If you veto this bill, Mr. President, the Congress will likely override it." Further cautioning him, Mr. Morgan added, an override of your veto will likely create more animosity from the Congress, weakening the modest power you currently enjoy. Despite John Morgan's warnings, President Burleigh vetoed the bill. The bill has now been sent back to Congress, where it's been fast-tracked for a vote. If it passes both houses with a majority of 70 percent, the president's veto will be overridden."

"You know Sheila, it's amazing that the president won't even consider the advice of his cabinet members."

"Yeah, he seems to have difficulty accepting counsel from any of his advisers."

After I finish my coffee, Sheila decides to have another cup. I say goodbye and head back to the gallery. As soon as I enter, I hear loud cheers, yells, and whistles emanating from the senate floor. I glance at the voting board and see the vote tally at 76 yeas, 23 nays, and 1 abstention. Immediately, I know that the president's veto has been overridden. Now the difficult task of secession from the United Nations will begin.

For the next couple of days, I spend time relaxing while working on the article about the United States withdrawal from the United Nations. During this time, I've been able to read about the panic-stricken atmosphere within the U.N. Delegates are bemoaning the withdrawal of the United States as a member and major benefactor of the organization. Leaks from the White House have found their way to various local and national newspapers, and radio outlets. Wild rumors with ridiculous disinformation concerning the U.S. withdrawal circulate the political and public arenas. Some articles allege that the General Assembly requested that the United States withdraw from the U.N., alleging that the U. S. had refused to remit dues for the year just elapsed. Exaggerated account after exaggerated account abound on television news and social media. One story outdoes another, with no facts to support any of the speculation.

According to one newspaper article, a pronouncement has been executed by the U.S. State Department and delivered to the U.N. secretary general for a meeting of the General Assembly to be scheduled on Thursday, just two days hence.

While watching a news program, I see a street reporter standing in front of the United Nations building. He says, "With Thursday quickly approaching, the phones to the White House and the State Department are buzzing 24/7. The phone calls have been nonstop since word broke about the United States' withdrawal from the U.N. In addition, the overwhelming public response has caused computer crashes at several government sites. Meanwhile, Ambassador Hanley and her delegation have been preparing all pertinent documents in anticipation of the upcoming U.N. session. A powerful speech has even been written to the members of the General Assembly, outlining U.S. dissatisfaction with the organization's proceedings and rulings."

After a short commercial break, he continues. "Behind the scenes, several U.N. representatives have been lobbying the White House and various congressional leaders, requesting that the United States reconsider the decision to withdraw. Understanding the financial loss to the United Nations, they are distressed and frightened about the future of the organization." He closes the report by saying, "Everyone appears to be unsure and panicked at the possible fallout emanating from the decision of the U.S. secession."

When Thursday arrives, I'm in attendance as a guest of the U.S. ambassador. At exactly 4:00 p.m., the General Assembly session commences while the attendees nervously await the arrival of the U.S. delegation. Once they arrive, the secretary of state leads the delegation into General Assembly Hall. When they take their seats in front of the assembly, the room is abuzz with chatter concerning the United States' action. Of the 193 members, only 191 are in attendance. Conspicuously absent are the delegations from the Republic of China and the Russian Federation.

Anxious to address the issue at hand, the secretary general quickly convenes the assembly. When he calls the U.S. ambassador to the dais, the chatter within the hall suddenly evaporates. The members focus their complete attention on Ambassador Hanley while she slowly makes her way to the microphone in front of the General Assembly. Gazing out at the delegations, the ambassador begins to cite the history of the United Nations, beginning with the League of Nations and continuing through the evolution of the organization's ninety year history. Continuing, she says, "The current state of affairs within this organization reflects a rebellious and contentious environment." Describing the view of the U.N.

from her country's perspective, she meticulously outlines the unfortunate disintegration of the principles upon which the U.N. was founded. Enraged, she raises her voice reflecting her obvious indignation. "The manipulation of the U.N. by certain renegade nations within the assembly has created animosity." Chastising the members, she adds, "The Security Council has exhibited an irresponsible voting record, especially on the recent vote concerning the Chinese and Russian intervention on U.S. soil." I silently cheer while she continues to present a meticulous description of the current crisis within the U.N.

While the ambassador is making her closing remarks, a quiet chant of "USA, USA" erupts from several of the western delegations. I listen as other delegations from Africa, Australia, and South America join in. In the midst of this, the chanting turns to cheers, creating a thunderous roar in concert with pounding feet, followed by loud clapping. Several delegations jeer while they exit the hall in protest of the tremendous support displayed for the United States. The Iranian and Venezuelan delegates are particularly disturbed by this demonstration. While withdrawing, many of them turn toward the assembly with thumbs down exhibiting their displeasure with their colleagues' affirmation of the United States.

When Ambassador Hanley finally announces the U.S. withdrawal from the U.N., a loud burst of panic and fear ignites throughout the hall. Understanding the impact of the U.S. action, the members certainly know that withdrawal of the United States will not only affect the U.N. financially, but will also create a leadership vacuum, resulting in major instability not only within the U.N. but worldwide. The last bastion of hope for the world will no longer participate in an organization rife with corruption, discrimination, and mistrust. I understand that the remaining members of the General Assembly must confront the issues causing fractionalization and outright subversion currently tearing at the very fabric of the United Nations. They'll be mandated to reform all aspects of the U.N., including the regulatory and economic organs.

After her speech, I join the ambassador when she descends the stairs near the dais. She approaches me and says, "Sean, we've made our statement. It's now up to the remaining members of the U.N. to right the ship." We walk toward the entranceway of General Assembly Hall. When we do, the international delegates swarm her, pleading for the U.S. government to reconsider their action. Begging, the delegates, to no avail, press the ambassador on the issue. Without any acknowledgment, we head through the front door and outside to a waiting limousine.

Digesting the events of the day, I know that the perils facing a rudderless United Nations will take a turn toward an unknown but frightening future. The perilous journey may lead to a conclusion that will ultimately threaten all aspects of world stability.

## CHAPTER 26

# RETRIBUTION

Early Saturday morning, I'm startled when the phone rings. I reach over Boynton's head and glance at the alarm clock display, which reads 5:00. I wonder who the hell could be calling at this time of the morning. After picking up the phone I hear John Errin's voice. Frantically rambling about an explosion at the newspaper building, his words are almost unintelligible. I try to calm him down enough so that I can understand what's taken place.

He tells me, "Sean, early this morning a bomb exploded in the basement of the newspaper building. The power of the explosion caused tremendous damage to the entire structure and caused a complete shutdown of the newspaper and several adjoining businesses."

Already knowing the answer, I ask John, "Did the police determine who may have carried out the attack?"

"No, they haven't, Sean, however, the bomb squad is investigating.

They're attempting to identify the responsible party, as well as the type of explosive device utilized."

"John, you and I both know the perpetrator is the Deutsche Christen paramilitary. We also know that C-4 plastic explosives were used."

"You're right, Sean. Dietrich's recent threat to destroy the newspaper leaves no doubt as to who did this."

"I assume the building is uninhabitable in its current state."

"Yeah, no one will be entering the building for a while. It's been completely cordoned off. Right now, we're going to have to relocate the newspaper operation to a temporary facility."

"I'm going to take a drive to the newspaper as soon as I get dressed, John. I want to see the damage and help you determine the next steps required to continue the newspaper operation. You can't do this alone."

"I'll see you when you get here. Goodbye, Sean."

I get out of bed, take care of Boynton, and get ready to drive to the newspaper. When I'm about to leave, Boynton is waiting by the front door. He knows I won't be home until late. Gently grabbing my hand with his teeth, he leads me into the kitchen and stops at his treat drawer. Reaching into the drawer, I extract two Milk Bones and place them on the floor. He begins chewing them while I head out the front door to my car.

When backing out of the driveway, I notice a black Mercedes SUV parked diagonally across the street approximately three hundred feet from my location. Inside the vehicle, I notice two men observing me. Putting my car in gear, I begin slowly driving down the street. I stop at the corner and glance in the rearview mirror. The SUV is pulling out from the parking spot. After proceeding through the intersection, I begin to speed up. In concert with this, the SUV likewise picks up speed.

A few minutes later, the vehicle begins tailgating me. Suddenly, the Mercedes rams the rear of my car, jolting me. I lose control and veer left, smashing into the side of a parked vehicle. Thank God there was no oncoming traffic; otherwise, a crash could have been fatal. Recovering, I press on the accelerator and zip ahead to avoid another encounter, but the SUV charges my vehicle again. Pulling alongside of me, it slams into the passenger side of my car, nearly driving me into an oncoming pick-up truck. I slam on my brakes. When the Mercedes pulls ahead, I begin to accelerate. Crashing into the rear of the SUV, I attempt to force it into one of the parked cars located along the street. Instead, the vehicle swerves to the right and spins out of control, angling into an oncoming taxi in the middle of a four-way intersection.

One of the men steps out of the passenger side of the Mercedes, pulls out a gun, and fires at me. I duck my head below the dashboard and slam down on the accelerator, driving my vehicle straight into the passenger side of the SUV. The gunman is immediately thrust against his vehicle. He drops to the ground as I back up and await the arrival of the police. Abandoning the gunman in the street, the SUV speeds away from the scene. I immediately hit the accelerator and follow.

Veering in and out of traffic for what seems to be an eternity, the

Mercedes suddenly crashes into an oncoming truck. The driver's side door of the SUV flies open, and the driver jumps out and begins running. I stop my car, jump out, and chase him. After charging into a private parking garage he runs past the barrier and up the ramp. I continue the chase, close the gap between us, and finally tackle him on the second level of the garage.

When he gets up, he takes a swing at me but misses. Throwing a left hook, I strike him on his right temple. He loses his balance and falls to the ground. He quickly gets to his feet, reaches inside his jacket, and he reaches inside his jacket and pulls a knife from a sheath that's strapped to his belt. Lunging at me, he attempts to stab me in the chest, but only manages to rip through the fabric of the jacket above my left shoulder. When he attempts to pull back, I grab his arm and bend it toward him, plunging the knife deep into his right chest cavity. He gags, stumbles, and then falls to the ground with blood oozing from his mouth and chest.

Just then, the police arrive and order me, "Put your hands above your head! Now, kneel on the ground and put your hands behind your back!" One of the officers clamps a set of cuffs on my wrists and pulls me to a standing position.

I ask, "Why am I being cuffed?"

The officer tells me, "Be quiet and don't cause any trouble." They then examine the assailant's body while the EMTs and several more squad cars arrive.

A police sergeant approaches and begins questioning me. "Who's the man you stabbed?"

"I don't know who he is, but he and his associate attempted to run me off the road and kill me."

The sergeant asks, "Why were they trying to kill you?"

I angrily tell him, "I have nothing more to say. Read me my rights."

When turning my head, I see Lieutenant Parisi exiting one of the squad cars. Once he sees me, he rushes up the ramp and has a hurried exchange with the EMTs. He then hurries over to me and orders the sergeant to remove the handcuffs. The lieutenant requests that the officers assist the EMTS. He asks, "Is this one of the men involved with the Deutsche Christen group?"

"He and his partner are the two trackers who, I believe, killed Jake Trexler."

"Are you sure they're the murderers?"

"I'm not 100 percent positive, but I feel pretty confident that they're guilty."

"We'll find out soon, Mr. Carrol."

"If these two men survive, Lieutenant, you may be able to interview them to ascertain their link to Deutsche Christen, and more importantly, determine who hired them to kill Jake Trexler."

"I'll keep my fingers crossed. The EMTs don't expect the second suspect to survive, however, the first guy you struck with your vehicle is in police custody at a local hospital and should recover. He sustained two broken legs, three shattered disks in his back, plus some cuts and abrasions."

While Parisi and I are talking, the EMTs move the assailant to a waiting ambulance. Within a couple of minutes, the ambulance, accompanied by two police cruisers, exits the garage and heads for the hospital. According to Lieutenant Parisi, the man is in serious condition.

The lieutenant informs me, "You'll have to file an incident report and provide a statement at the precinct." He adds, "Your car will be removed from the scene and driven to the station. You'll be free to go pending a complete investigation of the incident. Make sure that you don't leave the area, because we may have to talk to you again."

After providing a statement to the police at the precinct, I collect my keys from the desk sergeant and head to my car. Checking the chassis, I discover that the passenger side door is smashed in, the grill is cracked, and the rear bumper is slightly pushed in. In spite of the damage, the car is drivable. I'll have to see about repairs during the week.

It's now 1:00 p.m., and I still have to drive by the newspaper building to view the damage. When I get there, John Errins is standing in front of the building talking with two police officers from the Bomb Disposal Unit. I take a long look at the front of the building and see that most of the windows are blown out and that a large portion of the building's brick surface has been scorched from the explosion and the heat that arose from the ensuing fire.

After I exit my car, John signals for me to join him. He asks why I'm so late. I tell him about the incident, and he begins shaking his head in disbelief. Understandably, he appears stressed. After all, he's suffered a tremendous setback with the destruction of the newspaper building, and now he must begin the relocation process for the paper. No longer a young man at the age of sixty-four, he's facing a massive undertaking for the immediate future. I hope he's emotionally and physically up to the task.

We begin walking around the building while John explains the extent of the damage. He tells me, "The insurance adjuster estimates the building and business equipment loss at over five million dollars." John continues, "In an effort to help us restart the newspaper operation, the adjuster gave me a check to allow immediate purchases of printing presses, collators, computers, and paper stock. This will enable us to quickly begin operations and mitigate our business losses. The good news, if there is any, is that the newspaper will be temporarily relocated to a large warehouse just ten blocks from our current location. Unfortunately, the move can't be completed for at least two weeks."

In order to help John, I offer to provide my time whenever, night or day. We shake hands, and he thanks me. I tell him, "I need to start for home. I'll call you tomorrow."

CHAPTER 27

# CHINA'S THREATS AND ASPIRATIONS

Early the next morning, Boynton and I return home after taking our usual walk to the park. I head into the kitchen and turn on talk radio. The host, James Moore, is nervously reporting that the U.S. military has been placed on high alert. He says, "As a result of the confiscation of numerous Chinese and Russian merchant ships by the U.S. Navy, tensions have increased dramatically between the U.S., Chinese, and Russian governments."

Mr. Moore goes on to say, "In the Pacific region, anxiety and fear among several indigenous cultures has been intensified because of Chinese aspirations for hegemony in the area. China's sudden aggressiveness has created substantial political and military unrest, especially along the Pacific Rim. Forcibly expanding their influence throughout the region, the Chinese are impeding free trade among many neighboring countries. Their thuggish behavior has been reinforced by the proliferation of their military." The station then goes to commercial break.

Within a couple of minutes Mr. Moore returns for the conclusion of the report. He states, "Having created a blue-water fleet, China's aspirations of expansion have finally been realized. Beginning with a brown-water fleet in the 1950s, whereby their naval forces protected all inland waterways, and upgrading to a green-water fleet in the 1980s, which broadened the navy's role to include regional and coastal responsibilities, they have now come full circle. A major challenge to the Republic of China, of course, is the U.S. Navy. If this challenge were eliminated, China would have free rein in realizing its long-term ambition of becoming the sovereign power throughout the Pacific. With the evolution of their naval power, the Chinese can at long last exert their military muscle and challenge the United States."

I turn off the radio and pick up today's *New York Times*. The front-page headline reads, "End of an Era, Building to Be Sold." While reading the article, I'm in shock. The U.S. government has issued a directive to the United Nations ordering the secretary general to have the U.N. premises at 405 East Forty-Second Street vacated within the next twelve months from the current date of September 10. The building is slated to be demolished on September 12. The property will then be sold to a real estate developer who plans to build high-end commercial and residential condominiums. The U.S. government has clearly conveyed the message that there will be no delays. All personnel and property within the building are to be gone by September 10—no exceptions.

I reach for my cell phone and dial Colonel Gannon. "Hi, Colonel. It's

Sean. I understand from Stan that you're organizing our team to strike several of the Deutsche Christen camps. I'm sure things are chaotic right now, however, I'd like to volunteer for the mission. My sole purpose is to contribute to the defeat of this organization."

"Sean, are you sure this is what you really want to do?"

"Colonel, you know that Deutsche Christen has created nothing but turmoil for me and my family. They also represent a major threat to our country and the freedom we enjoy. As a member of the military there's nothing more important I can do than to help defeat Deutsche Christen."

"Sean, you'll have to get to Eglin by tomorrow, because we'll be flying to Ohio in mid-afternoon. There we'll join up with rangers from Fort Bragg and Delta Force who are arriving from several bases throughout the country. Our combined force of 320 have been ordered to attack and disorient the militia from the Marietta, West Virginia, and Gallipoli, Ohio, camps. Being the main East Coast drop-off points for weapons to Deutsche Christen, these sites are critical to the paramilitary. In conjunction with our campaign, two similar operations have been organized in the Midwest and far west. If our plan is successful, a confrontation with Deutsche Christen may be delayed. A delay will permit our military a window of opportunity to better prepare for the inevitable."

"Colonel, I'm going to organize my gear and meet you tomorrow at the base." I hang up the phone and head upstairs to prepare for the early morning trip.

# CHAPTER 28

# SPECIAL MISSION

It's now 9:35 a.m., and I've just arrived at Eglin A.F.B. After being driven to the main office building of the base, I walk into the lobby, drop my bag on the floor, and stand at the information counter awaiting assistance. While leaning against the front desk, I feel a tap on my right shoulder. When I turn, I see Lieutenant Hisan standing in front of me dressed in marine fatigues. He salutes and asks me to follow him. I haven't seen him since our mission to rescue my niece and nephew at the Wheeling camp. He looks well rested and fit. We climb the stairs to the second floor and hurry down the long, narrow hallway to the colonel's office. At the end of the hallway we enter and salute Colonel Gannon. He immediately stands and salutes us and requests that I sit down. Once again, Lieutenant Hisan salutes and then departs.

The colonel tells me, "We're scheduled to take off today at 1500 hours and fly to Wright-Patterson Air Force Base. There, we'll board six Chinook helicopters accompanied by two AH64 Apache Longbows.

Our plan is to land three Chinooks two miles north of the Marietta camp while the other three helicopters head to the Gallipoli camp. Sean, I need you to lead the team at Marietta, while I take command of the team for Gallipoli. Just so you know, satellite images we received from the NRO show peripheral weaknesses at both camps. Once we pass the periphery of the camp, however, the mission becomes extremely dangerous. Although the corners of each camp appear soft with one guard maintaining surveillance, the militia has reinforced the interior guard positions and doubled the machine gun nests, staggering them every two hundred feet.

"In order to maintain silence, we've drafted several elite special forces who are expert bowmen. They've all had extensive weapons training and are skilled in hand-to-hand combat. With their assistance, we should easily secure the periphery of the camp at the southernmost and northernmost positions. Once these are secured, we can quickly move toward the center of the camp, silently disposing of any militia posted along the way. In concert with our movement, we'll set explosives near any buildings suspected of housing weapons or munitions. Our objective is to destroy as many weapons as possible, thereby impeding the militia's effectiveness and delaying action by their forces. After completing our mission, all teams will then return to Wright-Patterson A.F.B."

It's now nearly 1400 hours and time to go to the gym area where we'll meet with our teams. Once everything is organized, the colonel and I head to the building's entrance where a Jeep is waiting.

*William Brazzel*

Still stinging from the previous mission that resulted in the loss of several team members, I hope that the specifics of this mission have been kept on lockdown. If not, we may lose many more forces. By tomorrow, I'll have my answer.

# CHAPTER 29

# SINO-RUSSIAN PLAN

It's 9:00 a.m., and the Beijing streets are bustling with people who are rushing to work while school children stoically march to class, toting backpacks and lunch pails as they walk along the sidewalks of the local streets. The city is alive with activity. Throngs of bicycles parade along the thoroughfares and side streets, moving past the numerous open street markets that are shadowed by skyscrapers reaching more than thirty stories above the city landscape, evidencing the contrast of the old and new worlds.

In the meantime, at the Pacific Place Center, a meeting of high ranking military officers is underway. Admiral Xu, the senior military leader of the Navy of the People's Republic of China, has just completed his report on the capability of the Chinese military to fight a major war on three fronts. While closing his remarks, the admiral orders, "Today all officers and staff will be in attendance at a meeting at 1500 hours. The meeting is to take place at the Bayi Building in central Beijing. This session is considered top secret."

Having joined the People's Liberation Army Navy in 1990 at the age of twenty, Admiral Xu is a seasoned and well respected military officer. Now at forty-seven, he's the overall leader of the PLA naval forces throughout China. As vice chairman of the Central Military Commission, he has proven to be the most skilled and tenacious officer of anyone currently serving. His meteoric rise during his twenty-seven year tenure is attributed to his keen managerial skills and foresight in designing and developing futuristic military weapons.

Extremely popular among his troops, he wields tremendous power, something the leaders of the Central Committee of the Communist Party view as a threat to their positions. Fearing that Admiral Xu may someday utilize his military influence to threaten and undermine their authority, they maintain tight reins on their power, while at the same time attempting to limit the admiral's influence and power.

At 1500 hours, the admiral and his staff enter the main conference room of the Bayi Building. By most standards, the room is luxurious, containing gold-trimmed chandeliers, ornate fine art glass vases, and ancient Chinese paintings from the Tang and Song dynasties, contrasted by finely crafted wooden chairs from Italy. In the center of the room rests a round cherry wood conference table large enough to accommodate thirty or more people. Bottles of water, along with decorative stemware, have been strategically placed at the center and edges of the table. Impressive to say the least, the room's contents are opulent but not gaudy.

Shortly thereafter, a large entourage, headed by General Boris Melenev of the Russian military, arrives. As chief of the general staff of the Armed Forces of the Russian Federation, General Melenev oversees operational management of all Russian military personnel, equipment, and supplies. This is the main command and supervisory body of the Russian Armed Forces.

At fifty-two years of age, the general has overseen the Russian military infrastructure for nearly ten years. Smart but headstrong, he's been a key ally of Admiral Xu, supporting him on most issues related to military and political tactics and strategies. General Melenev, along with the Russian premier, Vladimir Uransky, long for the days of the United Soviet Socialist Republic, when Russia ruled all of Eastern Europe and threatened to achieve world domination. He's intent upon reclaiming this glorious age of influence and power.

General Melenev and Admiral Xu greet each other while staff members mingle and converse with their counterparts.

Twenty minutes later, Carl Dietrich, accompanied by three Deutsche Christen board members and two bodyguards, enters the room and hurries to greet Admiral Xu and General Melenev. He respectfully bows and then shakes their hands.

A few moments later, the admiral claps his hands, a signal for all attendees to take their seats at the conference table. Name cards have been placed on the table in front of each seat, and leather folders containing plans and tactics for the upcoming operation have been provided for all.

When everyone is seated, the admiral begins speaking. "We've recently encountered difficulties while attempting to infiltrate the United States with weapons and personnel. Many weapons have been confiscated by the U.S. military, and stringent regulations have been imposed to protect against any further border incursions." Angrily, he informs the attendees, "The Japanese have once again betrayed us by extorting Colonel Xang. He was compromised while being photographed in a homosexual tryst with a Japanese diplomat. As a result, sensitive military information has been transferred to the United States by Ambassador Hinto." The admiral continues, "This action represents yet one more example of the Japanese government's betrayal of the Chinese people." The admiral's jaundiced view witnesses his hatred and bias toward the Japanese.

After his tirade, he requests that everyone open the folders provided. He announces, "The attack plans have been revised. Instead of a first strike attack upon the United States, as initially planned, we'll attack our historic enemy, the Japanese. Knowing they're a secondary challenge to our navy in the Pacific, we'll eliminate the Japanese military along with the supporting U.S. naval contingency in Japan, thereby allowing our forces to fight on one front, the United States."

Just then Mr. Dietrich asks, "When exactly will my troops begin the invasion of the interior of the United States, and what is your time table for completing the mission?"

"Your troops should be in place at the outset of hostilities. The invasion will be coordinated with the Russian military on the U.S. East Coast, and with our troops on the West Coast. This leg of our invasion won't be easy, but I estimate the hostilities to last at least two weeks from our initial attack to completion of cleanup operations."

"That sounds like an aggressive time frame Admiral. My knowledge of the U.S. military's capabilities tells me that you may be underestimating the duration of the hostilities."

"You may be right, Mr. Dietrich, but I believe our estimated time to be reasonable. In any event, I'm not concerned. If the conflict continues beyond that time frame, we have reserves of manpower at the ready."

Detailing the next steps of the plan, the admiral states, "After the attack upon Japan, we'll turn our sights on the Hawaiian Islands and the U.S. mainland. We'll split all naval and air forces into two separate contingents. The North Sea Fleet will attack mainland Japan, preceded by heavy missile fire. Our bombers and fighter jets, emanating from the Beijing, Shenyang, and Jinan military regions, will then bomb the main military installations in Yokohama, Sasebo, and Yokosuka. This action will soften up the enemy, allowing our ground troops to land unencumbered."

After a short break, we return to our seats. The admiral continues. "In conjunction with the attack on Japan, the East Sea Fleet and the South Sea Fleet will simultaneously target the West Coast of the United States. Launched from our aircraft carriers, jets from the Chengdu, Nanjing, and Guangzhou military regions will attack the U.S. West Coast, from Washington State to Southern California."

Once again, Mr. Dietrich signals the admiral that he has a question.

"Yes, Mr. Dietrich?"

"Admiral, I'm concerned about the depth of the air force's penetration into the U.S. mainland. If they strike too deep, then the result may be friendly fire. How far inland do you estimate they'll penetrate?"

"Most of the air battle will be contained along the coastal areas, but if required, the air force may have to strike a couple of hundred miles inside the mainland. This will occur only if heavy resistance is detected."

"Thank you Admiral."

Admiral Xu continues, "After completing the mission over Japan, our remaining naval and air forces will rendezvous while our army proceeds with the cleanup operation of the Japanese archipelago. With utmost urgency, our fleet will then sail to the Hawaiian Islands to attack and destroy the military installations embedded there. This segment of the plan will be of short duration. After the merger of our Japanese and U.S. contingencies, we'll then unleash an overwhelming onslaught against the U.S. military, destroying all of their naval, air, and ground defenses along the West Coast."

I know the Admiral, being disingenuous, has an underlying reason for his desire to attack the Japanese. Reflecting back, I recall our dinner meeting of last January at a local restaurant, where we were discussing delivery of weapons to my paramilitary organization. He told me, "Mr. Dietrich,

Deutsche Christen is an important element of the troika." Emphasizing our importance he told me, "Your organization will be instrumental in the attack upon the United States. The ground war for the heartland of the U.S. will ultimately determine the outcome of the war."

Continuing, he told me that all allies of the United States and, especially Japan, must be annihilated. Relating that his father had brainwashed him from early childhood about the Japanese invasion of China in 1937, he profiled the indignities and merciless treatment cast upon his people. This occurred just two years prior to Adolf Hitler's invasion of Poland.

He said that during the eight year period of Japanese occupation, the Rape of Nanking and Unit 731 occurred. Both events were horrific experiences for his people. He described the germ warfare experiments of Unit 731 that incorporated the use of various biological toxins and bacteria when experimenting upon the Chinese population. The Japanese subjected his people to batteries of horrifying germ warfare tests. Considered no more than guinea pigs, thousands of Chinese people died at the hands of this barbaric, contemptible, and cruel enemy. He said that through this experimentation, the Japanese hoped to create biological weapons powerful enough to be utilized against their U.S. adversaries, thereby leading them to win World War II.

Equally offensive was what he told me about the Rape of Nanking, the capital of China at the time, where unbelievable depravity was unleashed. Here, thirty-five thousand citizens and soldiers out of a population of sixty thousand died from beheadings and random shootings by Japanese soldiers. Worst of all, he said, Chinese men were used as field dummies to hone the attack skills of the Japanese soldiers. They were live targets used for bayonet training. With hands tied behind their backs, they were secured to wood posts and exposed to the charging troops, who leveled repeated blows to their bodies. This genocide reflected the Japanese's utter disregard for and abhorrence of his people. According to his description, the savagery displayed was like no other in history.

He went on to tell me about his grandfather, who had been targeted and murdered by the Japanese army. As a member of the Chinese defense forces, his grandfather led several hundred soldiers in their resistance against the Japanese invasion. Because of his leadership position, he was tortured in the most depraved manner imaginable. Stripped of all clothing, his hands and legs were nailed to a wood cross. The cross was laid flat on the ground while the Japanese soldiers cut a large $X$ in his chest cavity and stomach. Exposed to the elements, he would die within three or four hours, but this wasn't sufficient enough for the Japanese. Employing the use of gasoline, they poured it directly into the wound, knowing he would experience even greater suffering. The admiral related that his grandfather screamed for the remaining one hour of his life. At the climax of his life, his body displayed deep burn marks from having been exposed to the sun. The gasoline had accelerated his death while at the same time producing ulcers on the internal organs and ultimately complete desiccation. In his final remark, the admiral told me that he would exact vengeance against the Japanese for the merciless deaths of his grandfather and his people.

After illustration and explanation of the plan to attack Japan, Admiral Xu calls upon General Melenev, asking that he outline the ground attack. The general stands and states, "We'll be landing a massive force of over one million troops on both the East and West Coasts of the United States. While our forces push toward the interior of the country, Deutsche Christen will form a symmetry with our forces within the country's interior. Creating a pincer maneuver, we'll easily crush the U.S. forces. In conjunction with our navies and air forces, we'll destroy all coastal defenses, thereby neutering the U.S. military. Once this is complete, a massive cleanup operation will be implemented to ensure total victory."

After reviewing the plan several more times, Admiral Xu asks, "Are there any questions?"

A Chinese naval captain asks, "Why haven't you mentioned anything about air support to protect the transport ships?"

Gruffly, the admiral chastises the captain for not properly reviewing the contents of the folder. "Captain, plainly outlined under the naval guidelines regarding the U.S. invasion, you'll see that the Liaoning super aircraft carrier is configured as a major part of the operation. Carrying hundreds of jet fighters, the super carrier will provide the necessary cover to protect the troops and equipment while landing."

Appearing somewhat embarrassed, the captain withdraws his question and apologizes to the admiral.

Before ending the meeting, Admiral Xu states, "The target date for the attack upon Japan will be thirty days from today, October 14." After making this declaration, he ends the meeting.

While everyone is exiting the conference room, Mr. Dietrich approaches Admiral Xu and General Melenev. Acknowledging the critical role his militia will play in the upcoming U.S. attack, he requests that additional heavy armaments be supplied to his organization.

The general tells him, "Mr. Dietrich, we cannot ensure the delivery of more armaments. The U.S. military has tied a very tight noose around the periphery of their borders. We can't even smuggle a pistol into the United States, much less heavy armaments. You'll have to make do with the equipment you currently have."

Acknowledging the admiral's comment, Mr. Dietrich nods, turns, and exits the room.

Knowing the unpredictability of Carl Dietrich, General Melenev and Admiral Xu agree that Dietrich is an untrustworthy ally. Once hostilities are ended, they both concur that he must be disposed of.

CHAPTER **30**

# THE PLAN

The incursion plan within the Deutsche Christen camps is performed almost flawlessly. Facing light security, my Special Forces team is able to penetrate deep into the compound at the Marietta camp. While we hold steady, a scout from my advance party approaches me.

"Major Carrol, a large segment of the militia is absent, presumably performing maneuvers at another camp. Only light resistance was encountered, and we were able to eliminate any of the militia we happened upon. As a result, we've been able to investigate freely. Our scouting party has discovered several munitions and weapons storage facilities. In addition, some highly sophisticated weapons were uncovered, including Stinger missiles, tanks, and Russian shoulder-mounted MANPADS, or man-portable air defense systems."

I salute and say, "Thanks for the information; it'll help us tremendously." Because the opportunity has presented itself, I instruct my team, "Destroy as many weapons and munitions as possible. This action will seriously handicap the militia by diminishing their firepower."

We set explosives at a nearby storage building that houses small arms and munitions. After backing away from the scene, we then head deeper into the camp. As we continue, an old cottage with rotted shingles and faded paint is revealed just inside the perimeter of a cluster of dilapidated shacks. We cautiously approach the buildings with our guns at the ready. Splitting into groups of seven, we carefully investigate the structures. To protect the perimeter around our position, two groups of our team are posted. We check each building for tripwires but detect none. When entering, we look for weapons and militia who may be hiding within.

After securing the cottage, my group and I forage through boxes and scattered paperwork left on an old wooden pull-down desk and kitchen table. While checking the drawers of the desk, I notice a small plastic container. I open it and view a pile of plans and drawings. At the base of the container is a black leather folder. On its face in gold is a large Chinese dragon inscribed with what appears to be a military insignia. I think to myself, *Oh, God. These appear to be official documents of the Chinese military.* While leafing through the folder, I discover notations written in Chinese in the margins of several of the pages. Unusual as this seems, the folder appears to contain official Chinese military plans, but the language contained within is written in English.

After quickly reading some of the notes, I'm stunned at the reference to an attack upon Japan. This isn't something I expected. I thought that the United States would be the sole target of any attacks. After reviewing further, I become convinced that major portions of the battle plans are contained within these pages. *I've gotta get these documents to Colonel Gannon.* I store the documents in my backpack. After rushing out of the cottage, I gather my team, and we begin exiting the camp.

When departing, we encounter a small contingent of militia. Heavily armed, they immediately open fire on us while we withdraw toward the river bank. Without hesitation, I order my team, "Return fire—and don't hold back!" Our forces turn and unleash a devastating barrage of weapons fire, wounding or killing a large number of militia. The remaining forces disperse in several directions. While we head west to the waiting Chinook helicopters, a powerful explosion occurs within the camp. The explosives we'd planted in the munitions storage building erupt in a huge ball of fire, destroying not only the weapons but also the storage warehouse.

"Great job, guys. Our mission has been completed without any casualties. It's a miracle that no one was injured or killed." Happy about our success, we realize that we may have delayed the inevitable conflict, but we'll have to get the attack plans to Colonel Gannon as quickly as possible. I call the colonel's cell number and advise him of our findings. He says, "As soon as you land call me. We'll have to make arrangements to get the plans to General Stanton."

After departing the Marietta camp, I continue reviewing the plans. The massive battle zone reveals attacks within the Atlantic and Pacific arenas. The number of soldiers and the amount of material to be employed by the troika is overwhelming. I wonder whether our military is up to the challenge.

## CHAPTER 31

# STRATEGY FOR COMBAT

From Wright-Patterson A.F.B. I hitch a ride on a small twin engine military plane that's flying to Pittsburgh. As a favor to me, the pilot has re-routed his flight to Hebron, Kentucky, where I'll grab a commercial flight to meet the colonel. After landing at the Greater Cincinnati International Airport, I immediately head to the American Airlines ticket counter to schedule a flight to meet with Colonel Gannon. Before booking the flight I call him.

"Hi, Colonel. It's Sean."

"Where are you?" he asks.

"I'm at the Cincinnati International Airport booking a flight to meet you. I'm bringing the invasion plans that I advised you of. We'll have to get them to the proper military channels as quickly as possible. If this information is what I believe it to be, we have no time to waste."

"Sean, I'm going to contact General Stanton and discuss the proper channels for presenting the attack plans. However, I need to verify their credibility."

"You know where we obtained the plans, Colonel. The documents contain specific details of a step-by-step plan, beginning with an attack upon Japan. The documents themselves are replete with Chinese military insignia and notes. More important, the tactics are engineered so precisely that no one but a military expert or experts could have created such comprehensive plans."

"It sounds like the real thing, but l believe we have to get the plans to the proper authorities to verify their plausibility. I'll call General Stanton right away. Hold tight, and don't do anything until I call you back."

"Okay, Colonel."

Within twenty minutes, my cell phone rings. "Sean, its Colonel Gannon."

"Yes, Colonel?"

"I spoke to the general, and he's arranged for a military flight to pick you up at the airport. You'll be flown to Joint Andrews Air Force Base in Maryland, where I'll meet you. From here we'll be transported to the Pentagon."

After landing, I disembark and meet with the colonel who is standing on the macadam near a hangar about two hundred fifty feet away. Oddly, he's not wearing his military uniform. This is highly unusual, because the colonel is always in uniform. I've only seen him out of uniform once before.

When I approach him, we shake hands and exchange greetings.

The colonel hurriedly points to a waiting limousine that's located two hundred feet away. When the limousine pulls up, the military liaison,

Colonel Travers, steps from the vehicle, shakes our hands, and requests that we quickly climb in. Escorted by two military Jeeps armed with .50-caliber machine guns, we begin the forty minute drive to the Pentagon. Colonel Travers tells us, "A meeting has been arranged with General Stanton and a number of high-level military officers. It's been scheduled for 2145 hours, just forty-five minutes from now."

The most direct route into D.C. is Pennsylvania Avenue. This road will take us through the towns of Forestville and Suitland, Maryland, on our way to the D.C. border.

When nearing the border, I turn and catch a glimpse of a black SUV shadowing the second Jeep located directly behind our limousine. Curious, I watch as it creeps to the rear of the Jeep edging ever so slowly. When entering the neighborhood of Anacostia in D.C., our driver slows down for a signal light. Out of nowhere, a pickup truck charges from the intersection to our right and strikes our vehicle hard in the front passenger door.

"What the hell is this all about?" remarks Colonel Gannon.

"I'm not sure, but I believe someone from Deutsche Christen may have tapped into my cell phone and intercepted our conversation. They're now desperate to retrieve the plans."

In the meantime, the SUV rams the Jeep located behind us, causing it to roll over. Two men jump out from the SUV and fire machine guns at our vehicle. Not realizing that the limousine is fitted with bullet proof glass, I drop to the floor. When I do, our driver slams on the accelerator and crosses into oncoming traffic lanes. The SUV and the pickup quickly follow and once again fire at our vehicle. While negotiating our way through oncoming traffic, we nearly cause a head-on collision with a cab before crossing the Eleventh Street Bridge. Weaving in and out of traffic, we watch as the vehicles continue their pursuit.

In the meantime, police vehicles from the Metropolitan Police Department have been dispatched after, I believe, being notified of the incident from witnesses whose vehicles nearly collided with our limousine. Veering from the scene, we view the SUV and the pickup truck, which are attempting to escape pursuit by the police. Our driver asks, "Is everyone okay?"

Colonel Gannon responds, "We're all fine."

Proceeding, we arrive at the Pentagon, pass through the guard gate, and drive directly to the building entrance. Here we are met by two heavily armed marines who usher us through the front doors and to the second floor where we enter a large conference room. In attendance is General Stanton along with four generals, two colonels, and a major. They're seated at the conference table and are discussing the current military crisis. From what I can overhear, their main concern is the lack of adequate manpower to combat the Chinese and Russian battalions.

When he sees us, General Stanton rises from his chair and greets Colonel Gannon. At five feet ten inches tall and weighing nearly two hundred pounds, the general is a bulky but powerful-looking man. His short cropped gray hair and creased forehead and cheeks reveal a man in his sixties, while his deep set gray-blue eyes disclose a person of keen intellect. As a veteran of three wars, including those in Iraq and Afghanistan, he appears to be intense but confident. After shaking hands, the colonel then introduces me. "General, this is Major Carrol. He's one of my premier Special Forces officers."

"Great to meet you, Major. I've heard a lot about you." The general thanks me for attending and requests that the colonel and I take a seat at the conference table. After settling into the plush straight backed leather chair, I open my backpack, extract the plans, and hand them to General Stanton. Before I begin my explanation, the general questions the colonel and me. "I'm concerned about the credibility of the plans. It seems too convenient that they were discovered at a Deutsche Christen camp."

Answering the general I say, "Please take a look at the documents." I then tell him, "Check the margins of the pages. You'll see official Chinese military markings noted along the edges. This indicates to me that the plans emanated from the Chinese military. In fact, if you open the folder and turn to the last page, you'll notice an official military stamp with the signature of Admiral Aiguo Xu, the senior leader of the Navy of the People's Republic of China."

Although the attendees' confidence in the plans is questionable, General Stanton and his military experts have little alternative but to consider the information. I begin explaining the plans to those in attendance. While I outline the tactics of the enemy, the facial expressions of the attendees slightly contort, translating into bewilderment. My guess is that the military plans previously developed by the joint-chiefs-of-staff didn't anticipate many of the targets or tactics to be employed by the troika.

While I outline specifics of the Chinese and Russian involvement, a colonel from the army rangers argues about the validity of the plans. He says, "We have no solid proof that these documents are credible. Moreover, I for one am not inclined to redesign our current military tactics."

While further discussing the plans, I ask the general, "Do you have anyone within the Pentagon who is fluent in Mandarin and steeped in Chinese military protocol?"

The general picks up the phone and makes a call. Within ten minutes a marine captain enters the room. The general hands him the folder and asks that he review the plans. The captain quickly reviews them and informs us, "The symbols are official Chinese military insignias. In addition, the signature of Admiral Aiguo Xu appears to be legitimate, because only he would retain an official Chinese naval military stamp." Shock pervades the room.

Our discussions transform from complacency and doubt to urgency and panic. Based upon the tone of the conversation, I discern that a major overhaul of the U.S. military's offensive and defensive tactics is critical to the prospect of a military victory. Still, several of the officers in attendance have misgivings about the credibility of the documents. They argue that some portions of the plans are illogical.

General Campbell, the chief U.S. Army tactician, states, "The attack upon Japan will surely weaken the naval and army forces of the Chinese. Logic dictates that they should attack the United States first, thereby eliminating the big dog. Having destroyed the mainland forces of the

United States, they'll be able to easily turn their attention toward the destruction of their remaining adversaries."

General Stanton argues, "Attacking Japan is a critical step needed by the Chinese navy to protect its rear flank. If they don't carry out this attack, they'll be vulnerable to attacks from both Japan and the Hawaiian fleets." In the final analysis, the general states, "My ultimate concern is that the losing side will revert to the use of atomic weapons once they realize their plight. This is a second phase of the war not addressed in the plans. Although preventing the use of atomic weapons will be a serious challenge, the reality is sobering."

The meeting has dragged on for over an hour. The discussions have vaulted from military personnel, to heavy equipment defense, and ending with naval and ground fortifications.

Unfortunately, no concrete solution is presented. According to General Stanton, "The only guaranteed way to reduce casualties is by launching an early missile strike, employing ICBMs with nuclear warheads." None of the attendees favor this approach, however, they admit that this may be the only way to preserve the United States and its people.

Finally, after another hour and fifteen minutes of review and discussion, the general stands and thanks me for the invaluable information provided. He states, "A meeting of the joint-chiefs-of-staff and several military committees will commence shortly. The purpose of the meeting will be to further analyze the plans and formulate a more propitious defensive and offensive strategy for thwarting the Chinese and Russian aggressors." In parting, he says, "The military plans you provided are well formulated, indicating that the engineers of the plans are extremely skilled at military tactics. This alone lends credibility to the plans."

Before departing, the colonel and I speak with the general. During our conversation, he advises, "Two military jets have been fueled and prepped to transport you back home. I'll be in touch with you in a couple of days, Colonel." In the meantime, the general assures us, "The military strategists will reformulate their military plans. Hopefully, implementation of a new strategy can be quickly developed to establish adequate defenses against the enemy. If we fail, our future will be bleak."

After saying goodbye to the general, Colonel Gannon and I head to the entrance, where we are met by Colonel Travers. We're ushered into a limousine and transported back to Joint Andrews Air Force Base for our flights home.

Unsure of the ability of our military to defend against the overwhelming forces of the troika, I pray that General Stanton and his advisers find a means to overcome the enemy. Time is of the essence, and this constraint may result in planning errors that will impair success of the mission—and more important, jeopardize the lives of those defending our country.

## CHAPTER 32

# PREPARATION FOR WAR

Two days later, I arrive at the newspaper warehouse building to find John Errins signaling for me to come to his office. I open the door and enter. "Good morning, John."

"Hello, Sean. What do you think of our temporary newspaper facilities?"

"They seem fine, but I'd rather be at our old building. It had a more natural workflow and definitely contained more square footage."

"Unfortunately, it won't be possible for us to return for at least a year. The structural issues presented by the old building's foundation have set us back by more than six months."

"That's too bad. We'll have to deal with things as they are. Do you need me for something, John?"

"Yeah. I've just received some disturbing news from a colleague of mine concerning conflicts that have arisen at the United Nations. Since the United States withdrew from the organization, strong political blocs have formed within the U.N. A massive tug-of-war is developing, a movement that may ultimately destroy the U.N. My source tells me that China, Russia, Iran, Syria, Cuba, and Venezuela have formed a consortium dedicated to promulgating an agenda aimed at establishing their unchallenged control over the United Nations. All six nations have been thuggishly forcing their agenda upon the membership."

"What effect does this group of countries have on the U.N.?"

"As a result of their aggressive actions, I understand several countries have been bullied into withdrawing from the organization, and others are threatening to leave. As of today, the membership has dwindled to 150 participating countries from an all-time high of 193. Sean, I need you to get to the U.N. and do some investigating into what the hell is going on."

"I'll jump on it right away, John."

"Call me as soon as you obtain any additional information concerning the situation."

"I'll talk to you later."

I catch a cab and head over to the United Nations. I know several delegates from the British and German Consulates who'll definitely be able to provide some inside information concerning the turmoil taking place.

After entering the U.N. General Assembly Building, I head to the lower level where the information center is located. When approaching the information desk, I ask one of the guides if Ambassador Robert Quigley is in the building. She asks, "Who are you, and why do you wish to see the ambassador?"

"I'm an old friend of his and would like to talk to him regarding the current changes taking place within the U.N."

She checks my ID and makes a phone call to the ambassador's office. Requesting that I follow her to a second-floor conference room, she informs me that the ambassador is finishing up a staff meeting and will see me shortly. After entering the conference room, I take a seat at a large wooden conference table located in the middle of the room. Decorative and impressive, the room features deep maroon color walls, accented with dark wood ceiling trim, and Brazilian hard wood floors. Along the walls rest several cocoa leather couches and wing back tufted chairs. Within a few minutes, Ambassador Quigley arrives and takes a seat across from me. "Hello, Sean. It's been awhile since I've seen you."

"Yeah, Ambassador. It's been at least three or four years."

"What brings you over here?"

"I've been hearing rumors about some political problems that are taking place within the U.N. Can you shed any light on what's occurring?"

"Wait a second, Sean." The ambassador gets up, closes the door, and returns to his seat. "I don't know what you've heard, but I can tell you that the organization is imploding. There's a consortium of nations that are, let us say, playing hardball. Because of their actions, the U.N. is fracturing. These nations are diluting the effectiveness of the organization while degrading its once stellar reputation. As you may know, the collapse of the U.N. has been hastened by the withdrawal of the United States, which has been quickly replaced by a group of six outlaw nations. Quite honestly, little hope exists among the remaining membership for the survival of the organization."

Continuing, the ambassador states, "Stories have been circulating about the formation of a new international federation intended to replace the United Nations. This was unknown at the time of the United States' withdrawal, at which point the sole intent of the U.S. government was to create the new federation with the objective of isolating this consortium of pariah nations. Lead by the United States, ninety-four countries have already made overtures to become members. The purpose of this new organization is to create a movement toward democratization of all participating nations. With their joint economic and military power, they'll be able to strangle the economies of all six pariah nations, plus North Korea."

"My God, Ambassador, this situation is unbelievable."

"To say the least. But, Sean, this information is off the record. I need you to promise that you won't repeat any of this for a few days. My government is in the midst of withdrawing from the U.N. I don't want any repercussions at this time."

"You have my word that nothing will be said." I get up from my chair, shake the ambassador's hand, and rush out of the U.N. The information I've just received is compelling. A fiction novel couldn't have read any better. If the U.N. collapses, worldwide chaos will ensue resulting in military conflicts that will range out of control. These conflicts will involve many nations, causing death or injury to countless millions of people. Ultimately, the resultant devastation will wreak havoc upon the international community, thereby destroying all meaningful paths to peace. However, if the new federation becomes reality, then chaos may be avoided.

A few days later, on October 11, everything appears calm, but a tenseness permeates the air. In the last few days I've witnessed unusual movements of military equipment and personnel within the city and the nearby states of New Jersey and Connecticut. While traveling to the newspaper each day, I watch as a steady stream of military and civilian trucks and flatbed trailers transport equipment that is hidden under heavy canvas. The caravans of vehicles are primarily traveling northward, and their destination is unknown to me. In conjunction with this, I've seen major troop movements throughout the city. While riding to work, I've witnessed large groups of heavily armed troops boarding the New York subway system; they appear to be mobilizing for military action. The image is very unusual. Coincidental with the October 14 date, allegedly when the Chinese and Russian invasion plans are to be implemented, I know that these actions are somehow coincident with defense plans for the country.

While I'm digesting these recent events, my cell phone rings. After answering, I hear Colonel Gannon's voice. "Hi, Sean."

"Hello, Colonel."

"The reason for my call is to let you know that my special forces team has been assigned to the area southwest of Pittsburgh for defensive purposes. In fact, we're scheduled to fly to Pittsburgh today. I'm not sure if you're available, but we need a couple of additional team members. I was hoping that you could join up with us, because we need all the help we can get. For now, we've been ordered not to engage the Deutsche Christen paramilitary but to simply observe their movements near the Pittsburgh area.

"Colonel, I'd like nothing more than to participate with the team. I'll organize my gear and catch a flight. Count me in."

"Great. I'll meet you at the Pittsburgh International Airport today at 1500 hours. Report to the mezzanine area; it's been cordoned off exclusively for our use."

That afternoon, I arrive at the airport and hurry to join the special forces team. After saluting the colonel, I head into a large and rather stark green room, where I observe approximately one hundred troops sitting about awaiting instructions. Within a couple of minutes, the colonel enters and orders everyone to form a line and stand at attention. As we fall in line, he directs us to march to the awaiting Chinook helicopters located downstairs. Within ten minutes of boarding, we lift off and head to our destination. Our flight only takes twenty-five minutes, however, the entire team is nervous about the circumstances of the mission. The anticipation of our unknown path makes all of us feel imperiled.

CHAPTER 33

# HELL ON EARTH

My fleet journeys north in the East China Sea, while the obscuring haze of the ocean fog impedes our progress. Just three hundred nautical miles south of Japan, we're expected to arrive within fifteen miles of the southern tip of the country by 0500 hours. Unfortunately, the dense October fog is delaying our mission while at the same time creating havoc. Despite our best efforts, the *Kaifeng*, a Luda-class destroyer, grazed the side of the *Kunming*, a Luyang III destroyer, resulting in a slight tear to the lower section of the *Kunming* ship's hull. It's hoped that the incident, though inconvenient, won't prevent the *Kunming from participating* in the upcoming military actions, as we'll require every available vessel.

In the meantime, a message is received from General Melenev. "Admiral, our Northern Sea and Baltic Fleets are sailing toward the United States. They're currently 350 nautical miles northeast of the coast of New York. We should arrive there within seven and a half hours. Simultaneously, the Black Sea Fleet, emanating from Crimea, departed the Mediterranean about eight hours ago and is rapidly sailing toward the United States, where our fleets will rendezvous and prepare for the commencement of operations along the East Coast."

While aboard the *Guangzhen*, a Luyang-class destroyer, I observe as the fog slowly dissipates, creating a clear path for our journey. My first lieutenant approaches me, salutes, and says, "Admiral Xu, we're severely behind schedule. Unless we increase our speed, we may lose our advantage under cover of night, thereby exposing our position."

I call the communications officer and order, "Increase the fleet speed from twelve to twenty-two knots."

We're now nearly 250 nautical miles south of Japan; arrival at our destination is estimated at 0630 hours. Focused solely upon reaching our destination on a timely basis, I ignore defensive tactics essential for evasion of enemy attacks. Believing we have clear sailing ahead, I'm unconcerned about any impending danger. Passing orders, I tell my communication's officer, "Recall the picket ships from their scouting sectors, and change our station assignments to widen our fleet formation."

"Yes, Admiral."

When we cross the twenty-five mile mark, I radio central command, ordering the officer in charge, "Launch the first battery of missiles at our Japanese targets, and apprise me of the results." Understanding the importance of a first strike in preserving the fleet, I await news about the impact of the launch.

Suddenly, I hear tremendous explosions. Our fleet is being attacked by submarines! Torpedoes have struck several of our ships. Evidently aware of the route we would follow on our path to Japan, a submarine group has lain in wait for several days in anticipation of our arrival. I'm shocked, wondering how our plans were revealed. In spite of the attack, our fleet continues on.

I immediately order all destroyers to locate and destroy the submarines. Just then, a message is received from the communications officer at central command. "Admiral, the missile launch against Japan has failed. Only five missiles of the seventy-three launched struck their intended targets. Satellite images reveal that a battery of Patriot missiles are responsible for the failure of our missile attack. Unfortunately, the pre-attack satellite images didn't reveal the Patriot installation."

Panicked, I pass an order to my commanders. "Launch ship-based missiles, and fire cannons at the southern coast of Honshu." Once again, the missiles prove ineffective, but the artillery fire devastates the coast of the island.

In response to our attack, the Japanese military launch land based cruise missiles. Several warships are struck, resulting in the sinking of one frigate and one destroyer. In conjunction with the missile launch, the Japanese unleash a massive barrage of cannon fire. Fortunately, the damage is minimal.

Anxious to retaliate, I enter the bridge, push the communication officer aside, and grab the microphone. I contact Commander Zhiou, my second-in-command. "Deploy two squadrons of jet fighters to attack the Japanese defensive positions along the coast."

"Yes, Admiral."

When our jets strike the coast of Japan, they are met with heavy missile fire. Two jets are immediately shot down. Suddenly, three squadrons of U.S. fighter jets appear in the southern sky. The squadrons strafe our fleet and then turn toward the southern coast of Japan to attack our jets. Dogfights ensue, with both sides suffering heavy casualties. The Americans lose ten jets while twelve of ours are downed.

With the invasion plan faltering, I order my commanders, "Divide our forces and encircle the island." Desperate for a victory, I'm taking a gamble by stretching out the lines of our fleet, thereby creating dangerous defensive weaknesses.

Aware that our attacks have produced major damage to southern Japan, I'm confused and concerned about the lack of a naval response from the Japanese and U.S. naval forces. Curious, I order that two jet fighters be dispatched to perform a flyover of the harbors to ascertain the status of their naval forces.

Approximately twenty minutes later, I receive an urgent radio message from one of the pilots. "Admiral, the naval facilities contain many deactivated vessels. We did a low flyover and found that many of the vessels are small, nonmilitary boats or older ships anchored within the harbor."

I then realize that the military fleets have been swapped, substituting decommissioned and civilian vessels for the Japanese and American naval ships. I urgently sound the high alert. Believing that the Japanese and American fleets are shadowing us, I order my officers to expand our radar and sonar surveillance in order to detect any unwarranted approaches by the enemy.

In the meantime, reports from my Eastern fleet disclose that the East and West Coasts of the United States are under heavy attack from our forces, the Russians, and the Deutsche Christen paramilitary. The reports reveal that both our army and the Russian army have created beachheads on each coast near major cities such as New York, Baltimore, and San Francisco, and that they have begun movement toward the interior of the United States. Symmetrically, the paramilitary is moving from the interior of the country toward both coasts, rapidly destroying everything in their path. Facing little resistance from the U.S. military, they eagerly claim large swaths of land in the Midwest with ease. Almost unchallenged, the paramilitary is becoming overconfident—a strategic error.

In the meantime, battles in the states east of Kentucky and Ohio erupt sporadically with little push back from the U.S. military. The hotbeds of West Virginia and Pennsylvania are the most active areas, however, American troops have been ordered not to attack the enemy but rather to act as a defensive wedge temporarily holding their lines while U.S. offensive plans are being enacted.

CHAPTER **34**

# EMERGENCE

During attacks from the military forces of the troika, Colonel Gannon informs us, "Our forces have been slowly emerging from the safety of their remote sanctuaries in the northern and southern areas of the United States. Under cover of nightfall, they're quickly taking up positions along both coasts, preparing for a surprise counterstrike against the foreign invaders. According to military reports, our ground forces are being transported by planes, railcars, and trucks to strategic positions throughout the country. From bases in Canada, southern Texas, Alabama, and Florida, a massive movement of aircraft is underway by the air force and navy in a coordinated effort to attack the enemy's naval and ground positions. Emerging from the cover of darkness, our forces will catch them by utter surprise."

I ask Colonel Gannon, "Did the plans I provided to the military alter the initial plans developed by the joint chiefs?"

"Sean, what you provided caused the joint chiefs to overhaul their entire strategy for defending and attacking the troika. Because of those plans, our military has been able to anticipate the enemy's invasion tactics."

"What did our final military plans encompass?"

"The air force strategically relocated a massive number of fighter jets and bombers to Canadian airfields and bases deep in the southern United States. As part of the stratagem, privately owned commercial jets were flown into military bases located throughout the eastern, central, and western United States. This measure maintained the population of the airbases while simultaneously allowing diversion of military aircraft to safe havens. In conjunction with this, many of our troops were reassigned to remote areas throughout the United States and Canada, with plans to transport them to military hotbeds once the enemy positions were exposed."

"Colonel, that's genius."

"You're right, their plans are very creative."

As day evolves into night, the enemy attacks subside while they hold their positions. Tomorrow will be another day of combat. For today, however, the enemy troops are exhausted and hungry, unable to continue. Rest and food are sorely required, as is the replenishment of their military supplies.

Colonel Gannon and our special forces team have been monitoring the movement of the paramilitary and the Russian troops near Pittsburgh but haven't engaged the enemy. With nightfall arriving, we rendezvous with marine expeditionary forces from Camp Lejeune, North Carolina. Our combined forces now number 610.

Moving westward, we target paramilitary camps located east of West Virginia. Our special forces team eliminates all guard positions on the periphery of the camps. We covertly enter the camps, killing or capturing as many troops as possible and destroying all military equipment discovered. In spite of the fact that most of the paramilitary are in combat, the damage we do will definitely impede them. After moving farther west, we then head south, securing positions behind enemy lines. In tandem, twelve other military groups have created a symmetry of forces along the perimeter from Pittsburgh south to Tallahassee, Florida. Likewise, other military teams have been organized from Pittsburgh to Elizabethtown, New York.

Colonel Gannon informs me, "The special forces, marines, and army units in the Midwest have employed similar tactics. The combined efforts of the teams will not only disorient the paramilitary but also eliminate many of their pivotal positions throughout the country."

Recent radio reports confirm that our air force and navy are attacking aircraft and naval vessels of the Chinese and Russian fleets. Their main targets are aircraft carriers anchored off of both coasts. Coordinating a first-strike strategy, they destroy numerous aircraft, thereby inhibiting a counterstrike.

CHAPTER 35

# ATTACK UPON JAPAN

In the East China Sea, my Northern Fleet has partially encircled the large Japanese island of Honshu from northwest to Shimane, southwest to Nagasaki, and northeast to Nara.

The preparations for the attack upon Japan have finally been completed. As admiral of the Northern Fleet, I've ordered my officers to launch missiles and massive cannon fire from all battleships and destroyers. Unaware of any danger from the U.S. and Japanese fleets, I remain focused solely on the attack upon Japan. Impatient and angry, I scream at the communications technician, "Radio all fleet commanders, instructing them to create greater spans between their ships."

"Yes, Admiral."

Tactically, this will allow our forces to disperse heavy weapons fire and cause damage throughout a more expansive area of the island.

My military logic and sound judgment have been warped by my deep hatred of the Japanese. I'm aware that I am blindly barking illogical and unorthodox orders, thereby endangering my fleet. Understanding that persisting in this illogical emotional state will inhibit my ability to effectively lead our forces and ultimately realize the goal of destroying our U.S. and Japanese enemies, I'm nevertheless helpless to reel in my emotions.

Caught by surprise, the U.S. and Japanese fleets begin their attack upon our warships. Swarming into the Sea of Japan, their forces overwhelm our portional fleet located along the western coast of Honshu, surprising them with massive firepower. With determination and precision, they barrage our ships and stage a near total destruction of our fleet. Attempting to escape the onslaught of the U.S. and Japanese fleets, our ships head through the Korean Strait with the enemy navies in heavy pursuit. With only fifteen of our warships remaining, they are rushing to rendezvous with the remainder of our Northern Fleet, located in the East China Sea along the southern tip of Honshu. By conjoining our two forces, we'll increase our chances of survival.

While crossing through the Korean Strait, our portional fleet is met by an advancing fleet of U.S. and Japanese warships coming from the East China Sea. In a desperate attempt to avoid total destruction of our fleet, I order my officers to make a direct assault upon the enemy ships. As they continue cannon and rocket fire, the U.S. and Japanese vessels increase their speed in order to overtake our ships. Immediately, their warships begin an assault with artillery fire, destroying or disabling five ships of our Northern Fleet. Two of our remaining vessels manage to pierce the hulls of an American destroyer and a Japanese frigate. Our remaining eight ships quickly escape to rejoin our fleet at the southern tip of Honshu.

After rescuing the crews of both of their damaged ships, the U.S. and Japanese fleets sail toward our flotilla while we secure the southern tip of Japan in the East China Sea. When they approach, massive cannon fire erupts from our warships. Several of the approaching enemy vessels are struck, and their hulls ripped open, causing powerful explosions as the shells reach deep into the bowels of the ships. In response, the Americans and the Japanese open fire on our fleet. Ear-piercing cannon fire permeates the air. The sky is immediately filled with dark, heavy smoke billowing from the massive damage inflicted on both fleets. Submarines from our fleet finally enter the battle, launching torpedo strikes. Four ships from the U.S. fleet and three from the Japanese fleet are hit, disabling five vessels while sinking two. Likewise, three Chinese warships have been incapacitated, and two destroyers and one frigate have been sunk as a result of cannon and torpedo fire.

Realizing the peril we'll be subjected to by remaining, I order my officers, "Turn eastward and head toward the Philippine Sea." Hoping to rendezvous with our remaining fleet currently anchored off of the eastern coast of Honshu, we sail toward the North Pacific. While attempting to outrun the U.S. and Japanese ships, I order, "Proceed at full speed ahead."

When we approach the northern coast of Okinawa, we rendezvous with the remainder of our ships that are anchored east of the Okinawan coast. Our joint force, numbering twenty-eight battleships, destroyers, frigates, and submarines, begins steaming toward the Hawaiian Islands. My intent is to attack and destroy all military facilities on the islands. Mandated to defeat the U.S. fleet on Hawaii, I reflect upon the vulnerability of our fleet positioned off of the West Coast of the United States and the erosion of our Northern Fleet. Understanding that the combined Japanese and U.S. fleets are close behind, I reevaluate our plans and decide to bypass the Hawaiian Islands. Instead, I order my fleet to join the Eastern and Southern Naval Fleets located off the U.S. West Coast. Well aware of the weakness of our fleet and the powerful U.S. forces on Hawaii, I believe it wise to circumvent the original plans. We head directly to the U.S. West Coast. While steaming toward the United States, I believe that our naval forces along the West Coast, in conjunction with our Northern Fleet, can neutralize and subsequently destroy the naval forces of the U.S. and its allies.

When approaching the West Coast, I witness heavy naval and air battles in progress. From all appearances, the Eastern and Southern Fleets are in full control of the battle in spite of the presence of both the U.S. and Australian fleets. Based upon reports from my commanders, our forces have destroyed or disabled one-third of the enemy ships while having lost only 20 percent of our forces. With overwhelming air support, our military has battered the enemy, forcing their withdrawal from the conflict. The worry now is what we will encounter once the trailing U.S. and Japanese naval forces arrive.

Before rendezvousing with our Eastern and Southern Fleets, General

Melenev radios me concerning the situation on the East Coast. He relates, "Admiral, our forces have encountered stiff resistance and are being battered by the U.S. naval, air, and ground forces. In addition, a fleet of British and French vessels have entered the battle and begun attacking our forces from the north. They've managed to push most of our fleet south, just above the Delaware River inlet. By assaulting our navy with heavy weapons fire, the U.S. forces have regained the upper hand. Having lost more than one-third of our fleet, we're struggling to beat back the massive attacks from the enemy."

Just before signing off, the general states, "With sixty ships of our navy either destroyed or severely damaged, and twenty thousand troops and naval personnel dead or injured, I'm not sure how much longer we'll be able to hold off the allied forces. At this point, I don't have much hope of defeating them."

*CHAPTER* **36**

# THE FINAL CONFLICT

Our team is exhausted from the unending skirmishes with the militia over the past several days. Numerous firefights and other clashes have overwhelmed us. Realizing our team's emotional and physical condition, I tell Colonel Gannon, "The men are dog tired and need rest."

"Sean, you're right. I haven't paid much attention to their condition, because of the massive firefights we've encountered. The men definitely appear fatigued and require some rest. We don't need them collapsing in the field."

The colonel orders our team to seek refuge near a small stream situated in a heavily wooded area just southwest of Morganville, West Virginia. To ensure our security, I set up sentinels within wooded areas along either side of the stream and three hundred feet upstream and downstream. Because of the intensity and duration of the combat we've endured, a respite of several hours is needed. Unfortunately, reality dictates a much shorter time frame.

I listen to radio reports from headquarters, advising us that the situation on the East Coast has severely disintegrated for the Russians. At sea and on land, they're absorbing heavy casualties in manpower, equipment, and ships. In addition, ground forces of the U.S. Marines and Army have been crushing Deutsche Christen forces along the coast, pushing them back to Wheeling and farther west. Still, they continue to fight.

Meanwhile, on the West Coast, military reports reveal that crucial naval battles are taking place between U.S. and Chinese forces near cities along the coast and within large coastal inlets. Among the U.S. naval commanders, the hope is high that the Japanese and U.S. fleets from Japan will soon enter the conflict, helping to turn the tide in favor of the United States and its allies.

In conjunction with the naval actions, fierce ground battles are underway in California, Oregon, and Washington, where heavy casualties are mounting on both sides. According to the reports, crushing defeats incurred by the paramilitary in Arizona, Nevada, and Idaho have caused exposure of Chinese army positions along the California and Oregon borders. The impact of this setback has created vulnerability for the Chinese ground forces that are absorbing overwhelming attacks from both the U.S. ships along the coast and ground forces from the interior of the country.

After resting for a couple of hours, I'm awakened by Colonel Gannon, who tells me, "Sean, our sentries detected movement of troops heading in our direction from the east. Get everyone up, and form a defensive perimeter around the camp."

Hidden behind rocks and trees, we wait, anticipating the arrival of the intruders. Soon we glimpse a small band of soldiers approaching our position from two hundred feet away. Unable to determine their allegiance, we continue to observe. Once they're within one hundred feet of our position, we emerge with our weapons leveled at the strangers. Colonel Gannon screams, "You're surrounded. Halt and drop your weapons!"

Without hesitation, the band of seven drop their weapons and raise their hands in the air. Noticing that they are American soldiers, Colonel Gannon rushes toward them and asks who's in charge. A captain identifies himself and shakes the colonel's hand. Enthusiastically, our entire team greets them. We then head back to our camp and mingle while discussing the current state of military operations. From what we gather from the group, the Russian forces on the East Coast have been crushed. As a result, the allied forces have redirected their resources.

According to the captain, "The air force has been ordered to move several squadrons of jets to the interior of the country in order to provide cover for U.S. ground forces. Hoping to force a surrender by Deutsche Christen, they've been attacking the enemy wherever they're encountered. Frightened by the onslaught, the civilian population has abandoned their homes and businesses, seeking refuge at higher elevations and below ground. In fact, many towns have become ghost towns."

In the meantime, we decide to break camp and head toward Wheeling, where we're sure to encounter militia forces. We hope to destroy the remnants of Deutsche Christen once and for all, thereby ensuring victory and wiping out any threat to the U.S. government.

CHAPTER 37

# UNBEARABLE LOSS

Naval battles along the West Coast have temporarily subsided, and the U.S., Japanese, and Australian navies have withdrawn from the scene. This suspension of hostilities allows my naval forces, as well as the enemy, to regroup and plan for the ensuing battle. After inventorying our assets, I redirect our remaining resources and coordinate all efforts to guarantee victory. In a huddle with my staff, we discuss tactics and decide to implement some unorthodox flanking maneuvers intended to surprise the allies.

Just then, one of my officers informs me, "Admiral Xu, the enemy ships are underway and heading in our direction."

I order my commanders, "Get underway and proceed to the coast."

While we position our forces, a large flotilla of Chinese and Russian merchant ships appear on the horizon. These are the ships that were confiscated by the U.S. Navy during boarding operations intended to detect illegal shipments of weapons into the U.S. Coming from the coast, they're sailing directly toward our fleet. Displaying the national flags of both countries, the ships are a welcome and refreshing sight for our naval personnel. Cheering loudly, the crews begin waving to the approaching vessels. Unbeknown to us, the merchant ships have been programmed to ram our vessels. U.S. naval technicians created guidance software that enables them to control the speed and direction of the merchant ships remotely. Unimpeded, they approach our fleet at full speed.

Realizing that the approaching vessels are on a collision course with our fleets, the crews panic. They rush to their posts and begin firing artillery in an attempt to destroy the approaching ships and avoid the calamity that otherwise awaits us. Our ships' engines are quickly started in the hope of escaping the onslaught of the massive flotilla. Suddenly, explosions of our naval and merchant ships occur as our vessels are rammed. Five of our ships are sunk, and three are disabled.

No doubt, sensing an opportunity, the U.S. naval forces attack our fleets. With the hope of swinging the momentum in their favor, they unleash a massive barrage of artillery and missile fire. I realize that we've been trapped between U.S. forces and the blitzkrieg of the flotilla of merchant ships. We've clearly been caught flat-footed. While absorbing massive losses to our assets and personnel, I understand the unfortunate fate of my forces. As a result, I must attempt to preserve the residual assets of our fleets and ground forces. I grab the radio and order, "Rescue all ground forces, retreat, and sail for home."

During the rescue, our fleets suffer major setbacks to the remaining vessels. Clearly, sitting ducks we continue rescuing our troops. Three more ships are struck and sunk by incoming fire. In view of this devastation, I instruct my commanders, "Retreat immediately and head toward home." After abandoning nearly one hundred thousand troops, I'm overcome with grief. Feeling distraught and helpless, I collapse, emotionally frantic at this stunning outcome. I raise my hands, place them over my face, and weep uncontrollably, realizing the tremendous loss of not only our troops but also the war waged for the control and subjugation of the United States.

While we retreat, the U.S. Navy and their allies shadow our fleets and continue their bombardment of our ships. They're apparently hell-bent on following and attacking our fleets until we're rendered impotent.

In the meantime, radio reports from Central Command detail the battles on the East Coast. Devastated, the Russian military has been destroyed, forcing them to limp from the battle scene. Outlining the situation, the officer from Central Command informs us, "The Russians have absorbed devastating casualties and overwhelming damage to their fleets. With most of his chiefs of staff either dead or wounded, General Melenev has ordered the withdrawal of his forces. While withdrawing from the scene, the remainder of the Russian Navy is sailing toward the Black Sea in the hope of avoiding total destruction. As an unfortunate sideline, General Melenev was unable to rescue his ground forces, abandoning nearly fifty thousand troops."

When I arrive at the surface harbor of the Northern Fleet, I disembark my ship and head directly to my office. Bitter and angry over our defeat,

I've sworn revenge against the United States and its allies. I contact Central Command and inform them of the devastating outcome.

Angered by the results, one of the officers advises me, "Admiral, this matter must be referred to the Central Committee of the Communist Party."

Well aware that such an action will end my career, I open the drawer of my desk and extract a small revolver. After falling back into my desk chair, I lean forward and rest my elbows on the edge of the desk. While holding the pistol with both hands, I aim the barrel under my chin, angling it slightly. I slowly squeeze the trigger and fire. Instantly, my head is jarred back and then quickly launched forward, finding a resting place on the desktop. While I lose consciousness, the gun falls to the floor, landing in a pool of blood.

After hearing the gunshot, a naval officer from a nearby office rushes in. Upon entering, he witnesses the office awash in red. Repulsed at the horrific scene, he panics and rushes out to seek assistance from the medical staff.

**************

In the aftermath of the international conflict, I've witnessed the devastating destruction of our military. As the Russian general in charge of the East Coast invasion forces, I've not only failed to defeat the U.S. military, but have also tainted the Melenev family name. With our military power nearly destroyed, I'm still determined to defeat the United States. We understand our current vulnerability to a military takeover, and we've begun devising a plan to reclaim our honor while simultaneously crushing the United States.

With our limited military resources, only one option remains, and if implemented, it may sink the world into a cataclysm of boundless depths—something we're willing to chance. Desperate to avenge our defeat, Yang Quan, the chairman of the Central Committee of the Communist Party, and Vladimir Uransky, the premier of the Russian Federation, have arranged an emergency meeting in Moscow for tomorrow, October 25. Considered top-secret, the meeting will draw all senior governmental and military officials of both regimes. Given the critical nature of the meeting and the importance of any decision, I'm aware that urgency is paramount.

Nearly one hundred officials have arrived at the government building of the Russian Federation, also known as the Russian White House. They enter the main hall, where magnificent marble floors and stairs highlight the beauty of the massive entranceway. Accentuated by fifty foot high ceilings that are underscored by the bright lights emanating from the many overhead ceiling lamps, the room is spectacular. It's somewhat stark. With sharp linear angles of the ceilings and walls, the room exhibits a clean and cold geometric setting—something unique to Russian architecture.

I greet the representatives as they're ushered to the conference hall within the Presidium. This is the most prestigious room within the building. Here is where the pulse of the Russian government is monitored and decisions of the highest level are made.

Upon entering the room, the representatives greet me. Bowing with respect, Yan Quan says, "Good morning, General Melenev."

"Good morning, Chairman. Very nice to see you."

When each guest arrives, he or she is treated to a buffet breakfast featuring baked salmon, eggs, bacon, sausage, and a host of other foods, including fruits and breads. At 10:00 a.m., an announcement is made that the meeting will commence. When all representatives are seated, I convene the session. While presenting a short outline that discloses the purpose of the meeting, my voice assumes a tone of anger and irritability. I feel guilty at my inability to defeat and destroy the United States, and I subconsciously believe that if a final determination and attack upon the enemy is successful, my status among the hierarchy of the Russian government and military establishment will be resurrected.

I introduce Yang Quan, shake his hand, and clap along with the audience, welcoming him. After stepping to the microphone, Chairman Quan quietly but firmly begins outlining the only alternative we have to destroy the United States and its allies. He states, "Our military assets have been nearly depleted. We therefore have only one option for defeating the United States. That option requires the implementation and launch of nuclear missiles against our enemies. If we are to be successful, the attack must be carried out with the utmost urgency. If we delay, our chances of success will diminish. Therefore, it's imperative that we immediately undertake this bold step to ensure victory and reinstate our leadership within the world community."

While Chairman Quan steps from the dais, tremendous applause from the attendees greets him. The response unfortunately has set the tone for the decision to be sanctioned. In agreement with the chairman, Premier Uransky reinforces the call for the use of nuclear weapons.

Several Russian and Chinese officials rise and issue statements disagreeing with the proposal to utilize nuclear weapons. Proclaiming this plan to be assuredly disastrous, they plead that it be discarded; they are concerned about massive destruction and death worldwide. Unfortunately, their pleas fall upon deaf ears. With the military focused solely upon defeating the United States and its allies, they have no concern about collateral injuries or damage. What matters most is victory at all costs.

***************

CHAPTER **38**

# CONFRONTATION WITH DIETRICH

In the aftermath of the international conflict, pockets of enemy resistance continue while the U.S. military seeks out Deutsche Christen strongholds and the remaining Chinese and Russian troops scattered throughout the country.

Our team has been ordered to track down and destroy all militia situated within West Virginia. Our first target is the Wheeling camp. When Colonel Gannon and our team arrive at the perimeter of the camp, he tells me, "We'll move toward the center of the camp and then split our forces in two."

We slowly and cautiously enter the camp. Unsure of the threats we may be facing, our senses are heightened while we search and assess the military strength of the militia. After furtively moving into the body of the camp, our team is suddenly confronted by nearly one hundred fully armed troops wearing green and brown camouflage. Caught by surprise, the militia immediately unleashes massive rounds of machine gun and rifle fire, injuring five of our troops. In response, we overwhelm the militia with a barrage of heavy firepower. After killing thirty militia, the survivors drop their weapons and raise their hands above their heads.

Colonel Gannon tells me, "Sean, have the prisoners encircled and search each of them for weapons." After securing the remaining firearms, he orders the militia to sit on the ground in a circle while a small regiment of twenty special forces troops observe and guard them.

Colonel Gannon orders, "Split into two groups, capture or kill all remaining paramilitary within the camp, and destroy as many structures and weapons as possible." We move in, separate in northerly and southerly directions, and cautiously traverse deeper into the camp.

Upon discovering a large metal warehouse, I halt my team and instruct them, "Approach the building cautiously and check for booby traps." With guns pointed, we carefully open the large front doors and peer inside to view an enormous stockpile of small weapons and an array of ammunition.

I order my team to set explosives. Once these are planted and set, we quickly withdraw and detonate them. A thunderous blast rocks the entire area while the sky darkens with embers that morph into ash while slowly trickling to the ground. After observing the destruction of the warehouse, my team quickly retreats and continues exploring.

Penetrating deep into the camp, we encounter a group of twenty-five heavily armed militia. Much to my surprise, Carl Dietrich is leading the group. Although outnumbered by the militia, we'll be more than capable of subduing them. Withdrawing while firing, the militia quickly encounters the wrath of a barrage of weapons fire from our team. We launch grenades and rounds of machine gun fire and quickly bring the militia to its knees.

In the midst of the encounter, I notice Carl Dietrich attempting to escape into the nearby woods. Without hesitation, I pursue him through the heavy overgrowth and brush. Aware that I'm close behind, Dietrich turns and fires his weapon. I dive behind the trunk of a nearby maple tree and return fire. After he fires two quick rounds, Dietrich's weapon jams. He drops his gun and races toward a nearby creek.

I jump from the bank and tackle him as he reaches the near side of the water's edge. When I get to my feet, Dietrich punches me in the temple, jarring me. His facial expression reveals his deep hatred for me and his compelling desire to kill me. I rush at Dietrich and strike him in the chest with a powerful jump kick, knocking him to the ground. While getting up, he reaches into the top of his boot and extracts a combat knife with a long, narrow blade. While waving the knife, he charges and attempts to stab me. I drop to the ground and sweep his legs, bringing him down with a heavy thud. The knife then disappears in the rushing current of the creek and washes downstream.

When Dietrich gets up, I tackle him and furiously punch him. Releasing my long pent-up anger, I continue pummeling him. His face is bleeding profusely. Suddenly, I stop my attack, realizing I may kill him. With Dietrich unconscious, I get up and walk to the edge of the creek. I bend down to rinse my face and hands while enjoying the soothing coolness of the water.

Just then, I'm struck from behind. Forcing his arm around my throat, Dietrich squeezes. I'm gasping for air, unable to dislodge Dietrich's arm, and I begin losing consciousness. In desperation, I wrap my forearm around Dietrich's head, turn my body inward, and flip him into the creek.

When I kneel to catch my breath, Dietrich gets up and lands a kick to my gut. After following up with a punch to my head, he drags me into the creek and submerges my face, attempting to drown me. Reacting quickly, I grab Dietrich from under his right arm and roll his body, flipping him. I get to my feet and strike him with two punches to the side of his head. Stunned, he stumbles but then charges at me. When he does, I land a jump kick to his chest. He falls back into the creek, motionless. His body floats onto the rocky, and muddy surface of the bank.

I walk from the creek and drag Dietrich's body onto the wet dirt surface just beyond the bank of the creek. I check his vital signs and confirm that he's dead. When I begin to cry, I realize that the trauma and stress of the past few months have finally surfaced, overwhelming me. Though I'm happy at his demise, I'm still cognizant of the people who have unnecessarily died at his hands.

When I get up, a group of special forces troops approach. They help remove Dietrich's body and return me to my team. Colonel Gannon greets me and then says, "Dean Balstral was found in an old barn located just down the road. He hung himself from a large support beam. Before the defeat of the militia, he must have felt that his safety was guaranteed here, believing that the U.S. military would be easily defeated."

"I guess you're right, Colonel. I really would have preferred capturing him alive. We could then have meted out a punishment befitting his crimes."

"I'm with you, Sean. However, things worked out this way for a reason. In any event, I'm concerned about the ultimate outcome of the war. I know that the Chinese and Russians still maintain a battery of atomic weapons. Realizing that they have lost most of their ground, naval, and air forces, they may resort to the use of nuclear weapons."

## CHAPTER 39

# ODIN

Subsequent to our recent encounter with the militia, a meeting of politicians, military leaders, and prominent but influential citizens is arranged. I arrive at the White House, rush through security, and head directly to the briefing room, where I've been invited to attend a closed-door meeting. When I enter, I'm met by a collective of officials and reporters. While observing their behavior, my senses detect an atmosphere of uncertainty and apprehension concerning the purpose of today's gathering.

I look around the room before the meeting convenes and catch a glimpse of Sheila Hanley, the former U.S. ambassador to the United Nations. After pushing my way through the crowd, I tap her on the shoulder. "Good afternoon, Sheila."

"Hello, Sean. I didn't expect to see you here."

"Yesterday afternoon, I received a phone call from John Morgan's office requesting that I attend the meeting."

"Congratulations—you're among many of the elite leaders in Washington. The administration must think very highly of you."

"Sheila, are you aware of the reason for today's meeting?"

Replying, she says, "Not completely, but I know our intelligence services are concerned about several recent reports hinting that the Chinese and Russians are planning to employ nuclear weapons against us and our allies."

"My God. If this is true, it may be our Armageddon."

"Sean, everyone is on edge, unsure of what to do to defuse the situation. The only other alternative we have, though bleak, involves a preemptive strike."

"Oh, God. The thought of such a horrific act makes my blood turn cold."

While we're talking, the meeting is called to order, and everyone begins taking their seats. I say goodbye to the ambassador and grab a third-row seat.

Overseeing the meeting is Secretary of Defense James Halsberg. A tall man at six feet three inches, he presents an imposing figure and projects the image of an authoritative, no-nonsense leader. He states, "Ladies and gentlemen, I know that you're anxious to know why this meeting has been convened. To get right to the point, we've received information from the C.I.A. that the Republic of China and the Russian Federation are planning to utilize atomic weapons against us and our allies. If these weapons are employed, our world, as we know it, will be eviscerated. It's therefore our obligation to take whatever steps are necessary to deter, and at the very worst destroy, our adversaries. In order to explain the reality of the current situation and to outline alternatives to prevent an attack, I'd like to call upon General Stanton."

I watch intently as the general rises and approaches the secretary. With quick, deliberate steps, he walks to the dais and shakes the secretary's hand. The general picks up the microphone and glances out over the audience. Strangely, he refers to Odin, the most powerful Norse god and the god of war. "Odin is an example of leadership, strength, and overwhelming power. His is a name that brought fear to the hearts of his enemies." The general asks, "Has anyone heard this name used in a current military context?" Only Secretary Halsberg indicates that he has. General Stanton begins outlining what is known as the ODIN Project. "The project began in early 2003. Space Command, a special wing of the air force with the authority to launch and control military satellites, was responsible for its development. In conjunction with NASA scientists, they commissioned several independent aerospace contractors to help design and build a prototype satellite. The satellite was created with the capacity for evasion, and it was equipped with a force field capable of deflecting missile attacks. It contains eight nuclear missiles specially designed and installed within capsules in its aft section. The obvious purpose of this project is to provide a space defense shield for the protection of the United States."

"In mid-2006 the prototype was completed, and by early 2012 the final version of the satellite was ready for service. It wasn't actually launched into orbit until June of that year. Carried by a Titan IV rocket, the satellite was successfully launched. Under the auspices of the United States National Weather Service, the satellite was slated to replace the GOES-12 weather satellite scheduled for decommission in August 2013. Unlike the GOES-12, which was set in a geostationary orbit, ODIN was developed for an asynchronous orbit at five thousand miles above the orbit of the GOES-12"

"The missiles on board ODIN can destroy the earth three times over. The destructive power of each of these missiles is over one thousand times more powerful than the Little Boy atomic bomb dropped over Hiroshima during World War II. As you can see, ODIN is a major weapon to be employed in the event of a nuclear attack. Unknown to all but a few senior military officers and high ranking government officials, the project is still top secret. The activation of this weapon system may only be implemented with the authority of the president. Based upon our current intelligence reports, we may be mandated to employ this weapon to defend and protect our country."

After the secretary of state closes the meeting, people rush from the briefing room aware of the catastrophe that may await us. Shaken by the announcement, I immediately stand and rush to secure a cab to transport me to the airport. After catching a flight back to New York, I decide to contact my family and friends to caution them concerning what may be about to take place.

In the meantime, at the Presidium, after the premier's sanction of the use of nuclear missiles against the United States and its allies, the attendees of the nuclear conference listen as loud cheers explode within the building. The hawks have won, allowing the Chinese and Russians to proceed with a plan to attack their enemies with nuclear weapons. The launch has been scheduled for October 28 at 0500 hours. The complete arsenal of Chinese and Russian missiles will be activated. In spite of the warnings repeated by the group of antinuclear officers, the world will be under a cataclysmic threat.

At exactly 0200 hours on the twenty-eighth, all Russian and Chinese military crews are at their stations preparing for the attack. While awaiting the countdown, all systems are checked for launch preparation. Once the countdown clocks are synchronized, the launch sequence is begun.

CHAPTER 40

# FINALITY OF WAR

A couple of hours later, I arrive at the White House with General Stanton and Colonel Gannon to meet with Chief of Staff John Morgan. The general introduces me to Mr. Morgan. "John, this is Sean Carrol, a veteran special forces major and reporter from the New York International News. I believe you know the colonel."

I listen as the general advises Mr. Morgan that the Chinese and Russian silos have been activated. Mr. Morgan then asks, "General Stanton, what stage is the Chinese and Russian launch at?"

"According to our intelligence, the missiles have been targeted at the United States and several of our allies. The time of the launch, however, has not been determined. At this point, we have no alternative other than to prepare our defenses. It's now imperative that we obtain the president's permission to activate ODIN."

While we stand near the doorway to the Oval Office, I overhear Mr. Morgan's conversation with the president. "Mr. President, the Chinese and

Russians have activated their missile silos. We need your authorization to activate ODIN and our missile defense systems." I can hear President Burleigh arguing with Mr. Morgan and whining about the necessity for negotiations with the Chinese and Russians.

Mr. Morgan finally erupts, saying in an angry voice, "The Chinese and Russians have activated their arsenal of missiles. If you don't act immediately, you will be jeopardizing the lives of our citizens and those of our allies. In order to prevent a disaster, you must authorize the launch of the satellite missiles at once!"

We look at each other in confusion. It's hard to understand how the president can be so indecisive concerning such a critical and potentially catastrophic threat.

In spite of the gravity of the situation, the president exhibits his usual ambivalence, displaying his inability to make a decision. Once again, I hear Mr. Morgan screaming at the President, imploring him to take action.

Obviously frustrated and frightened, I see Mr. Morgan grab a gun from one of the nearby Secret Service agents. In spite of their responsibility to protect the president, I believe their inaction communicates their understanding of the gravity of the current world threat. Watching as the Secret Service agents turn their back to the president, I see Mr. Morgan point the gun barrel at the president's temple. He cocks the pistol and threatens to pull the trigger. While shaking, President Burleigh falls to the floor, begging for his life.

Mr. Morgan picks up the phone receiver, dials General Forrester at

Space Command in Colorado, and hands the phone to the president. In a low, quivering voice, President Burleigh says, "General Forrester, this is President Burleigh. I'm authorizing you to activate ODIN."

"Mr. President, in order to activate the system, I need your sequence codes."

While cowering, he asks, "Are you ready, General?"

"Yes, Mr. President."

"The sequence is alpha, omega, fourteen, seven, forty-four, five, whisper, johnnie."

I then head to the White House Command and Observation Center along with General Stanton and Colonel Gannon to observe the satellite activation process.

After re-verifying the codes, General Forrester turns the keys to the control panel and enters his and the president's codes into the display. Within sixty seconds the electronic instruction boards within the facility begin flashing, signaling authorization for the countdown. Beginning at number twenty, the countdown commences. Once complete, a visual of ODIN is displayed on the large overhead monitors. While I watch, the satellite rotation is in progress. Within ten minutes, the rotation is complete, and the dark black backboard of the satellite is visible.

From the center of the backboard, a thin opening appears. As it widens, the eight missile capsules are exposed. Meanwhile, I watch as the technicians at Space Command configure the missile trajectories. After entering the coordinates, General Forrester informs us that everything has been activated. General Stanton initiates two phone calls, one to Premier Uransky of Russia and the second to Chairman Quan of China.

It's now 0451 hours, just nine minutes preceding the scheduled launch of the Chinese and Russian nuclear missiles. While firmly addressing the two leaders, the general informs them that their missiles must be deactivated immediately. Laughing, Chairman Quan states that the United States has no choice other than to surrender. He says, "General, within a few minutes, the launch will be initiated."

General Stanton angrily warns them, "If you refuse to deactivate and surrender your nuclear missiles, we'll have no choice but to decimate your countries." He informs them, "There are eight nuclear missiles aimed at your countries. Capable of destroying the world three times over, they have been activated from a U.S. space satellite. Once again, I advise you to deactivate your missiles." The general provides both leaders with a five minute window in which to carry out his order.

Unfazed and doubtful of the general's threat, Chairman Quan emphatically states, "Your president is weak on military action, and I'm confident that you're bluffing."

The Chinese continue the launch countdown. The Russians, on the other hand, know of the general's resoluteness and honesty. Having negotiated with him on several previous occasions, General Melenev is aware of his unwavering determination and believes the threat to be authentic. As a result, they halt their countdown.

At exactly 0500 hours, we're informed that three Chinese WU-14 hypersonic nuclear missiles have been launched from Delingha in central China. This launch is intended as a precursor to the launch of the remaining battery of missiles that will constitute the second phase of the Chinese attack. Aimed at France, Great Britain, and the United States, the hypersonic missiles fly at ten times the speed of sound—7,860 miles per hour. Newly developed and tested, they signal a high level of weapons development. By flying close to ground level they're impervious to land-based missile attacks, thereby exposing the vulnerability of the allies' defenses. In addition, the fact that the ODIN missiles are unable to be precision targeted eliminates our option to destroy the Chinese missiles. Our only remaining hope is to employ the use of combat jets. There are, however, no conventional military jets that approach the speed of the WU-14 missiles. The missiles are expected to reach their European targets within one hour, and the United States in less than two and a half hours. As a result, the U.S. military is scrambling to find a solution to destroy the missiles.

Though untested, the Falcon hypersonic unmanned HTV-2 jet may be the only option. Capable of flying up to thirteen thousand miles per hour, it will be able to catch and destroy the Chinese missiles. Unfortunately, only two prototypes exist, and there is no data to support their performance. In desperation, the U.S. Air Force quickly commandeers both jets. The Falcons are each armed with four heat-seeking missiles and have the capacity to fly up to ten thousand miles without refueling.

In the meantime, authorization is provided to launch a satellite-based nuclear missile. Targeting Delingha, the missile is launched and quickly approaches the target. Impact is expected within twenty minutes. Regrettably, this attack will claim the lives of at least 1.2 million Chinese.

We've just been advised by Pentagon officials that the Falcon jets have been flown to Shaw Air Force Base in Sumter, South Carolina. They've been fueled, and all mechanical and electronic systems have been fully inspected. From Central Command, I listen to the air traffic controllers at Shaw as they inform us of the preparation of the jets for takeoff. Once prepped, the jets begin taxiing down the runway. When the all- clear is provided from the tower, both bolt north eastward, one heading for Great Britain and the other heading for France. Traveling at full speed, the jets rush toward their targets. Within thirty minutes, ground control experts at Shaw inform us that they will quickly intercept and destroy the three WU-14 Chinese missiles. Nervously, they guide the jets and finally locate the missiles nearly three hundred miles northwest of their position off the coast of Great Britain.

I continue to listen as the ground controllers activate the missiles aboard the Falcons and lock on to their targets. Suddenly, the controllers panic and begin yelling loudly after a huge explosion occurs. They inform us that one of the Chinese missiles has unexpectedly failed and exploded in Western Europe. Tracing the point of impact, they determine that central Belgium is the victim. In spite of this, two Chinese missiles are still headed for Great Britain and France.

After the first U.S. missile strike, Chairman Quan makes an urgent call to General Stanton, begging that he rescind any orders for launching additional missiles. He promises to surrender China's entire stockpile of nuclear weapons. Panicked by the devastation to his country, he is frantic to stop the destruction. Knowing that a second satellite missile has already been launched, the general informs the chairman, "You're response is too late."

Meanwhile, Belgian officials have informed us that the unexpected Chinese missile explosion has resulted in the destruction of the city of Roeselare, wiping out the population of 60,999. The devastation stretched to the west coast at Koksijde and as far north as Bruges. According to their report, hundreds of thousands of people have been killed from the direct hit of the missile. However, many thousands more will die because of the fallout from the atomic blast.

The second U.S. missile is quickly approaching its target. Shenyang, formerly known as Mukden, is a Chinese industrial center housing a population of 8.1 million. Hosting the Shenyang Sujiatun military airbase, this target, along with the entire northeast of China, will effectively be destroyed. The fallout from the missile blast will also impact many cities and towns throughout eastern and central China, including Beijing, claiming many more millions of lives.

While monitoring the crisis, we watch from the command and observation center as the two remaining Chinese missiles bear down on Great Britain and France. With time running out, the ground controllers at Shaw Air Force Base activate the missiles on the Falcon jets. Suddenly, one of the jets begins losing altitude. The technicians at the Colorado control center panic while attempting to detect and correct the problem. With limited time remaining, they turn their attention to the surviving Falcon jet, while still attempting to pilot the first jet into an unpopulated area. I nervously observe as they fire a missile from the second jet, targeting the Chinese missile currently descending upon Paris. Within twenty seconds the missile from the Falcon jet hits the WU-14 missile, creating a tremendous explosion that produces a confetti-like field of debris descending upon the villages and towns below. In the meantime, we receive news that our disabled jet has crashed in the northern Atlantic Ocean.

Activating a second missile from the Falcon jet, the control center technicians fire at the remaining Chinese missile. Within one hundred miles of the coast of Great Britain, the missile strike is imminent. Frightened because of the limited window of time for destroying the last missile, we nervously await its impact. While it approaches London, I grit my teeth. The Chinese missile begins descending. Suddenly, the U.S. missile clips the left rear corner of the Chinese WU-14, without causing an explosion. Vacillating erratically, the Chinese missile begins pitching to the left, veering in a southwesterly direction. I watch as the missile changes course, diverting toward northern Spain. Impact is calculated at twenty-five minutes. With two missiles remaining aboard the Falcon jet, the technicians at the Colorado control center hurriedly configure the missile trajectories and fire. Midway between the jet and the WU-14, the missile explodes.

With Spain in the crosshairs of the Chinese missile and time running out, the control center launches the last missile from the Falcon. People at the center hold their breath and pray as they wait for impact. Finally, the WU-14 is struck, causing a massive explosion in the Spanish sky. The entire control room staff scream and clap, knowing they have prevented a catastrophe. Miraculously, the Falcon jet has performed beyond expectations and has single-handedly preserved millions of lives.

From the command and control center, I weigh the results of the worldwide devastation, overwhelmed by the tremendous loss of life. As a member of the military establishment, I'm extremely distressed by the unfortunate and unnecessary devastation. The power-madness of our so-called world leaders has resulted in the loss of more than 250 million people, not to mention the millions who are injured and homeless. How regrettable.

In the aftermath of the war, I'm elated that all nuclear weapons have been surrendered and destroyed. This action brings about a new hope for peace, engenders a general sense of tranquility, and provides a promise for a brighter future. I understand that the loss of so many lives and the massive destruction throughout the world has been an unnecessary cost for coming to understand the meaning of peace and the benefit of harmony. What a difficult lesson we've had to learn.

While at my home, I'm surrounded by my family, Stan, and Betty. Sitting next to Linda, I'm observing how everyone is interacting. Relieved at the finality of the war, I'm hopeful about the prospects for the future. Realizing how difficult the ordeal of the past several months has been, I'm hopefully embracing the idea that somehow people will understand the meaning of cooperation and peace without resorting to a military solution. From the abduction of my niece and nephew through the final world conflict, my experiences have transformed my entire perspective concerning personal relationships and interpersonal priorities, and my worldview of the dangers associated with power-hungry individuals and governments.

While I'm sitting on my living room couch, Stan slowly wanders over with his cane in hand. He's come a long way since being shot during our mission to the Deutsche Christen camp. I'm just thankful that he survived. He asks Linda and me, "How are you both feeling?"

Linda says, "We're relieved that the conflicts are over. More important, we're happy that our family and friends are safe, even though they've experienced some harrowing incidents."

I say, "It's been trying, to say the least, but we all survived."

Stan nods. "Right now, I'm gonna grab a beer. Talk to you both in a little while."

Reflecting further, I understand that the personal relationships I've developed amid recent events have become sacred to me. My family above all has become the critical focus in my life, forcing me to realize the significance of strong unconstrained family love and support. Philosophically, I believe that peace is earned and subjected to constant struggle. It's not something inherited and passed on from generation to generation, expected to continue simply because we desire it.

While I listen to Danny and Amanda speak about their school classes and the forthcoming holidays, I feel emotionally rejuvenated, knowing that through their eyes tomorrow will be brighter. In spite of this optimism, I know that we must be ever vigilant, aware of threats that may imperil peace and our way of life. Never again can we trust our future to people such as Carl Dietrich—people who seek power purely to subjugate others. In reality, I know that somewhere down the road, we'll be challenged by the emergence of another figure like Dietrich, who may thrust our world into peril once again.

In spite of this, I'll do everything I can to educate people—and more important, to live my life enjoying and supporting my family and friends.

# About the Author

William Brazzel has worked as an insurance agent for thirty-five years. In his three-year endeavor to create a truly different and exhilarating story, he spent many hours researching history, geography, and current events. William currently resides in Morris Plains, New Jersey. Conflux is his debut novel.

Printed in the United States
By Bookmasters